STITCHED

charmz™

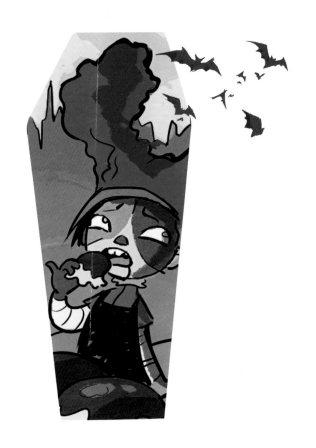

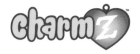

STITCHED

#2 "Love in the Time of Assumption"

Story by Mariah McCourt
Art by Aaron Alexovich

NEW YORK

STITCHED

by Mariah McCourt and Aaron Alexovich

STITCHED #2
"Love in the Time of Assumption"

MARIAH McCOURT – Story
AARON ALEXOVICH – Art and Cover
BRYAN SENKA – Lettering
DREW RAUSCH – Color

DAWN GUZZO – Production
MARIAH McCOURT – Editor
JEFF WHITMAN – Assistant Managing Editor
JIM SALICRUP
Editor-in-Chief

Charmz is an imprint of Papercutz.

PB ISBN: 978-1-62991-860-0
HC ISBN: 978-1-62991-861-7

Printed in India
September 2018

Charmz books may be purchased for business or promotional use.
For information on bulk purchases please contact Macmillan
Corporate and Premium Sales Department at
(800) 221-7945 x5442

Distributed by Macmillan
First Printing

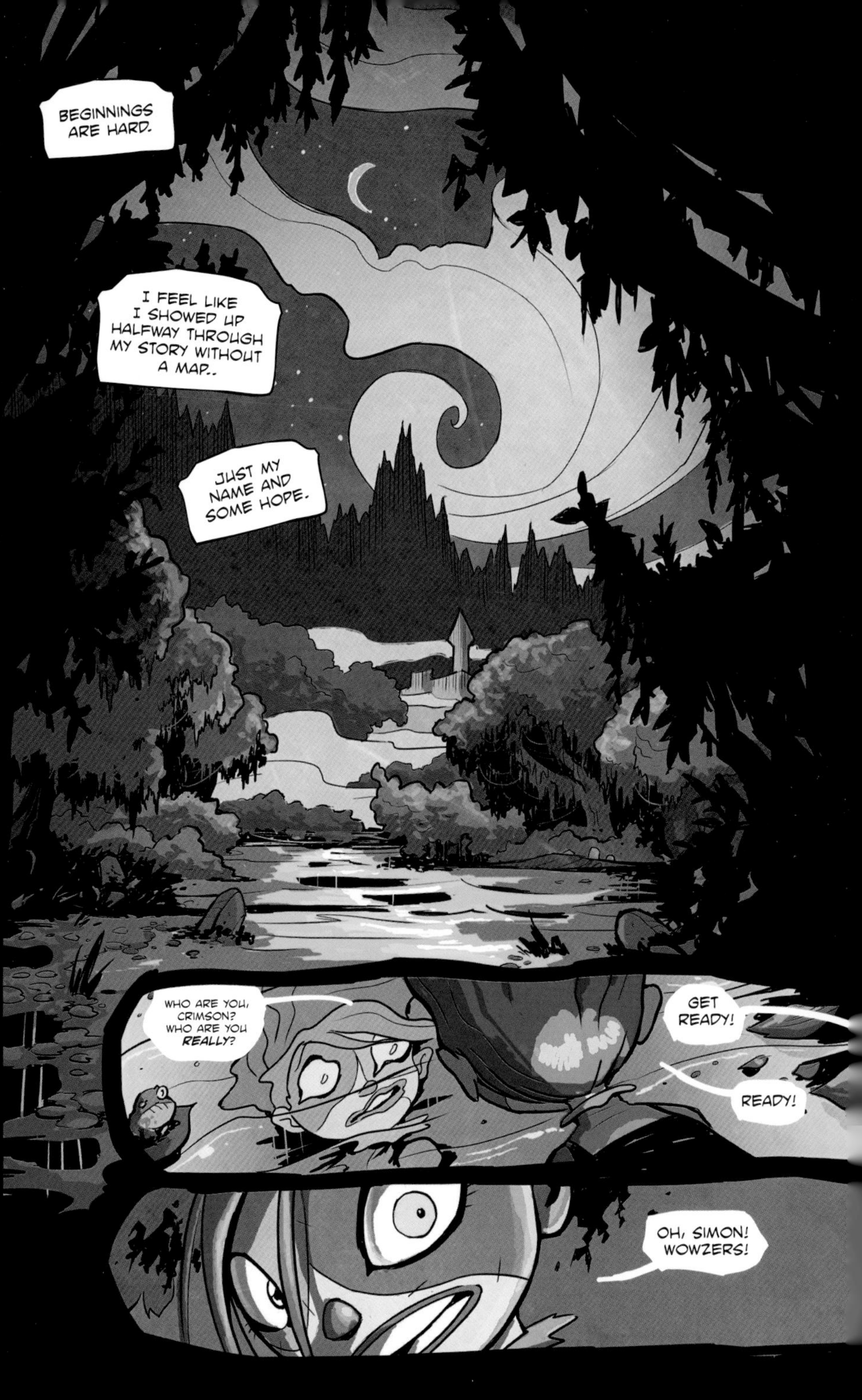
BEGINNINGS ARE HARD.
I FEEL LIKE I SHOWED UP HALFWAY THROUGH MY STORY WITHOUT A MAP..
JUST MY NAME AND SOME HOPE.
WHO ARE YOU, CRIMSON? WHO ARE YOU *REALLY*?
GET READY!
READY!
OH, SIMON! WOWZERS!

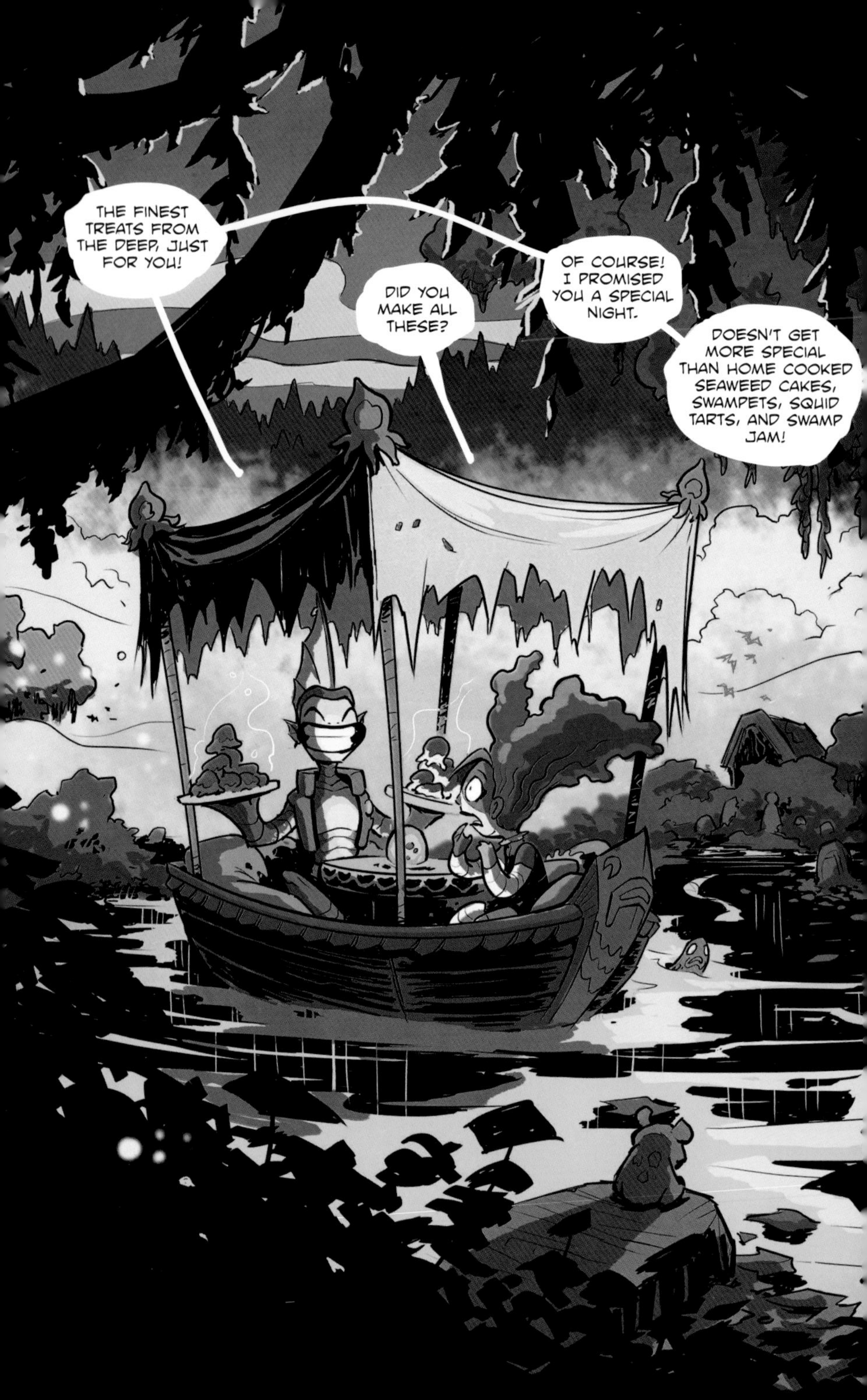
THE FINEST TREATS FROM THE DEEP, JUST FOR YOU!
DID YOU MAKE ALL THESE?
OF COURSE! I PROMISED YOU A SPECIAL NIGHT.
DOESN'T GET MORE SPECIAL THAN HOME COOKED SEAWEED CAKES, SWAMPETS, SQUID TARTS, AND SWAMP JAM!

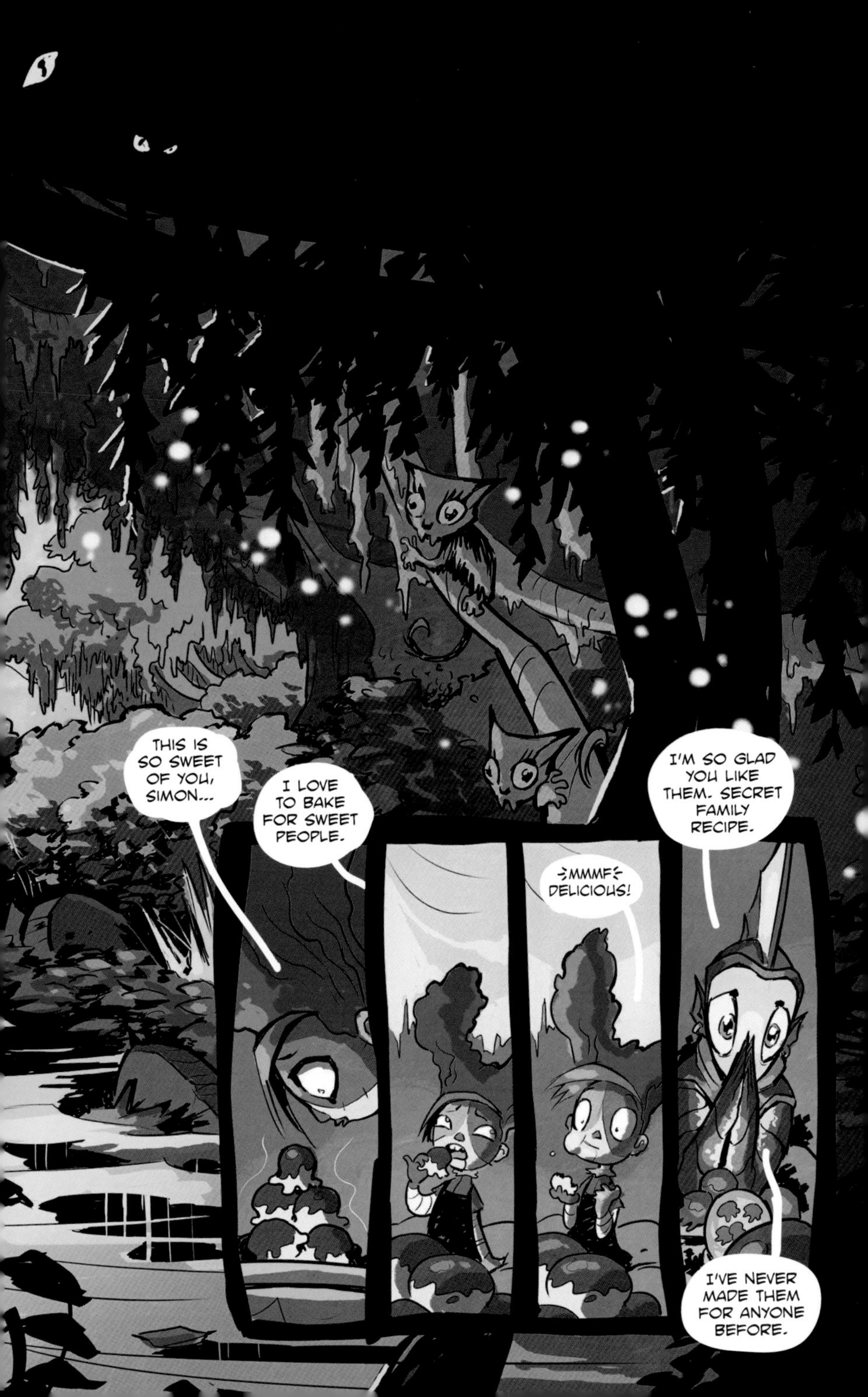
THIS IS SO SWEET OF YOU, SIMON...
I LOVE TO BAKE FOR SWEET PEOPLE.
MMMF DELICIOUS!
I'M SO GLAD YOU LIKE THEM. SECRET FAMILY RECIPE.
I'VE NEVER MADE THEM FOR ANYONE BEFORE.

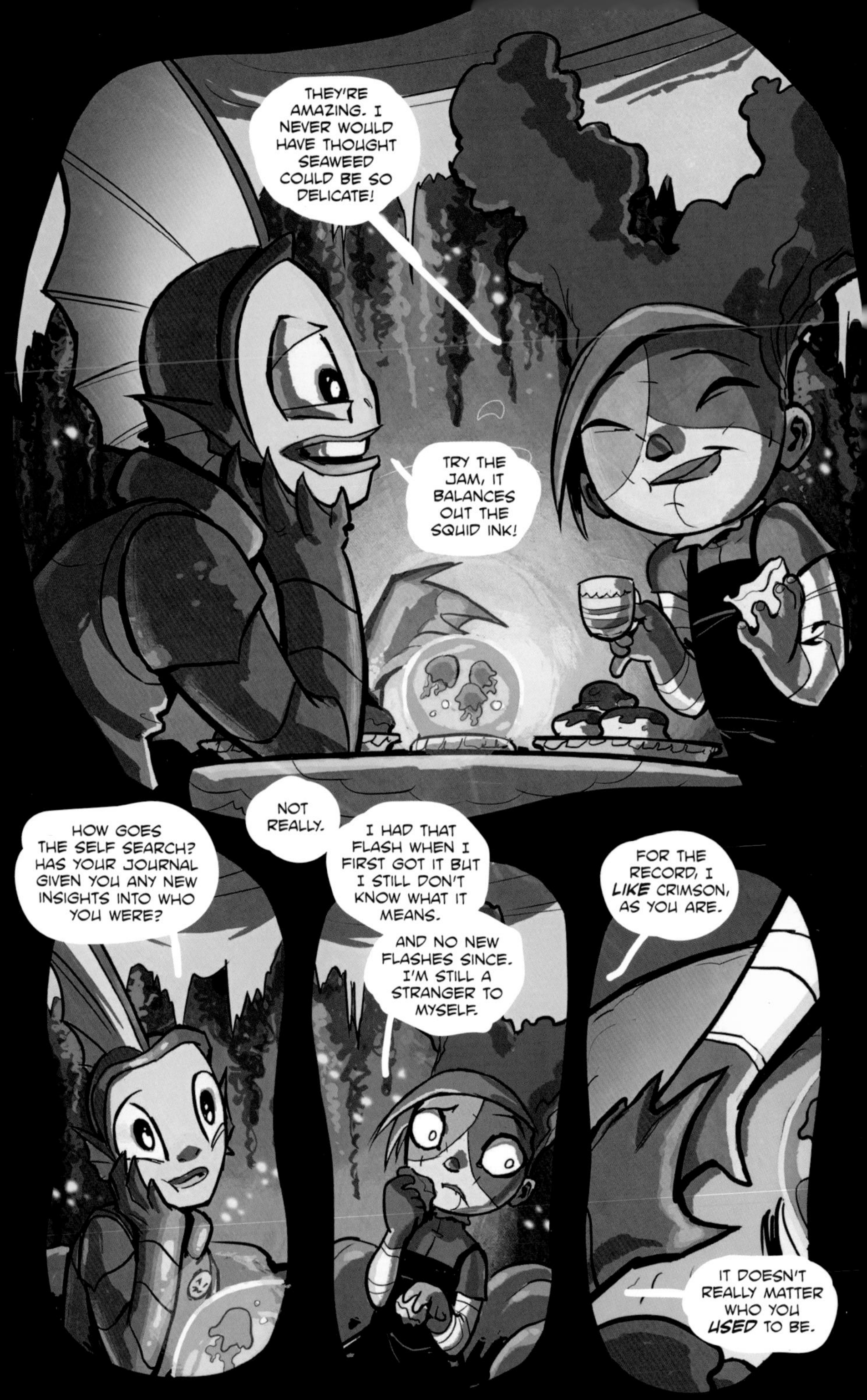
THEY'RE AMAZING. I NEVER WOULD HAVE THOUGHT SEAWEED COULD BE SO DELICATE!
TRY THE JAM, IT BALANCES OUT THE SQUID INK!
HOW GOES THE SELF SEARCH? HAS YOUR JOURNAL GIVEN YOU ANY NEW INSIGHTS INTO WHO YOU WERE?
NOT REALLY.
I HAD THAT FLASH WHEN I FIRST GOT IT BUT I STILL DON'T KNOW WHAT IT MEANS.
AND NO NEW FLASHES SINCE. I'M STILL A STRANGER TO MYSELF.
FOR THE RECORD, I LIKE CRIMSON, AS YOU ARE.
IT DOESN'T REALLY MATTER WHO YOU USED TO BE.

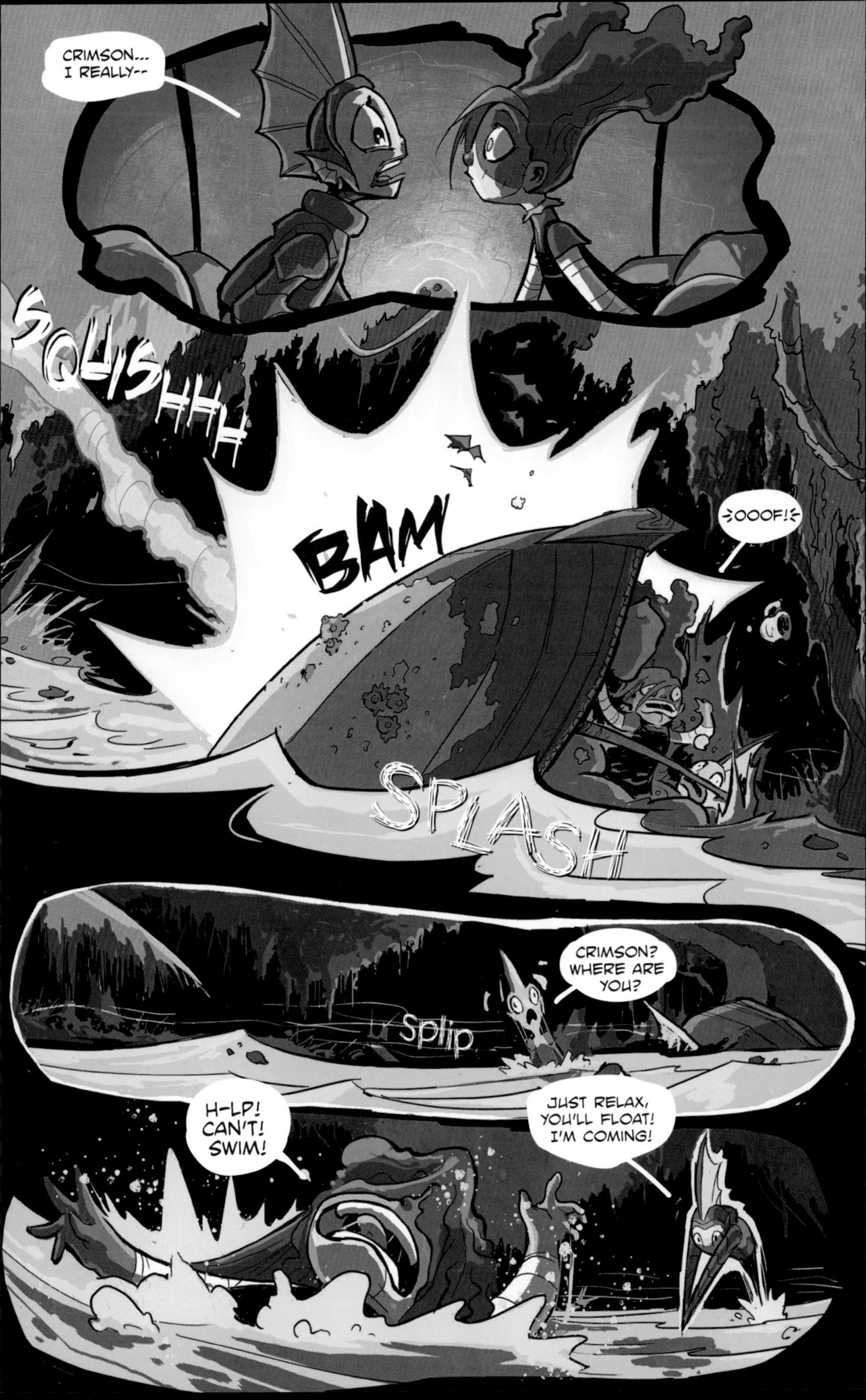
CRIMSON... I REALLY--
SQUISHHH
BAM
OOOF!
SPLASH
CRIMSON? WHERE ARE YOU?
Splip
H-LP! CAN'T! SWIM!
JUST RELAX, YOU'LL FLOAT! I'M COMING!

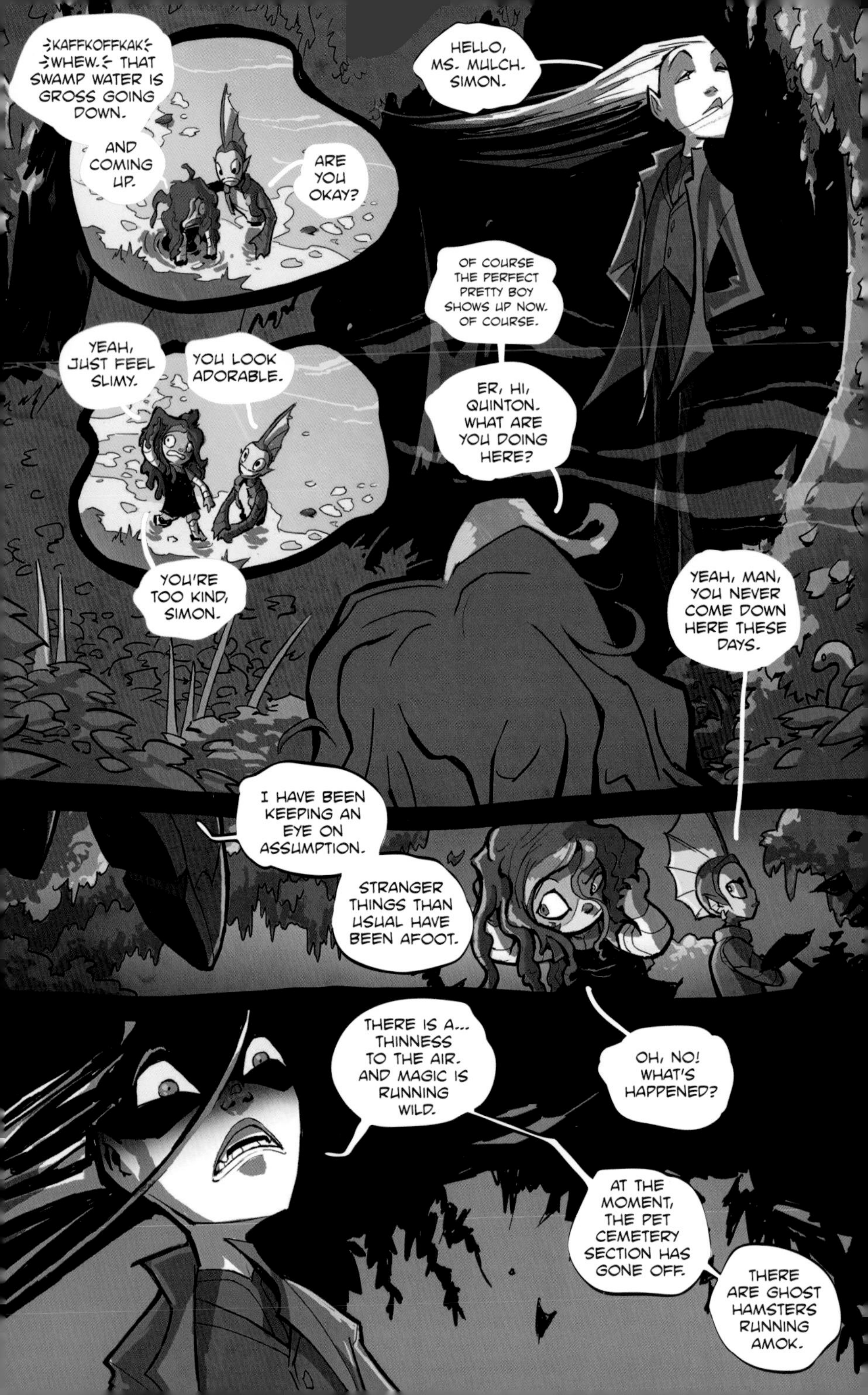

KAFFKOFFKAK WHEW. THAT SWAMP WATER IS GROSS GOING DOWN.
AND COMING UP.
ARE YOU OKAY?
HELLO, MS. MULCH. SIMON.
YEAH, JUST FEEL SLIMY.
YOU LOOK ADORABLE.
YOU'RE TOO KIND, SIMON.
OF COURSE THE PERFECT PRETTY BOY SHOWS UP NOW. OF COURSE.
ER, HI, QUINTON. WHAT ARE YOU DOING HERE?
YEAH, MAN, YOU NEVER COME DOWN HERE THESE DAYS.
I HAVE BEEN KEEPING AN EYE ON ASSUMPTION.
STRANGER THINGS THAN USUAL HAVE BEEN AFOOT.
THERE IS A... THINNESS TO THE AIR. AND MAGIC IS RUNNING WILD.
OH, NO! WHAT'S HAPPENED?
AT THE MOMENT, THE PET CEMETERY SECTION HAS GONE OFF.
THERE ARE GHOST HAMSTERS RUNNING AMOK.

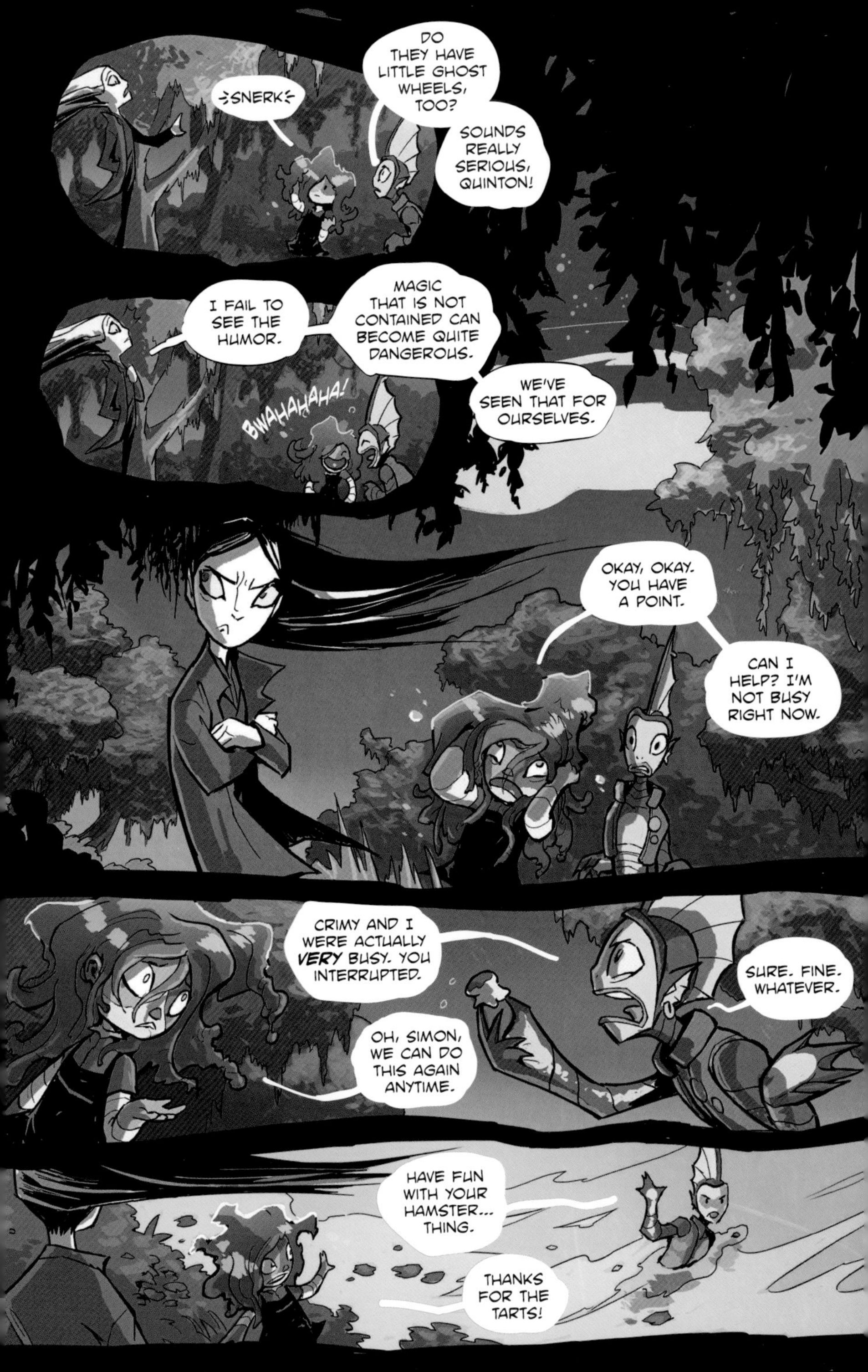

≈SNERK≈
DO THEY HAVE LITTLE GHOST WHEELS, TOO?
SOUNDS REALLY SERIOUS, QUINTON!
I FAIL TO SEE THE HUMOR.
MAGIC THAT IS NOT CONTAINED CAN BECOME QUITE DANGEROUS.
BWAHAHAHA!
WE'VE SEEN THAT FOR OURSELVES.
OKAY, OKAY. YOU HAVE A POINT.
CAN I HELP? I'M NOT BUSY RIGHT NOW.
CRIMY AND I WERE ACTUALLY **VERY** BUSY. YOU INTERRUPTED.
SURE. FINE. WHATEVER.
OH, SIMON, WE CAN DO THIS AGAIN ANYTIME.
HAVE FUN WITH YOUR HAMSTER... THING.
THANKS FOR THE TARTS!

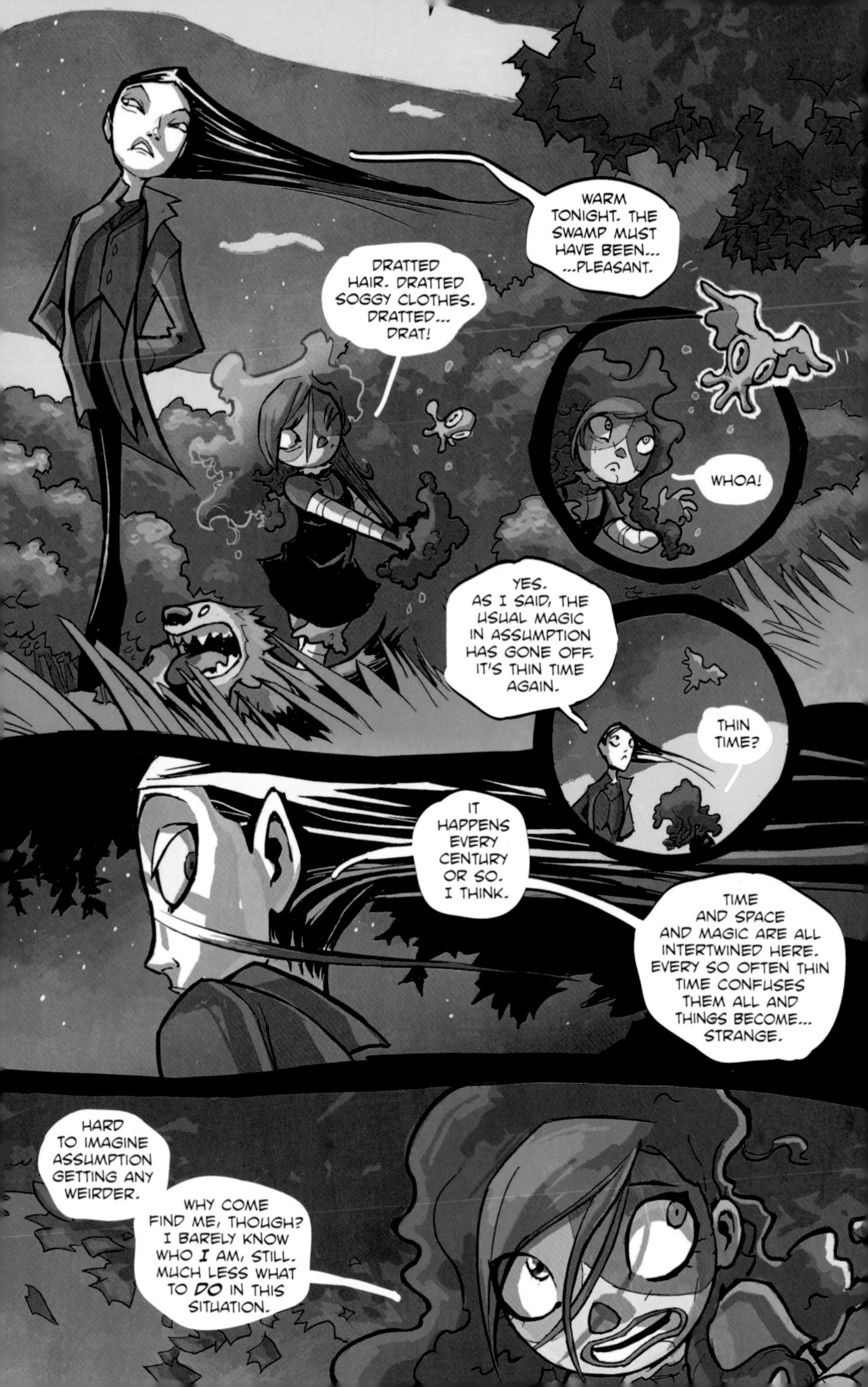
WARM TONIGHT. THE SWAMP MUST HAVE BEEN... ...PLEASANT.
DRATTED HAIR. DRATTED SOGGY CLOTHES. DRATTED... DRAT!
WHOA!
YES. AS I SAID, THE USUAL MAGIC IN ASSUMPTION HAS GONE OFF. IT'S THIN TIME AGAIN.
THIN TIME?
IT HAPPENS EVERY CENTURY OR SO. I THINK.
TIME AND SPACE AND MAGIC ARE ALL INTERTWINED HERE. EVERY SO OFTEN THIN TIME CONFUSES THEM ALL AND THINGS BECOME... STRANGE.
HARD TO IMAGINE ASSUMPTION GETTING ANY WEIRDER.
WHY COME FIND ME, THOUGH? I BARELY KNOW WHO I AM, STILL. MUCH LESS WHAT TO DO IN THIS SITUATION.

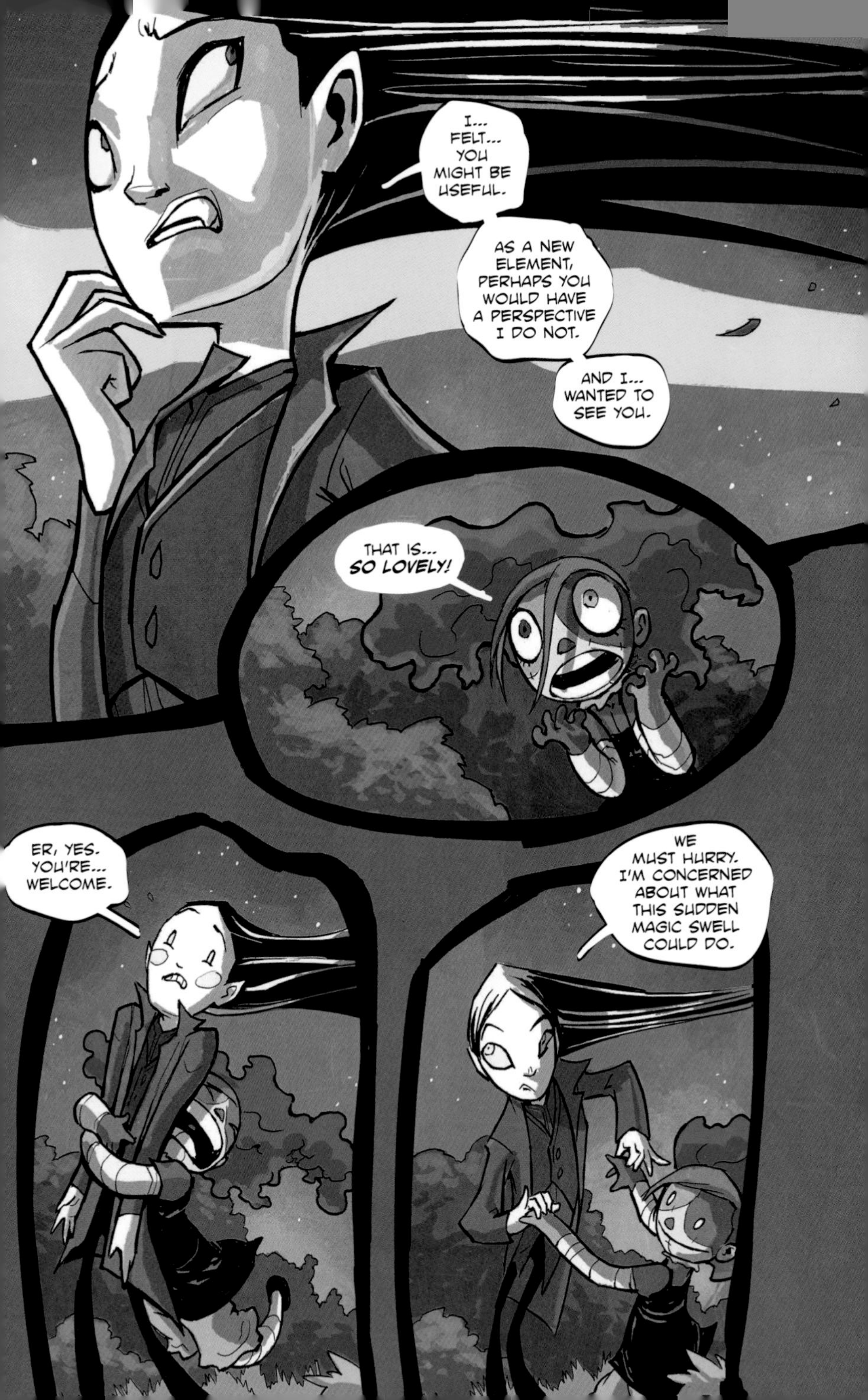
I... FELT... YOU MIGHT BE USEFUL.
AS A NEW ELEMENT, PERHAPS YOU WOULD HAVE A PERSPECTIVE I DO NOT.
AND I... WANTED TO SEE YOU.
THAT IS... **SO LOVELY!**
ER, YES. YOU'RE... WELCOME.
WE MUST HURRY. I'M CONCERNED ABOUT WHAT THIS SUDDEN MAGIC SWELL COULD DO.

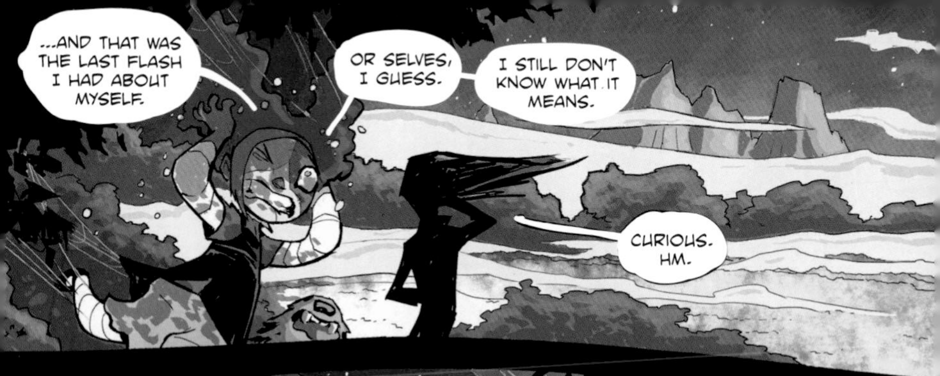
...AND THAT WAS THE LAST FLASH I HAD ABOUT MYSELF.
OR SELVES, I GUESS.
I STILL DON'T KNOW WHAT IT MEANS.
CURIOUS. HM.

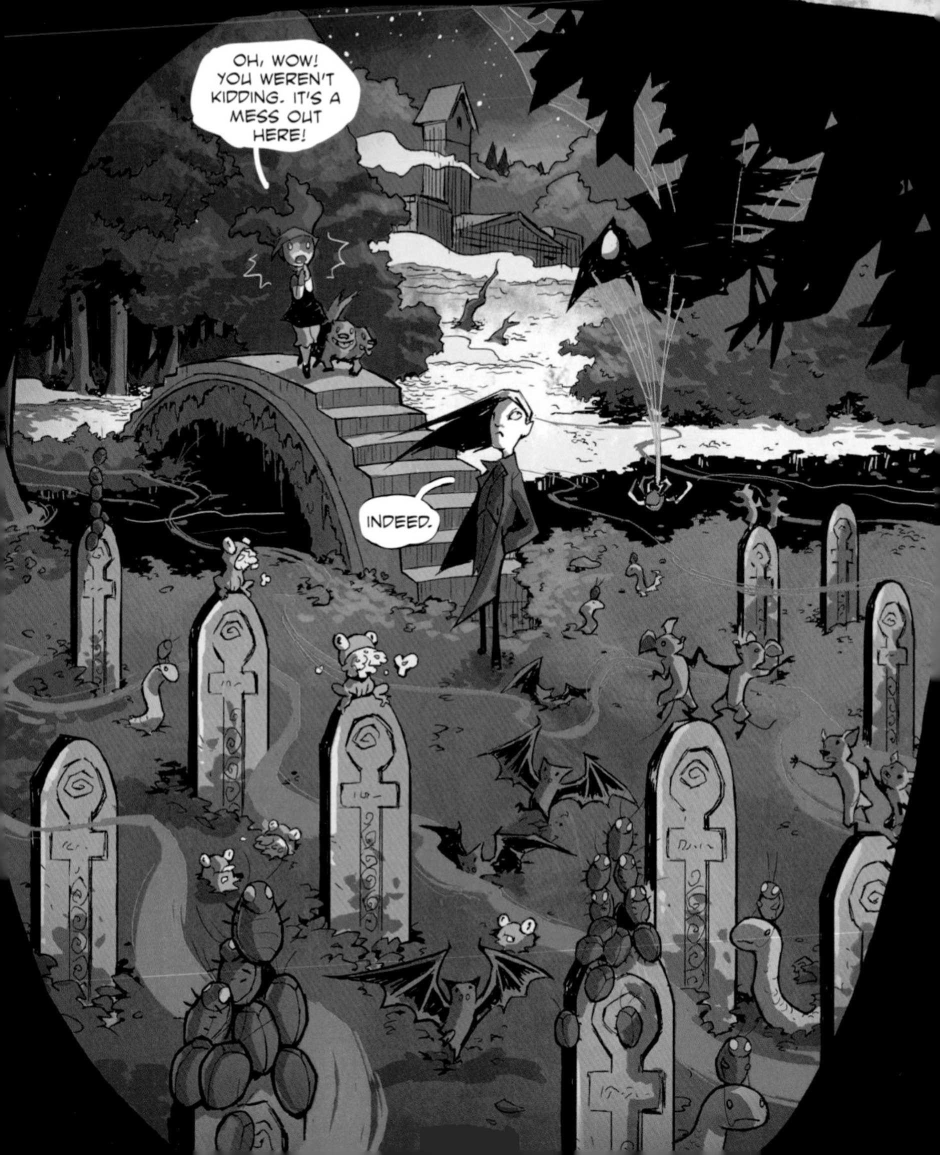
OH, WOW! YOU WEREN'T KIDDING. IT'S A MESS OUT HERE!
INDEED.

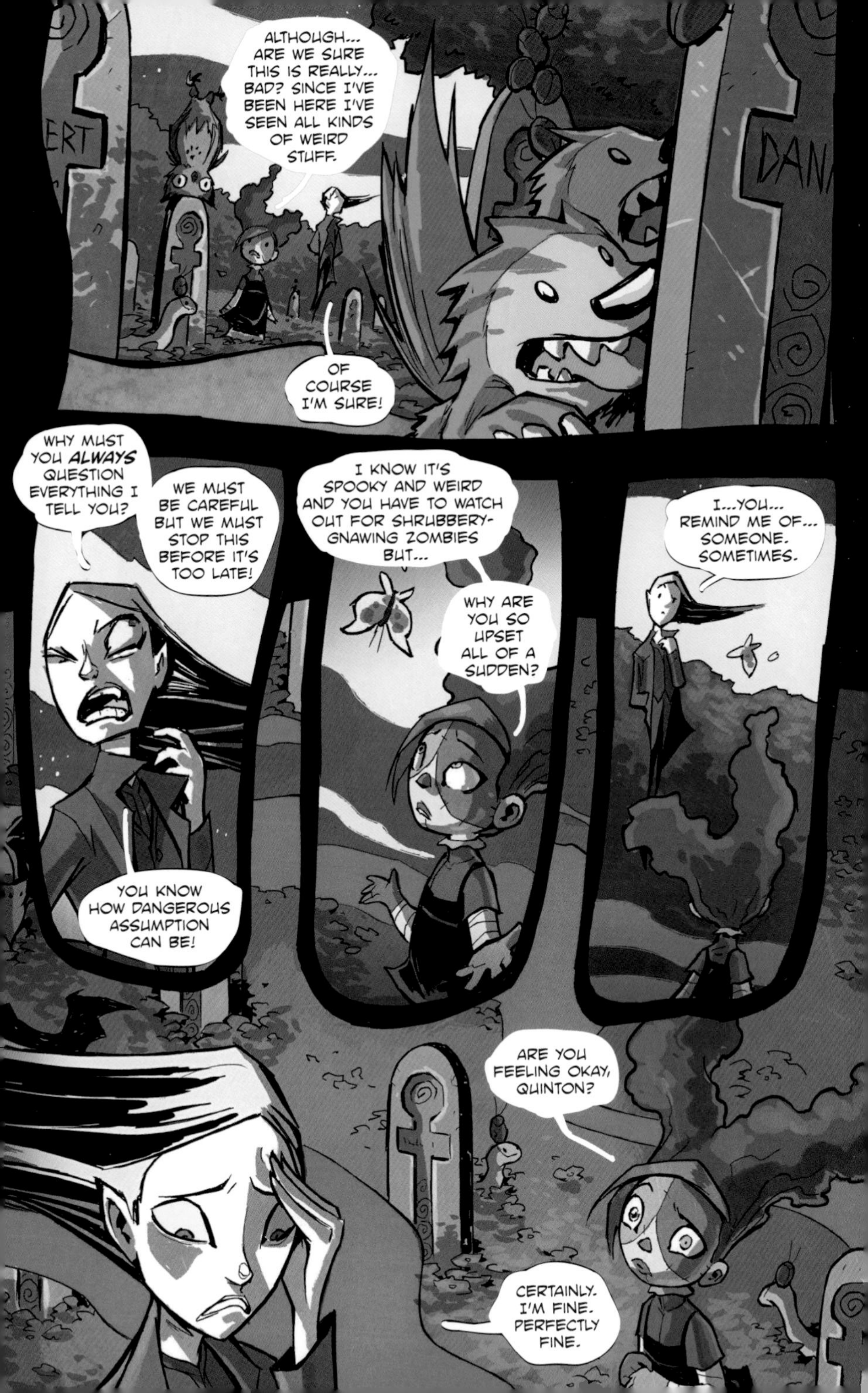
ALTHOUGH... ARE WE SURE THIS IS REALLY... BAD? SINCE I'VE BEEN HERE I'VE SEEN ALL KINDS OF WEIRD STUFF.
OF COURSE I'M SURE!
WHY MUST YOU **ALWAYS** QUESTION EVERYTHING I TELL YOU?
WE MUST BE CAREFUL BUT WE MUST STOP THIS BEFORE IT'S TOO LATE!
YOU KNOW HOW DANGEROUS ASSUMPTION CAN BE!
I KNOW IT'S SPOOKY AND WEIRD AND YOU HAVE TO WATCH OUT FOR SHRUBBERY-GNAWING ZOMBIES BUT...
WHY ARE YOU SO UPSET ALL OF A SUDDEN?
I...YOU... REMIND ME OF... SOMEONE. SOMETIMES.
ARE YOU FEELING OKAY, QUINTON?
CERTAINLY. I'M FINE. PERFECTLY FINE.

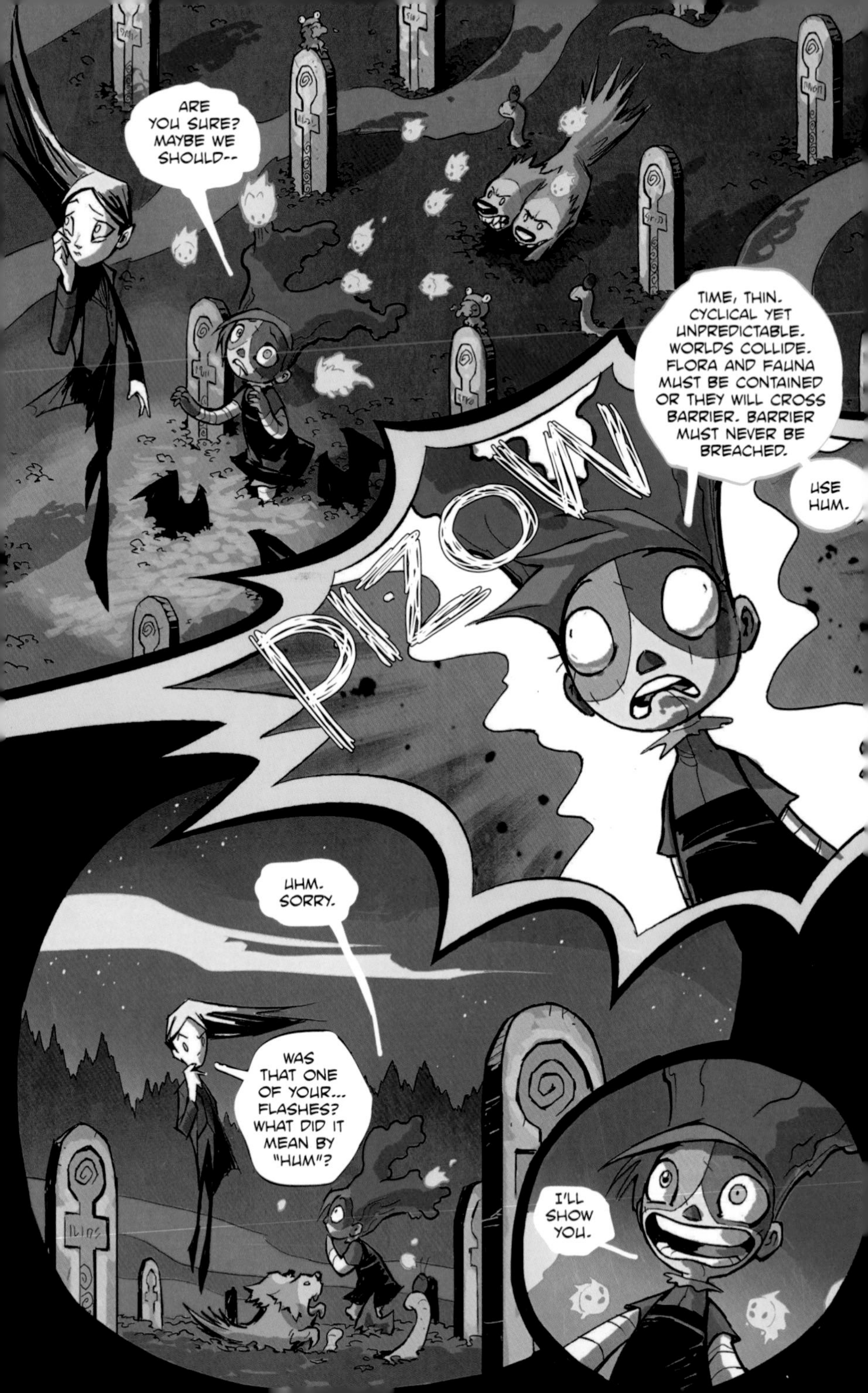
ARE YOU SURE? MAYBE WE SHOULD--
TIME, THIN. CYCLICAL YET UNPREDICTABLE. WORLDS COLLIDE. FLORA AND FAUNA MUST BE CONTAINED OR THEY WILL CROSS BARRIER. BARRIER MUST NEVER BE BREACHED.
USE HUM.
PIZOW
UHM. SORRY.
WAS THAT ONE OF YOUR... FLASHES? WHAT DID IT MEAN BY "HUM"?
I'LL SHOW YOU.

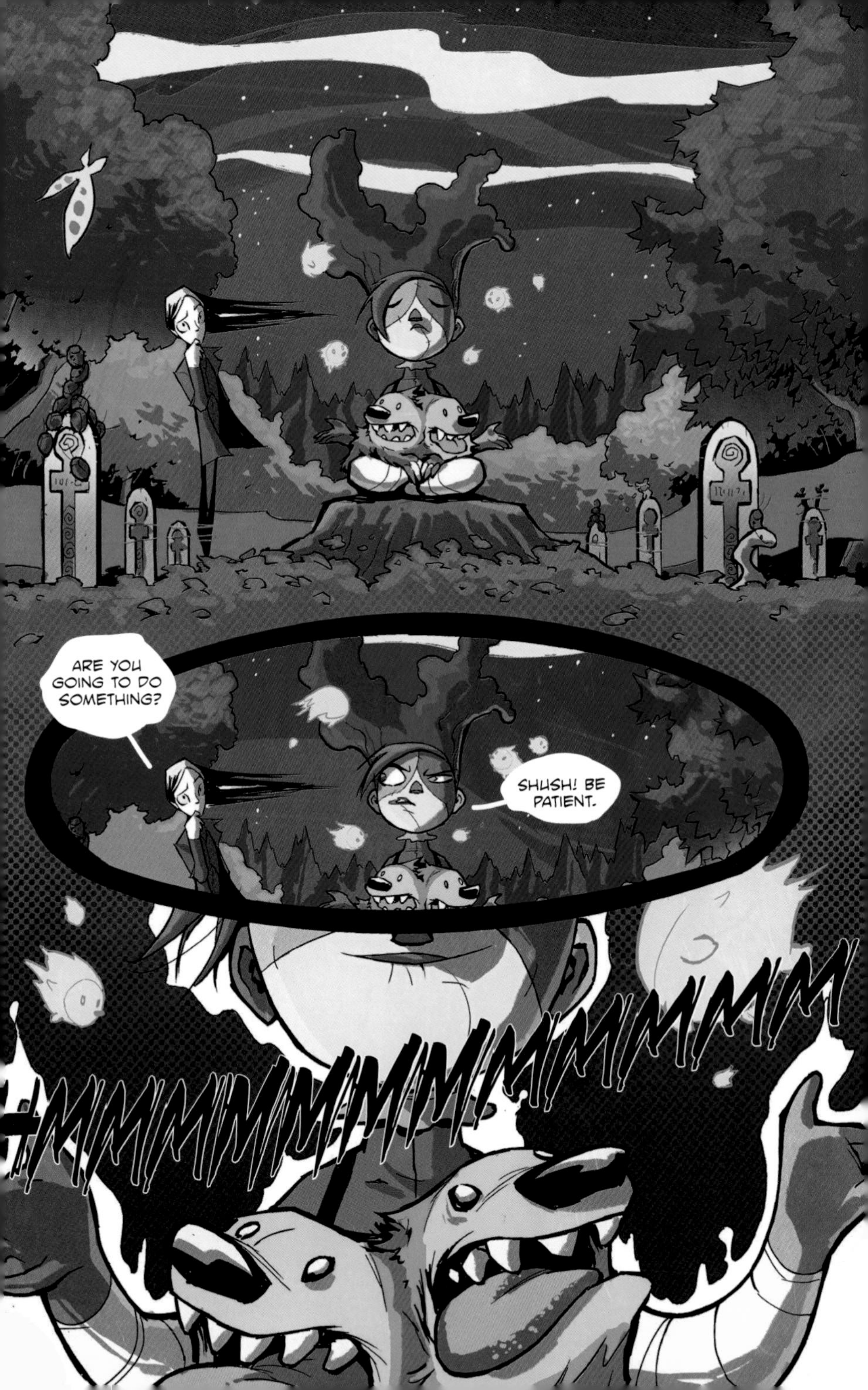
ARE YOU GOING TO DO SOMETHING?
SHUSH! BE PATIENT.
HMMMMMMMMMMMMMMMMMMM

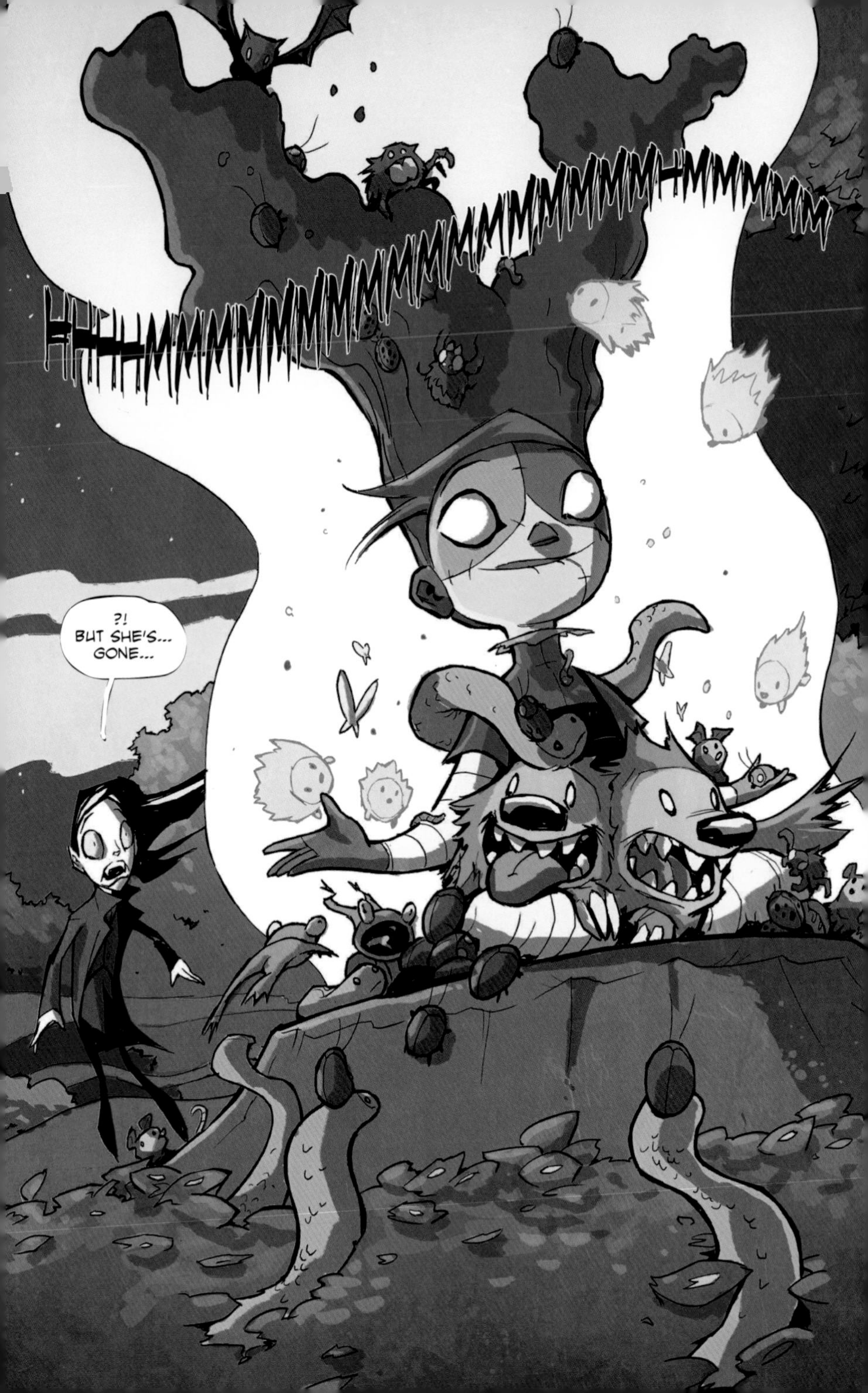
HHHMMMMMMMMMMMMMMMMMMMMMMMM-MMMMMM
?!
BUT SHE'S...
GONE...

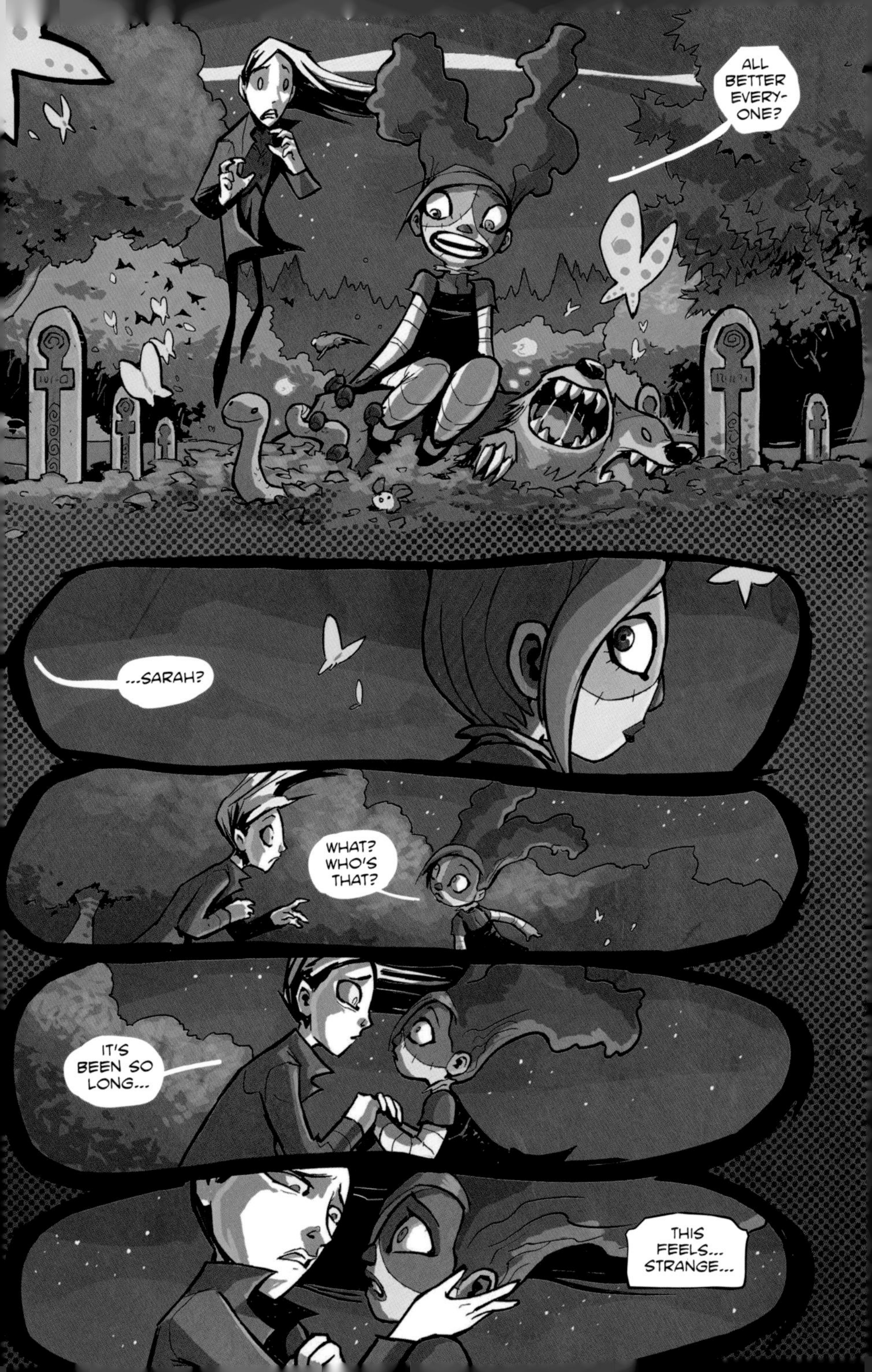
ALL BETTER EVERY-ONE?
...SARAH?
WHAT? WHO'S THAT?
IT'S BEEN SO LONG...
THIS FEELS... STRANGE...

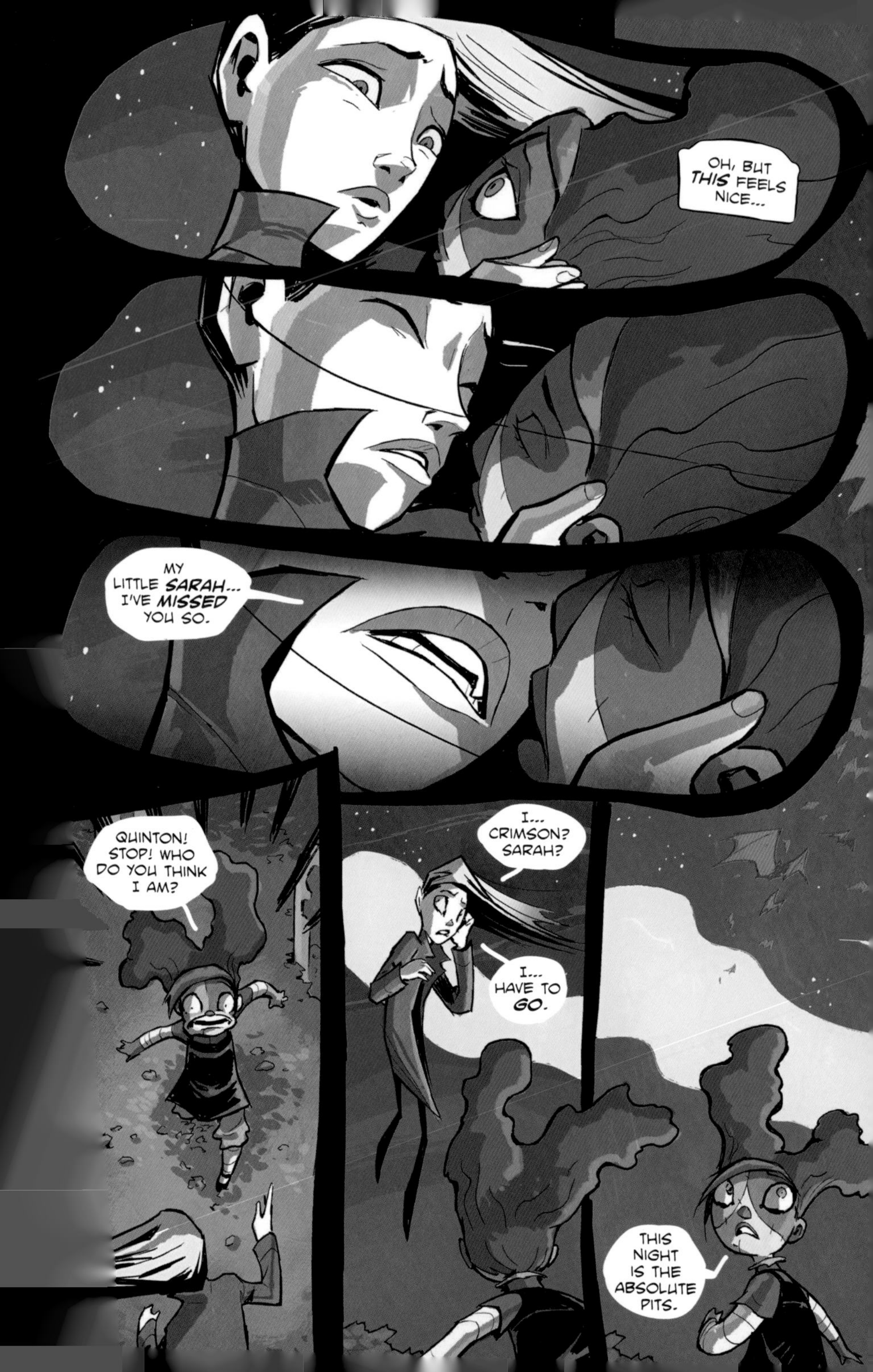
OH, BUT THIS FEELS NICE...
MY LITTLE SARAH... I'VE MISSED YOU SO.
QUINTON! STOP! WHO DO YOU THINK I AM?
I... CRIMSON? SARAH?
I... HAVE TO GO.
THIS NIGHT IS THE ABSOLUTE PITS.

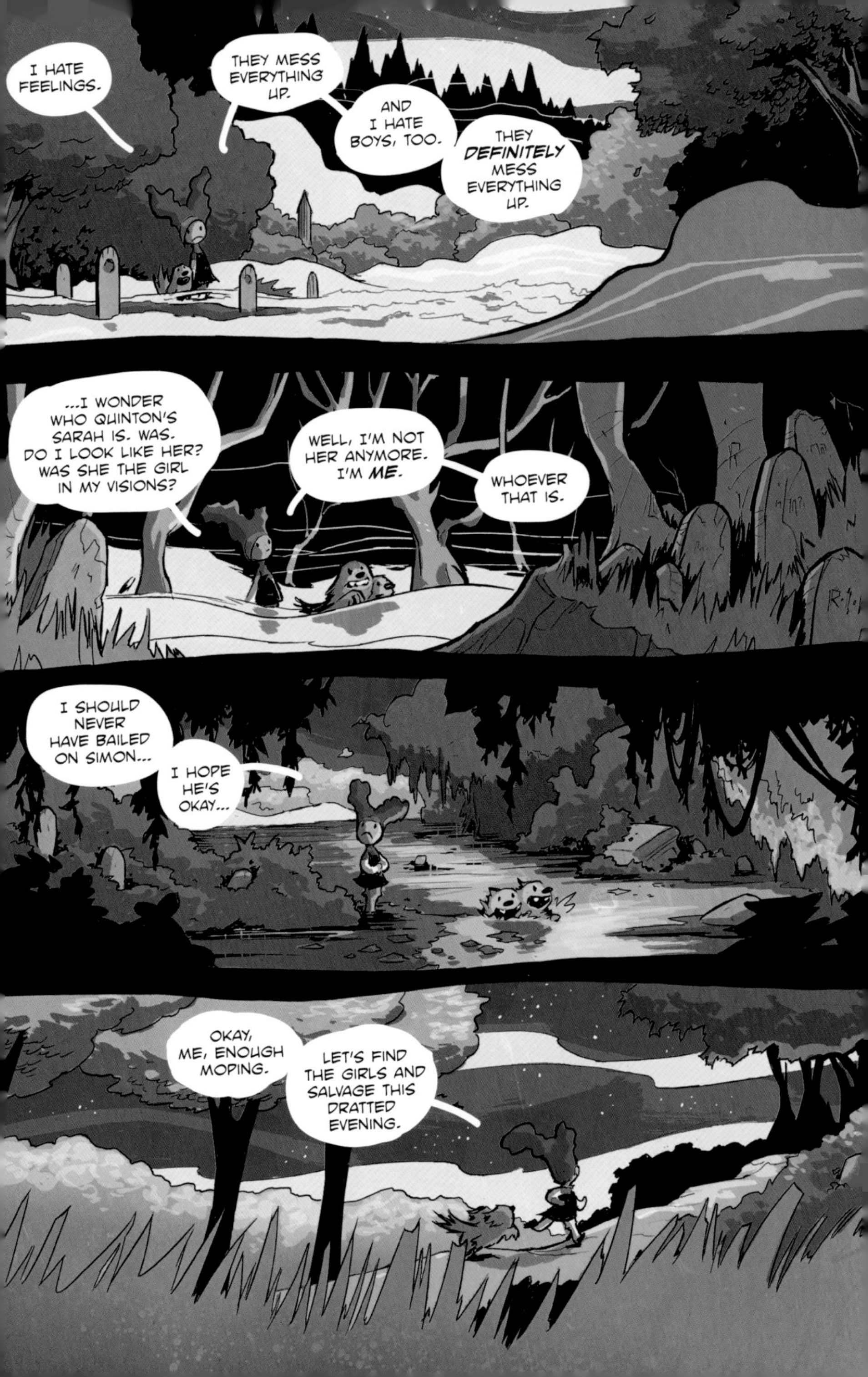
I HATE FEELINGS.
THEY MESS EVERYTHING UP.
AND I HATE BOYS, TOO.
THEY *DEFINITELY* MESS EVERYTHING UP.
...I WONDER WHO QUINTON'S SARAH IS. WAS. DO I LOOK LIKE HER? WAS SHE THE GIRL IN MY VISIONS?
WELL, I'M NOT HER ANYMORE. I'M **ME**.
WHOEVER THAT IS.
I SHOULD NEVER HAVE BAILED ON SIMON...
I HOPE HE'S OKAY...
OKAY, ME, ENOUGH MOPING.
LET'S FIND THE GIRLS AND SALVAGE THIS DRATTED EVENING.

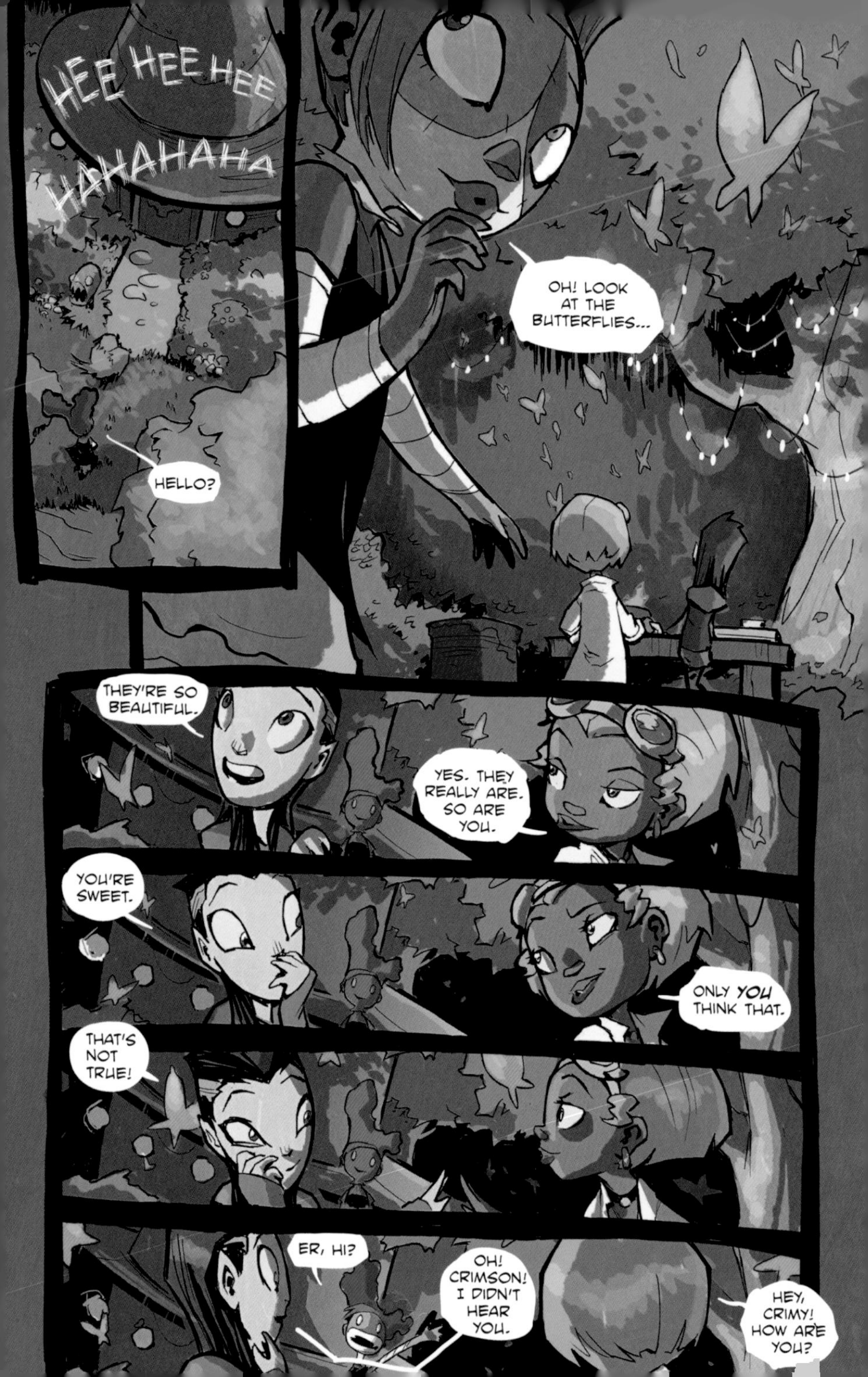
HEE HEE HEE
HAHAHAHA
HELLO?
OH! LOOK AT THE BUTTERFLIES...
THEY'RE SO BEAUTIFUL.
YES. THEY REALLY ARE. SO ARE YOU.
YOU'RE SWEET.
ONLY YOU THINK THAT.
THAT'S NOT TRUE!
ER, HI?
OH! CRIMSON! I DIDN'T HEAR YOU.
HEY, CRIMY! HOW ARE YOU?

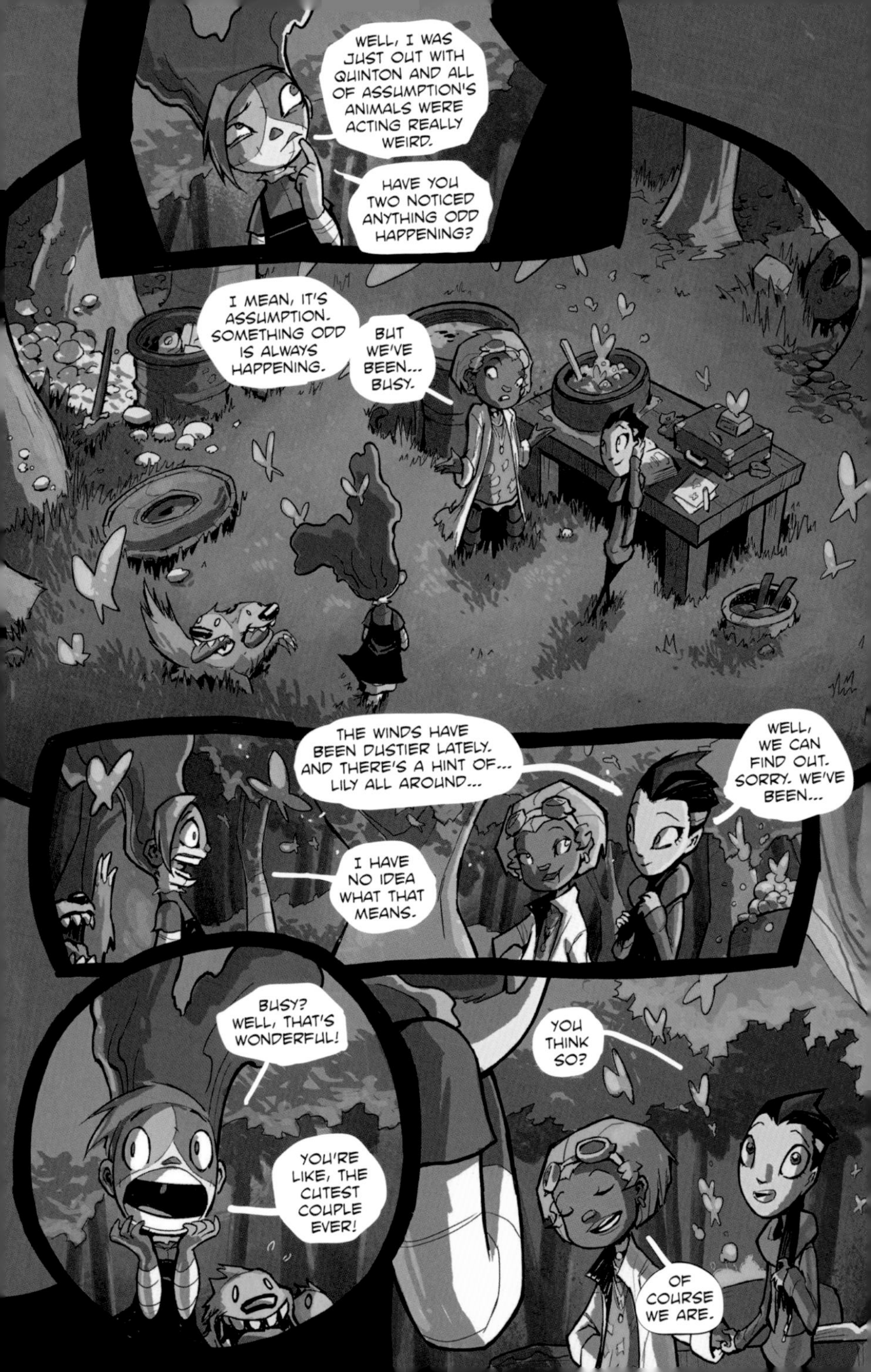
WELL, I WAS JUST OUT WITH QUINTON AND ALL OF ASSUMPTION'S ANIMALS WERE ACTING REALLY WEIRD.
HAVE YOU TWO NOTICED ANYTHING ODD HAPPENING?
I MEAN, IT'S ASSUMPTION. SOMETHING ODD IS ALWAYS HAPPENING.
BUT WE'VE BEEN... BUSY.
THE WINDS HAVE BEEN DUSTIER LATELY. AND THERE'S A HINT OF... LILY ALL AROUND...
WELL, WE CAN FIND OUT. SORRY. WE'VE BEEN...
I HAVE NO IDEA WHAT THAT MEANS.
BUSY? WELL, THAT'S WONDERFUL!
YOU'RE LIKE, THE CUTEST COUPLE EVER!
YOU THINK SO?
OF COURSE WE ARE.

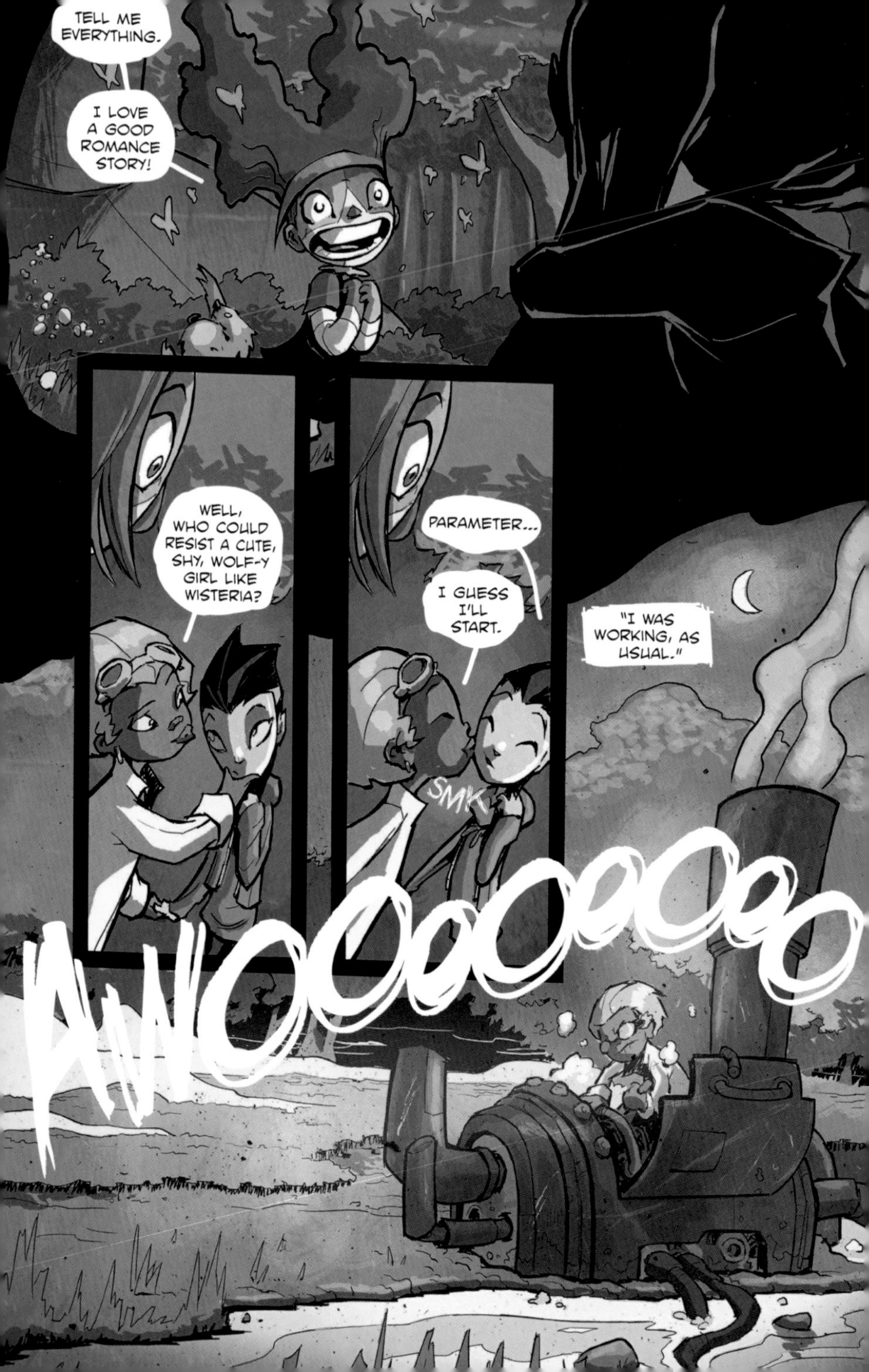

TELL ME EVERYTHING.
I LOVE A GOOD ROMANCE STORY!
WELL, WHO COULD RESIST A CUTE, SHY, WOLF-Y GIRL LIKE WISTERIA?
PARAMETER...
I GUESS I'LL START.
SMK
"I WAS WORKING, AS USUAL."
AWOOOOOOOOO

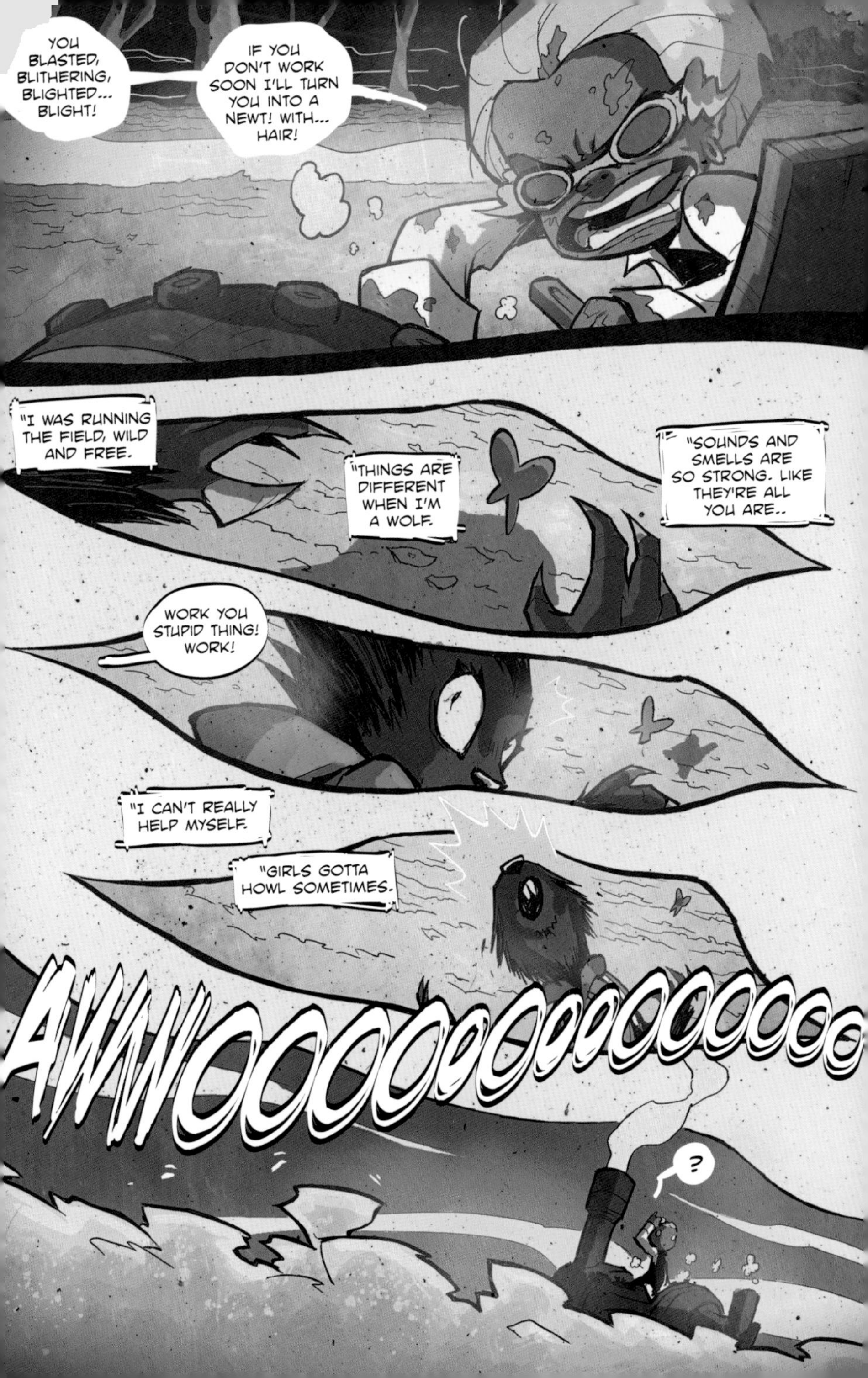
YOU BLASTED, BLITHERING, BLIGHTED... BLIGHT!
IF YOU DON'T WORK SOON I'LL TURN YOU INTO A NEWT! WITH... HAIR!
"I WAS RUNNING THE FIELD, WILD AND FREE.
"THINGS ARE DIFFERENT WHEN I'M A WOLF.
"SOUNDS AND SMELLS ARE SO STRONG. LIKE THEY'RE ALL YOU ARE..
WORK YOU STUPID THING! WORK!
"I CAN'T REALLY HELP MYSELF.
"GIRLS GOTTA HOWL SOMETIMES.
AWWOOOOOOOOOOOOOOOOO
?

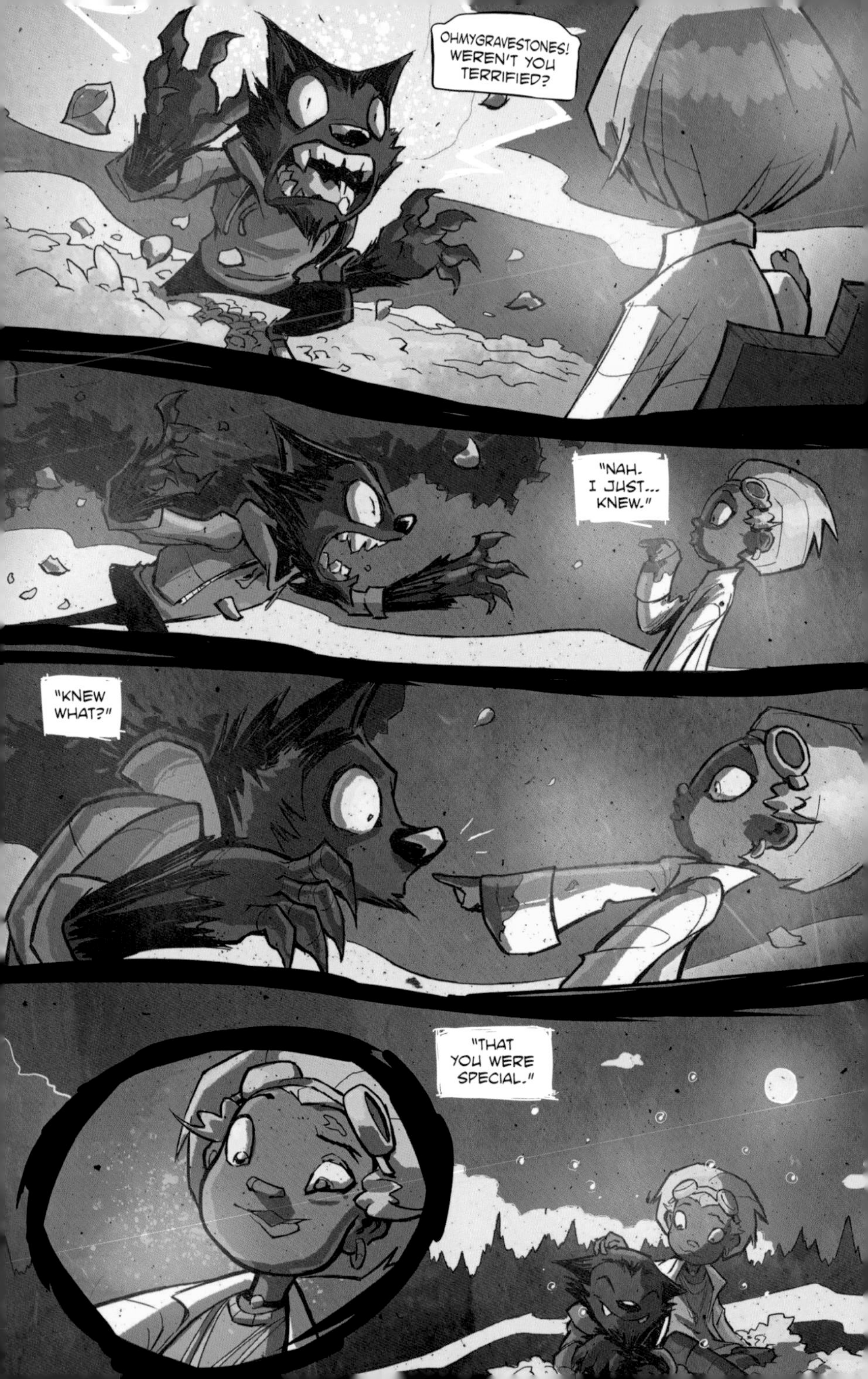
OHMYGRAVESTONES! WEREN'T YOU TERRIFIED?
"NAH. I JUST... KNEW."
"KNEW WHAT?"
"THAT YOU WERE SPECIAL."

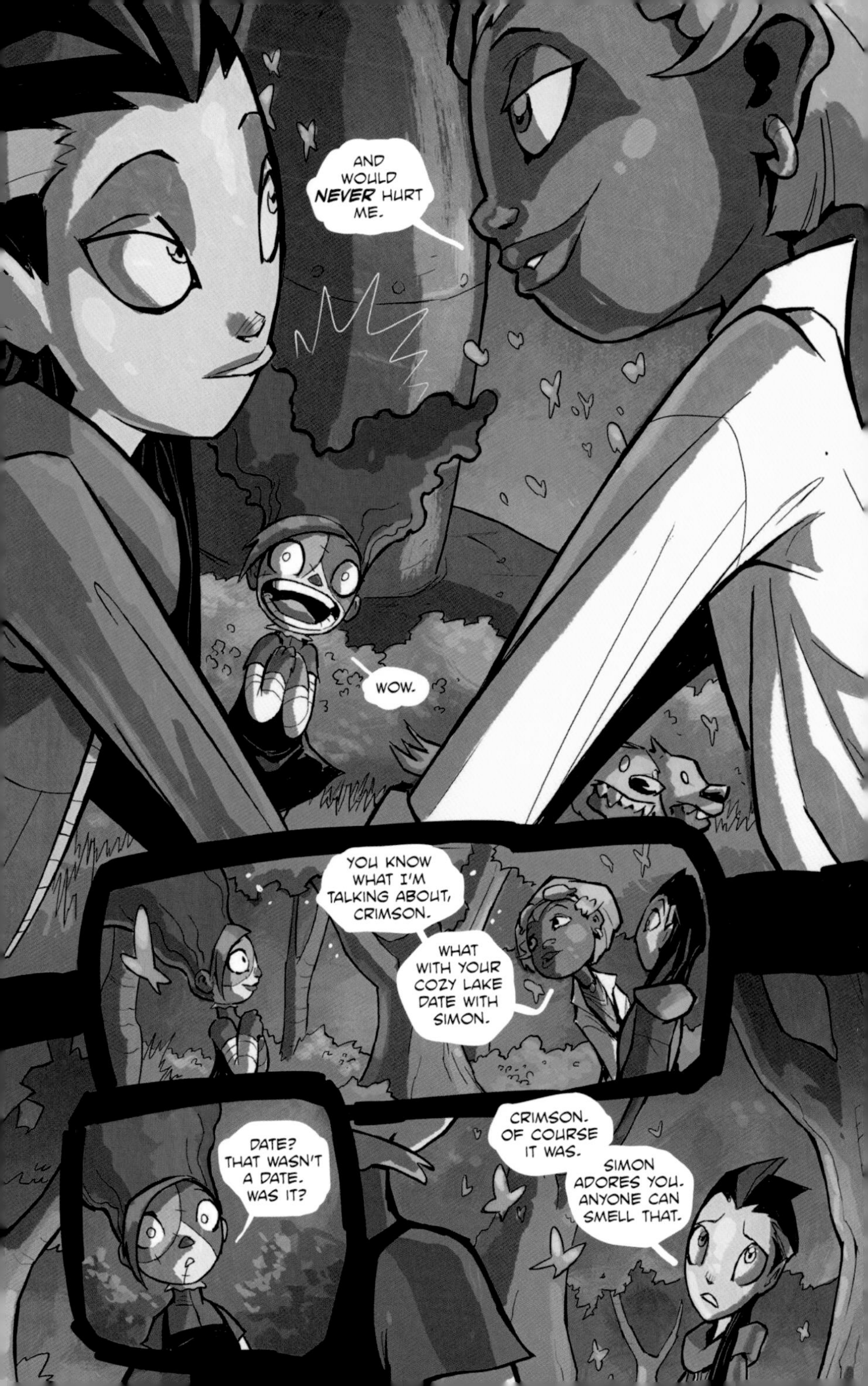
AND WOULD NEVER HURT ME.
WOW.
YOU KNOW WHAT I'M TALKING ABOUT, CRIMSON.
WHAT WITH YOUR COZY LAKE DATE WITH SIMON.
DATE? THAT WASN'T A DATE. WAS IT?
CRIMSON. OF COURSE IT WAS.
SIMON ADORES YOU. ANYONE CAN SMELL THAT.

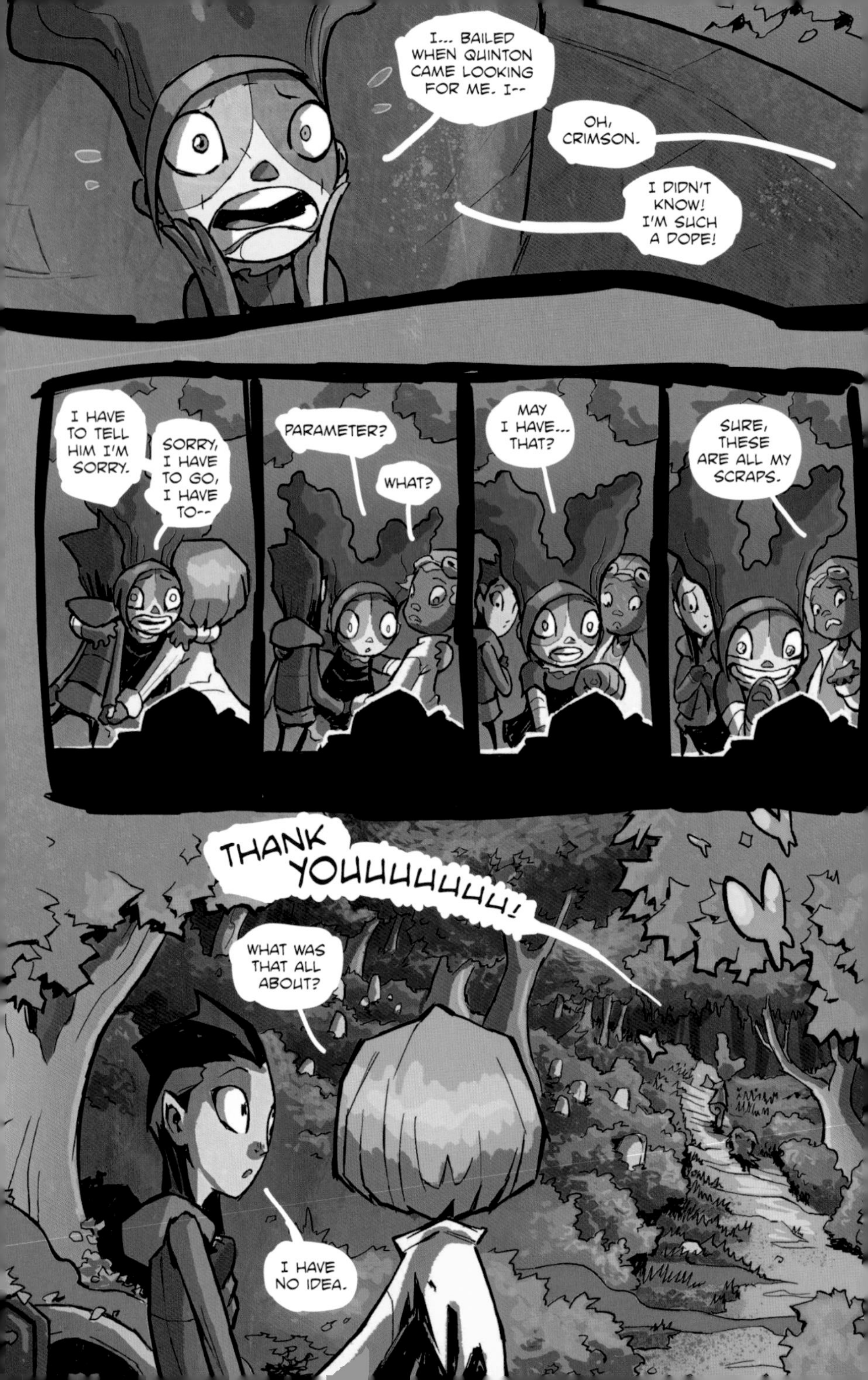
I... BAILED WHEN QUINTON CAME LOOKING FOR ME. I--
OH, CRIMSON.
I DIDN'T KNOW! I'M SUCH A DOPE!
I HAVE TO TELL HIM I'M SORRY.
SORRY, I HAVE TO GO, I HAVE TO--
PARAMETER?
WHAT?
MAY I HAVE... THAT?
SURE, THESE ARE ALL MY SCRAPS.
THANK YOUUUUUUU!
WHAT WAS THAT ALL ABOUT?
I HAVE NO IDEA.

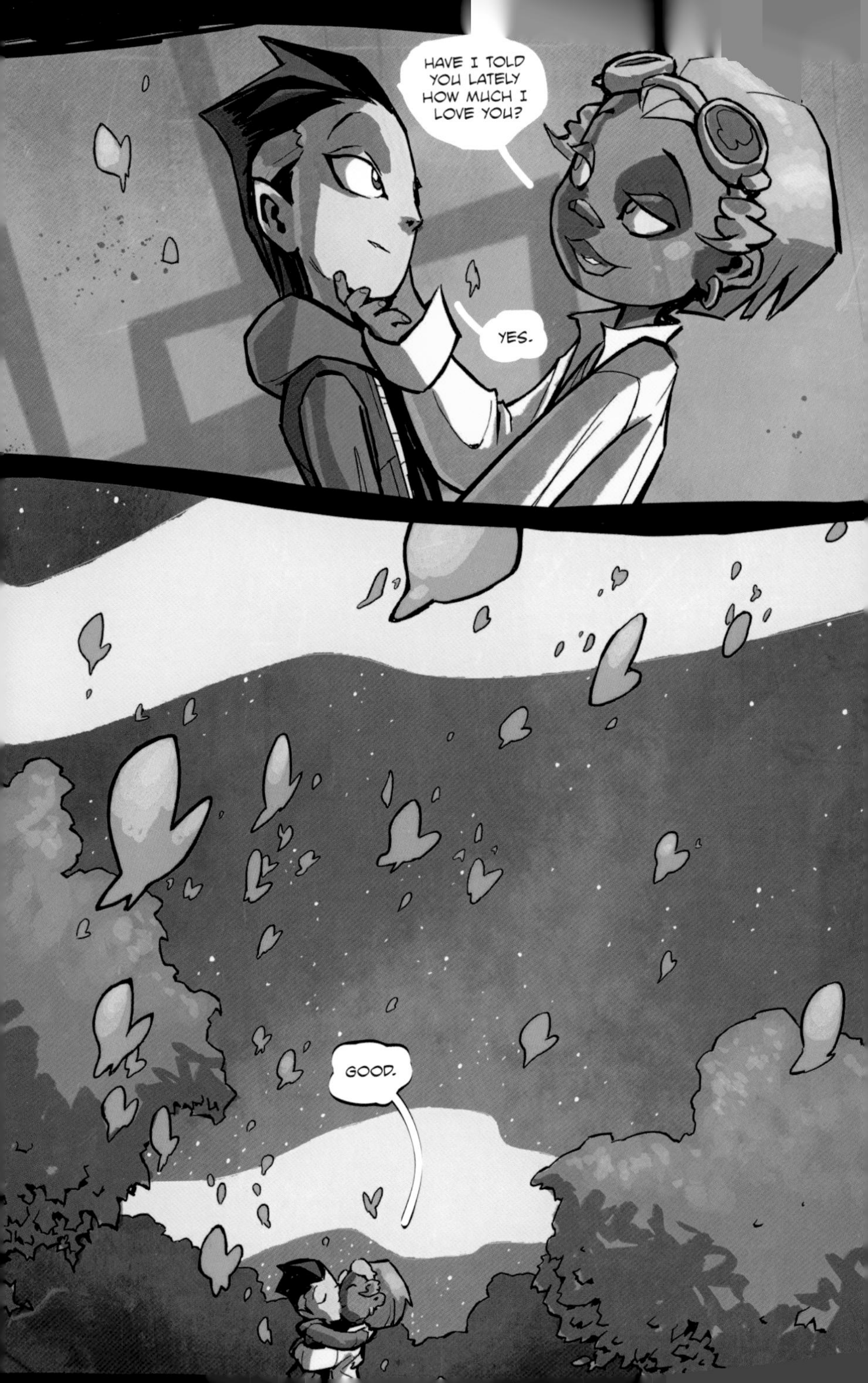
HAVE I TOLD YOU LATELY HOW MUCH I LOVE YOU?
YES.
GOOD.

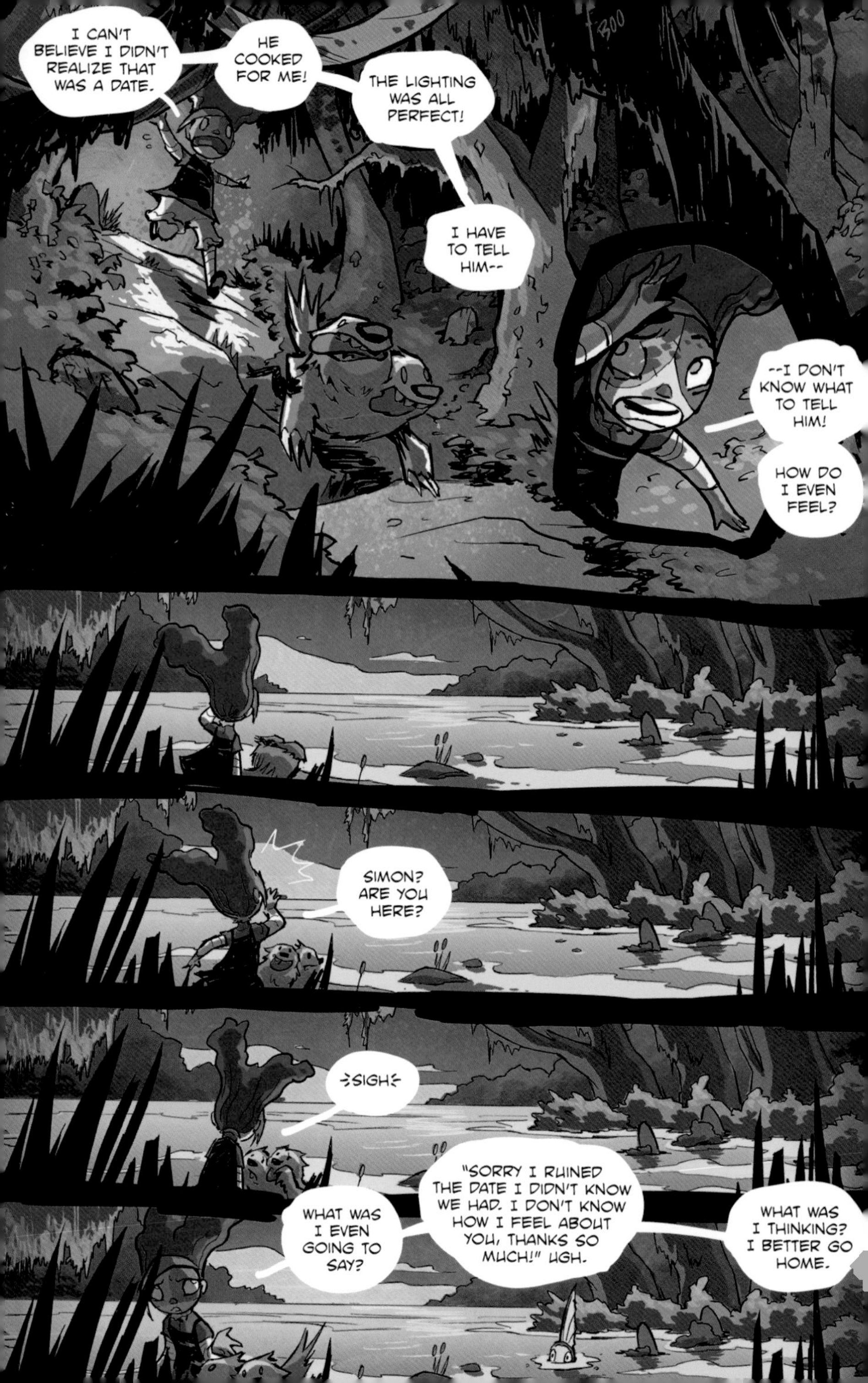
I CAN'T BELIEVE I DIDN'T REALIZE THAT WAS A DATE.
HE COOKED FOR ME!
THE LIGHTING WAS ALL PERFECT!
I HAVE TO TELL HIM--
--I DON'T KNOW WHAT TO TELL HIM!
HOW DO I EVEN FEEL?
SIMON? ARE YOU HERE?
-SIGH-
WHAT WAS I EVEN GOING TO SAY?
"SORRY I RUINED THE DATE I DIDN'T KNOW WE HAD. I DON'T KNOW HOW I FEEL ABOUT YOU, THANKS SO MUCH!" UGH.
WHAT WAS I THINKING? I BETTER GO HOME.

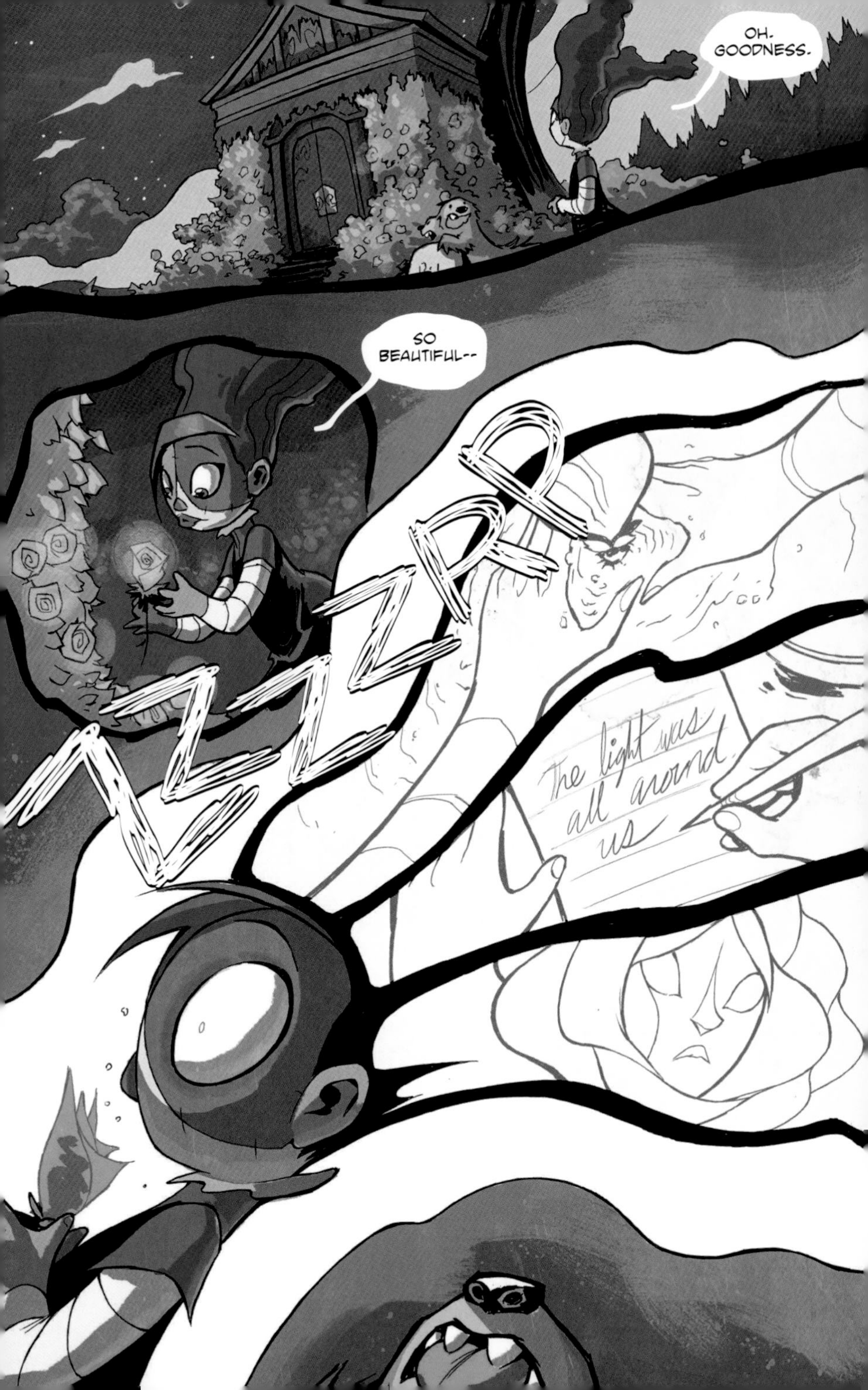

OH. GOODNESS.
SO BEAUTIFUL--
ZZZZZAP
The light was all around us

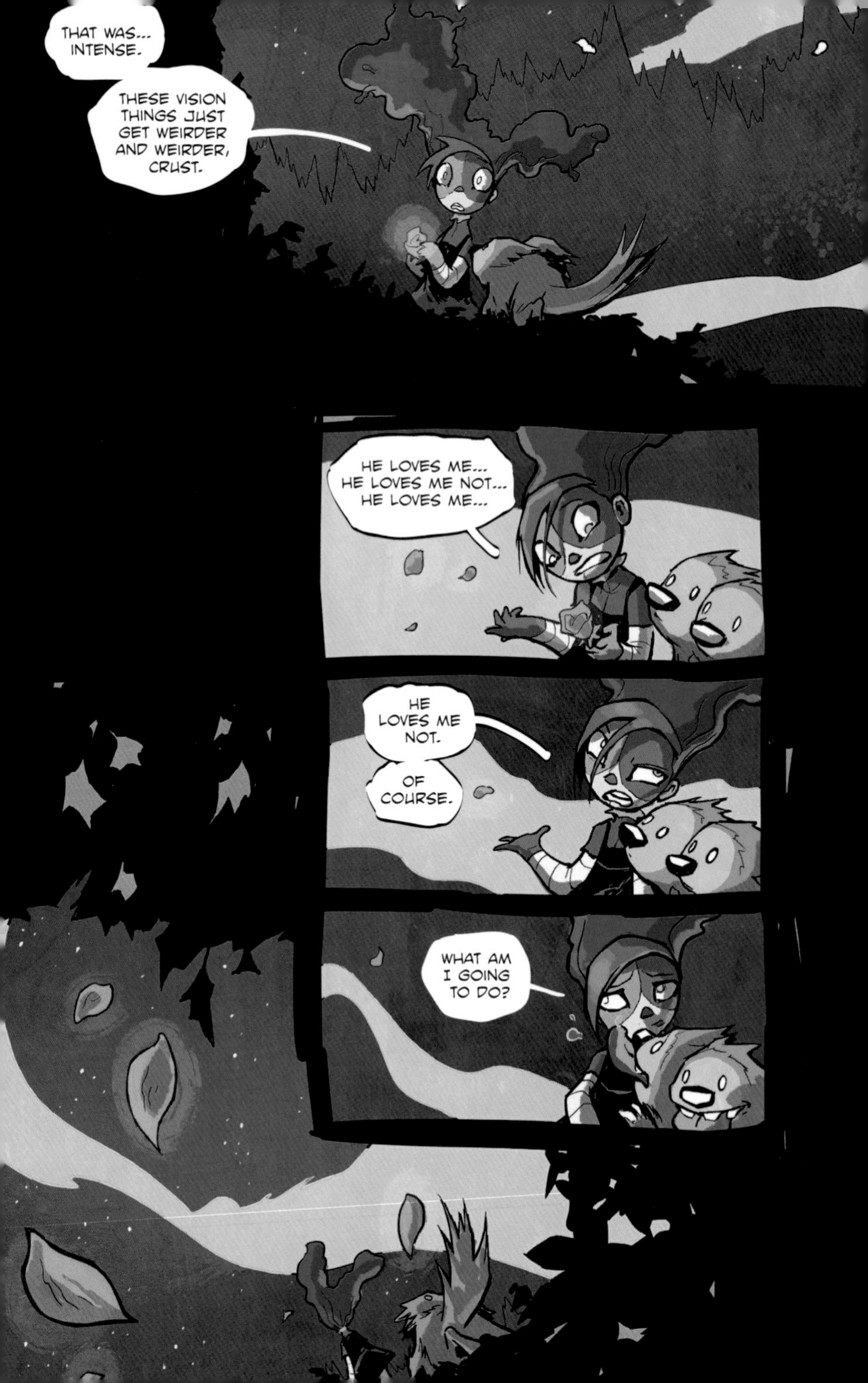
THAT WAS... INTENSE.
THESE VISION THINGS JUST GET WEIRDER AND WEIRDER, CRUST.
HE LOVES ME... HE LOVES ME NOT... HE LOVES ME...
HE LOVES ME NOT.
OF COURSE.
WHAT AM I GOING TO DO?

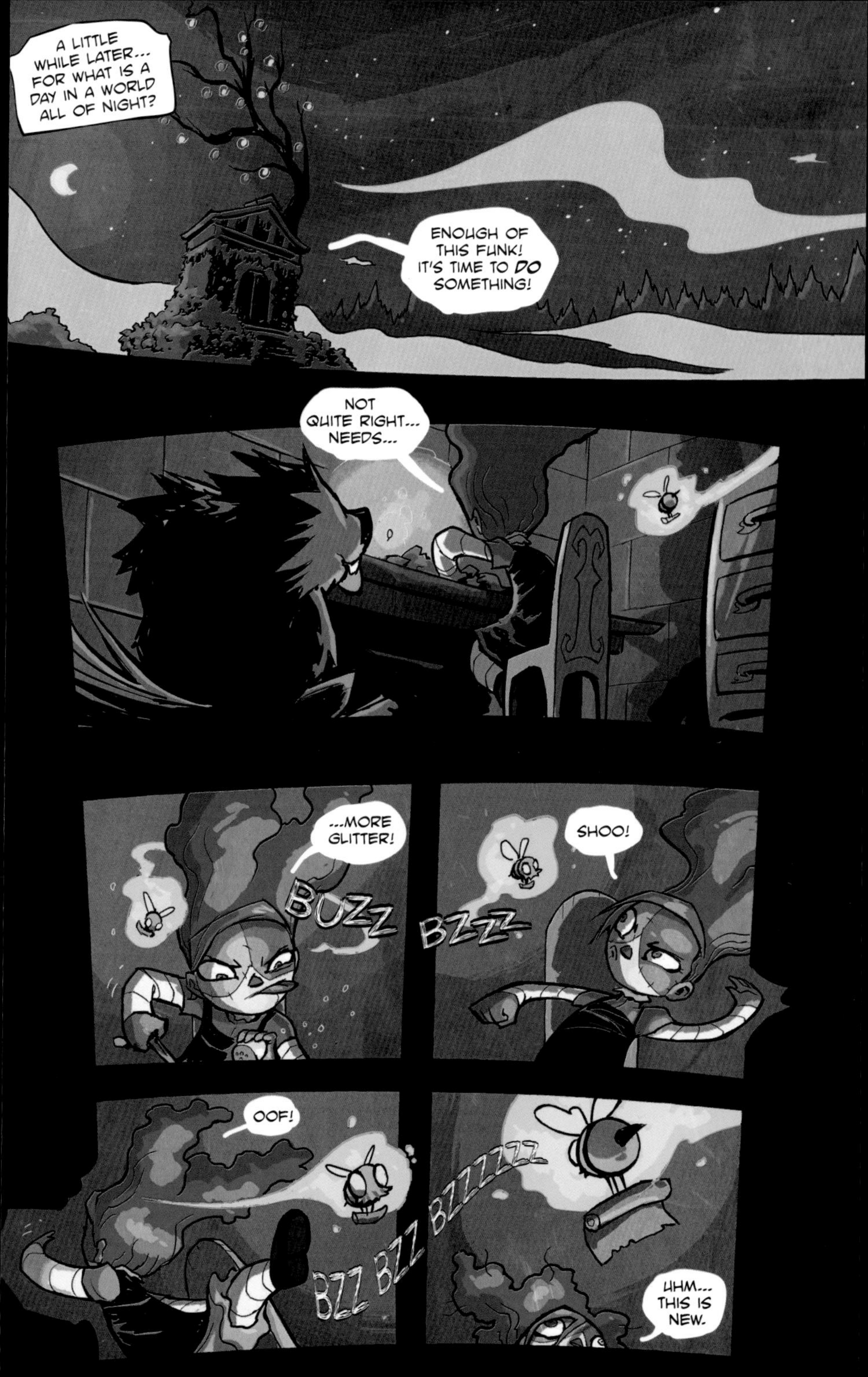
A LITTLE WHILE LATER... FOR WHAT IS A DAY IN A WORLD ALL OF NIGHT?
ENOUGH OF THIS FUNK! IT'S TIME TO *DO* SOMETHING!
NOT QUITE RIGHT... NEEDS...
...MORE GLITTER!
BUZZ
BZZZ
SHOO!
OOF!
BZZ BZZ BZZZZZZZ
UHM... THIS IS NEW.

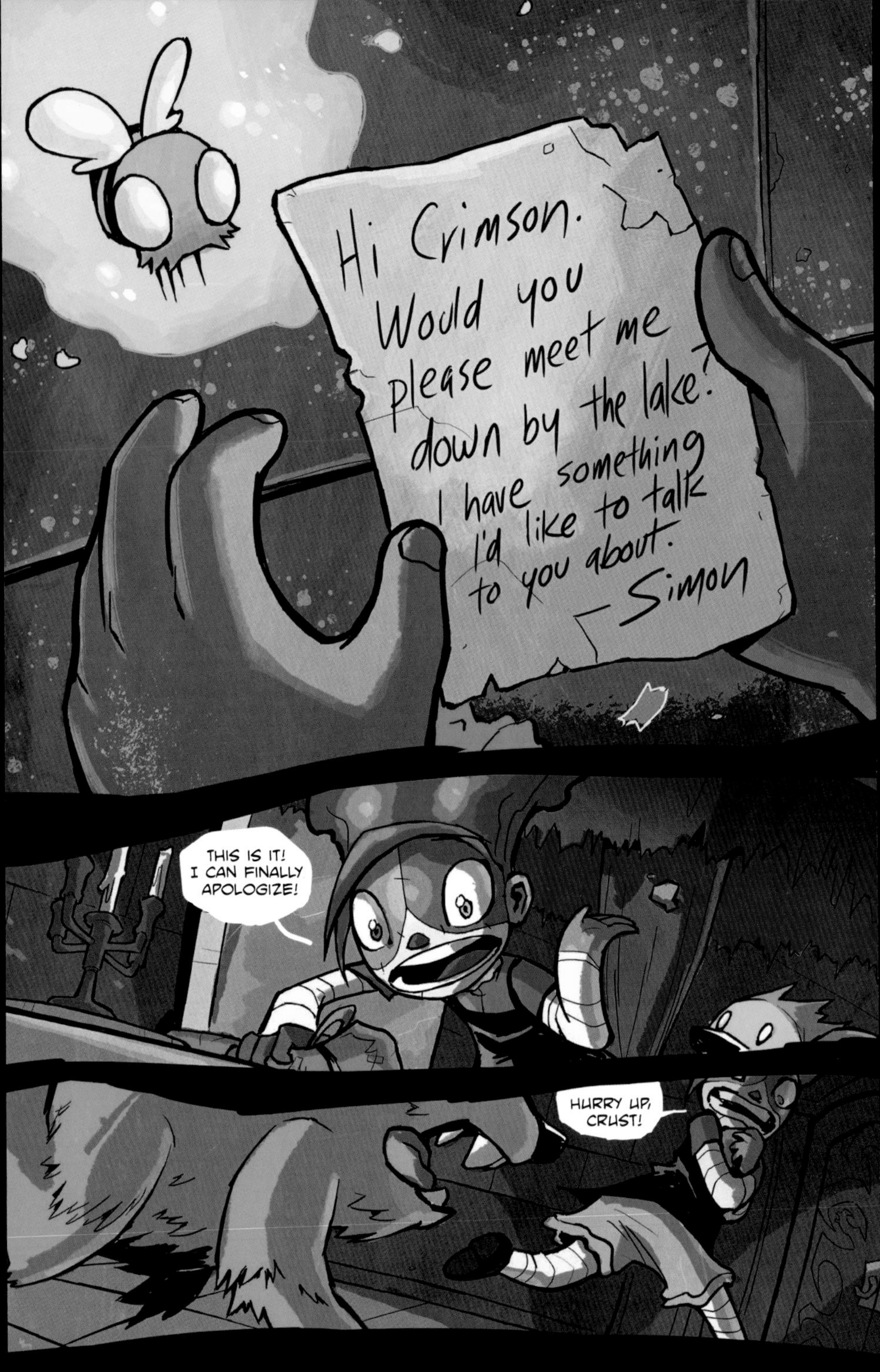
Hi Crimson.
Would you please meet me down by the lake?
I have something I'd like to talk to you about.
— Simon
THIS IS IT! I CAN FINALLY APOLOGIZE!
HURRY UP, CRUST!

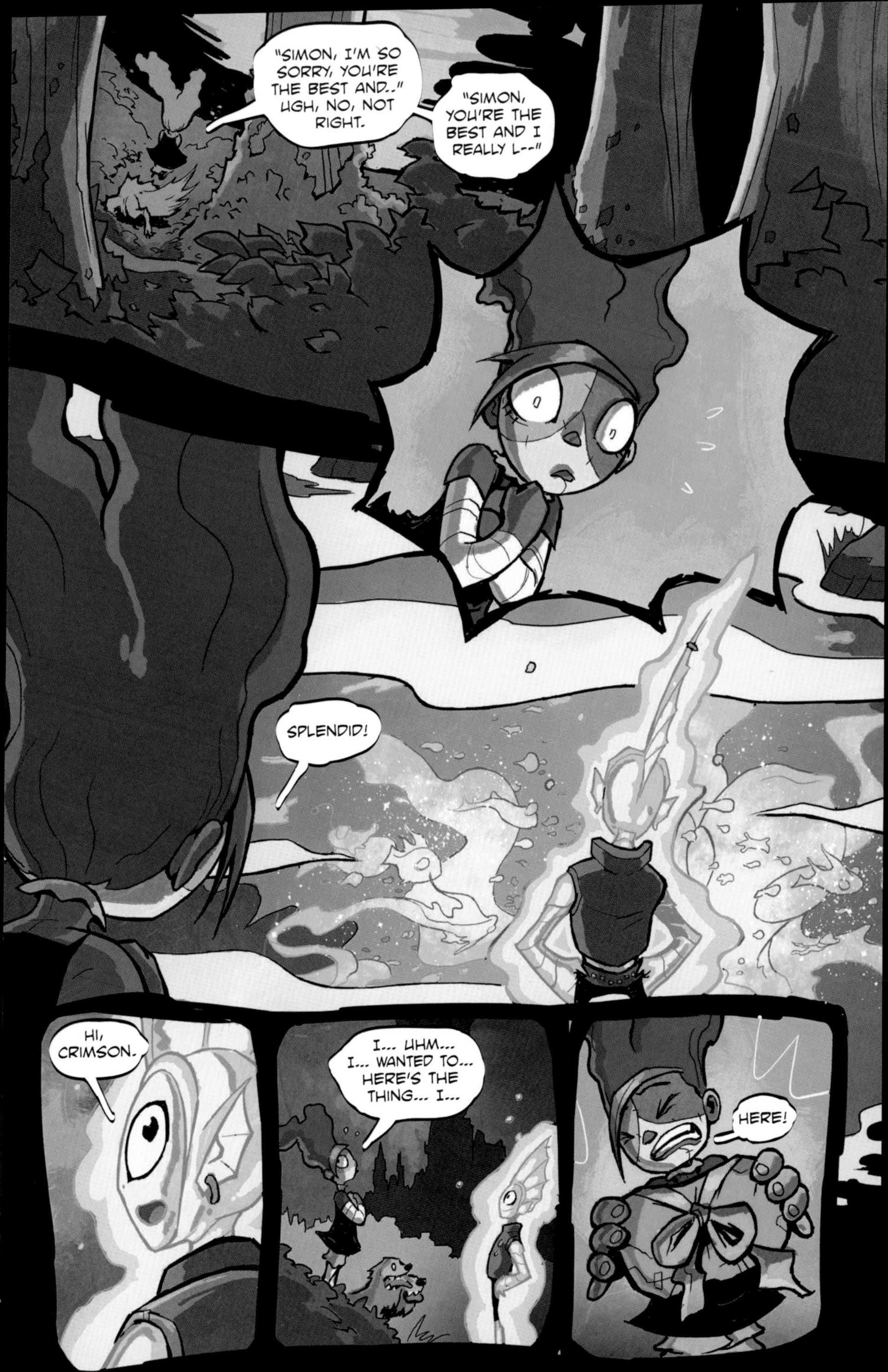
"SIMON, I'M SO SORRY, YOU'RE THE BEST AND.." UGH, NO, NOT RIGHT.
"SIMON, YOU'RE THE BEST AND I REALLY L--"
SPLENDID!
HI, CRIMSON.
I... UHM... I... WANTED TO... HERE'S THE THING... I...
HERE!

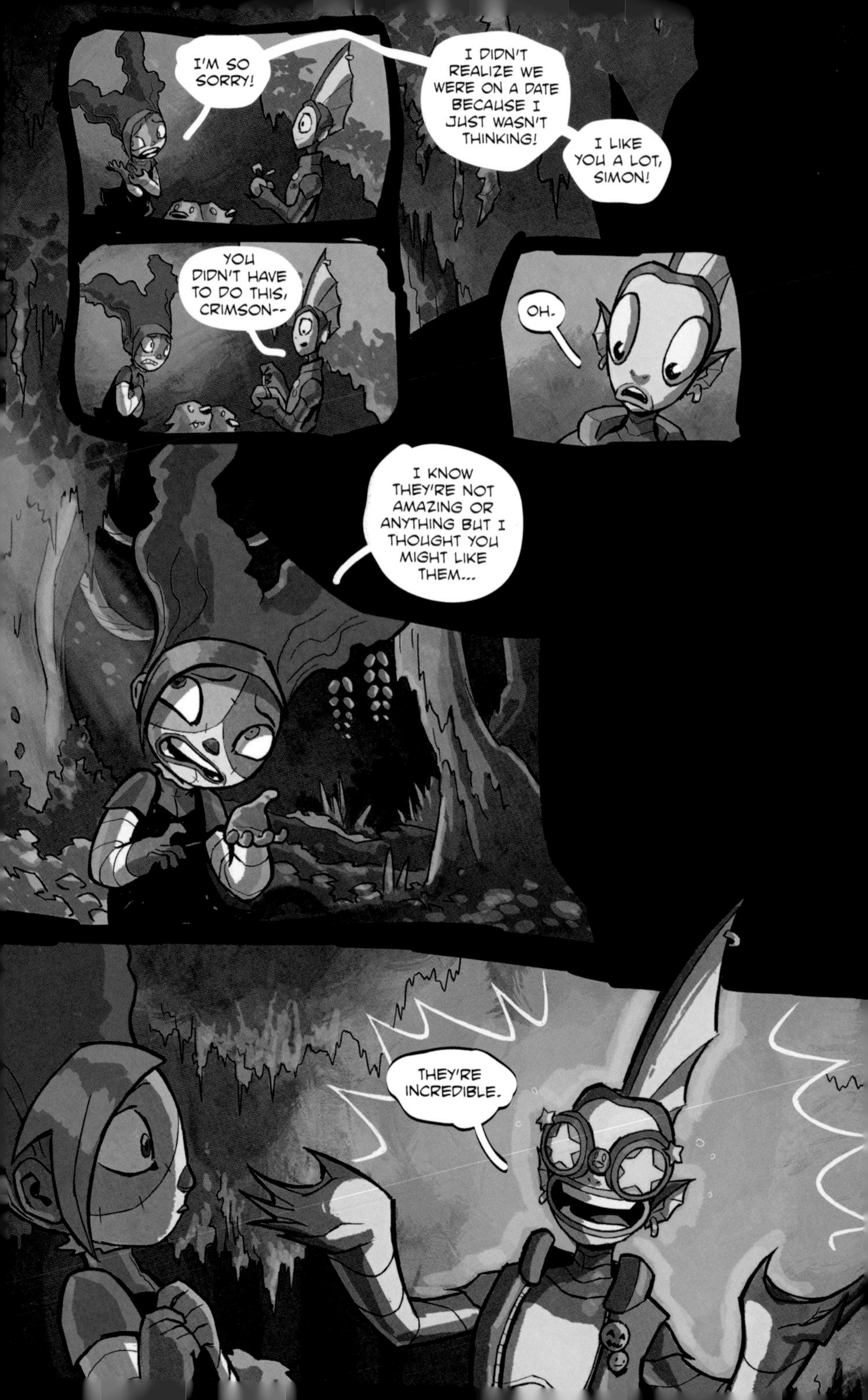
I'M SO SORRY!
I DIDN'T REALIZE WE WERE ON A DATE BECAUSE I JUST WASN'T THINKING!
I LIKE YOU A LOT, SIMON!
YOU DIDN'T HAVE TO DO THIS, CRIMSON--
OH.
I KNOW THEY'RE NOT AMAZING OR ANYTHING BUT I THOUGHT YOU MIGHT LIKE THEM...
THEY'RE INCREDIBLE.

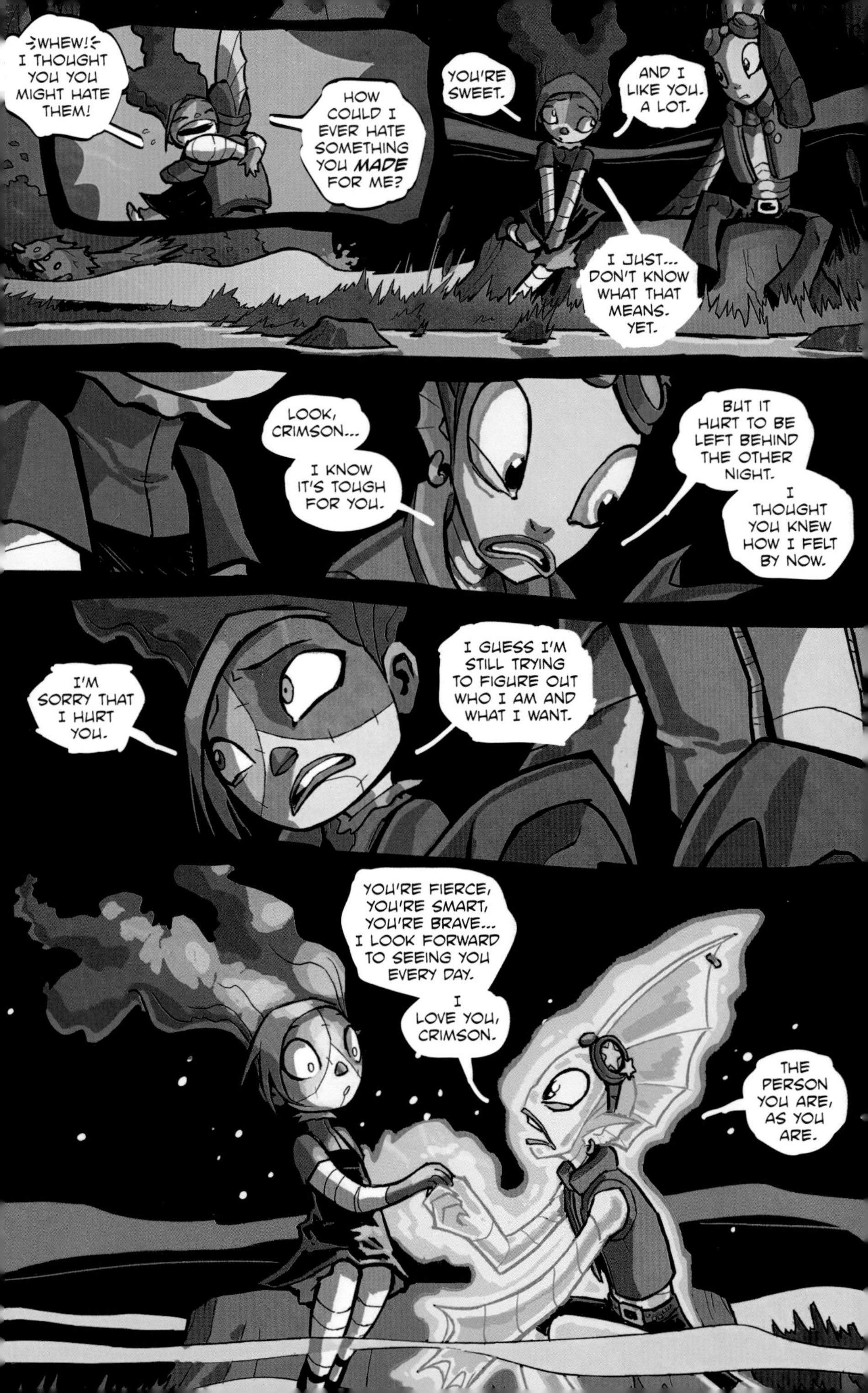

WHEW! I THOUGHT YOU YOU MIGHT HATE THEM!
HOW COULD I EVER HATE SOMETHING YOU *MADE* FOR ME?
YOU'RE SWEET.
AND I LIKE YOU. A LOT.
I JUST... DON'T KNOW WHAT THAT MEANS. YET.
LOOK, CRIMSON...
I KNOW IT'S TOUGH FOR YOU.
BUT IT HURT TO BE LEFT BEHIND THE OTHER NIGHT.
I THOUGHT YOU KNEW HOW I FELT BY NOW.
I'M SORRY THAT I HURT YOU.
I GUESS I'M STILL TRYING TO FIGURE OUT WHO I AM AND WHAT I WANT.
YOU'RE FIERCE, YOU'RE SMART, YOU'RE BRAVE... I LOOK FORWARD TO SEEING YOU EVERY DAY.
I LOVE YOU, CRIMSON.
THE PERSON YOU ARE, AS YOU ARE.

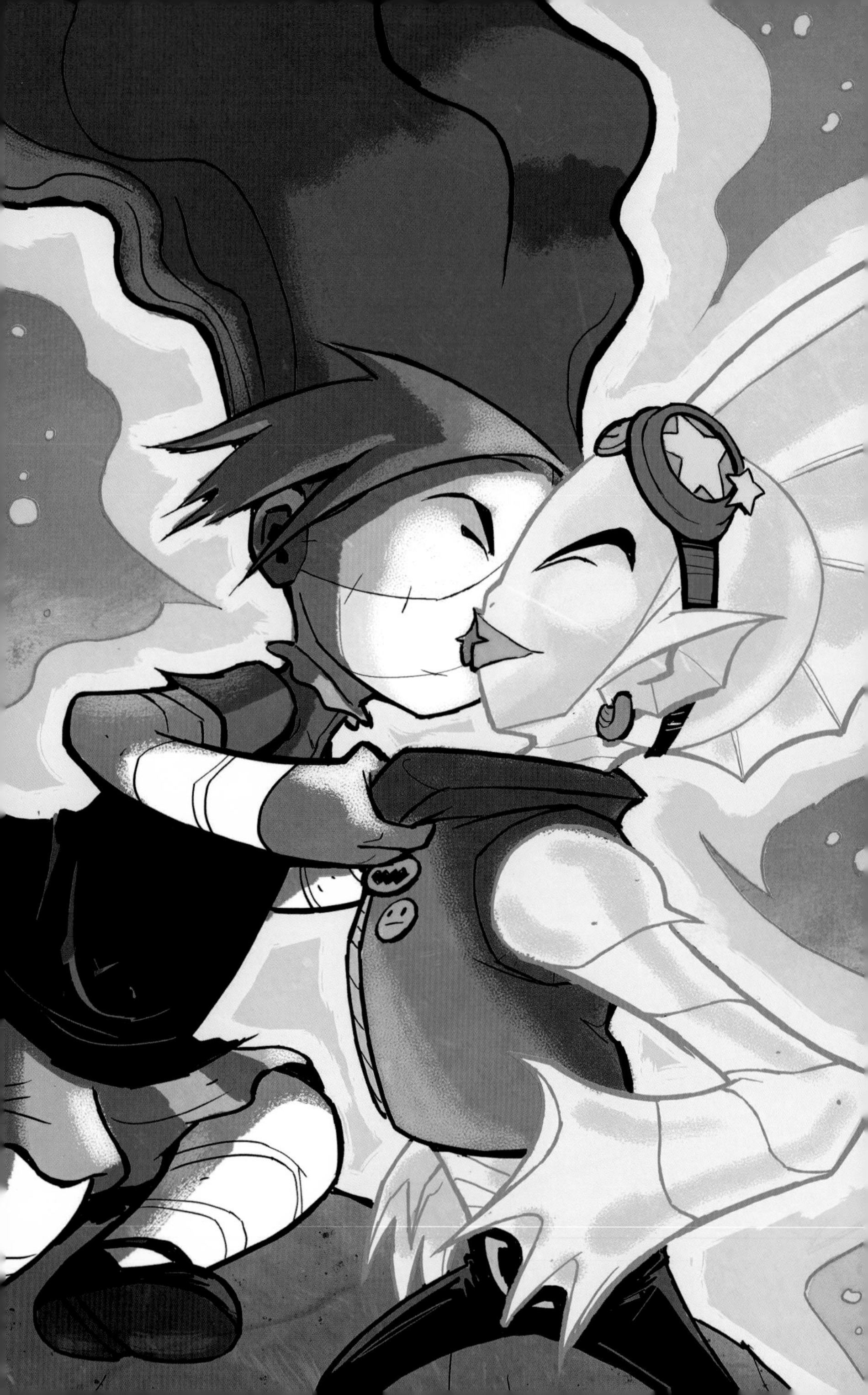

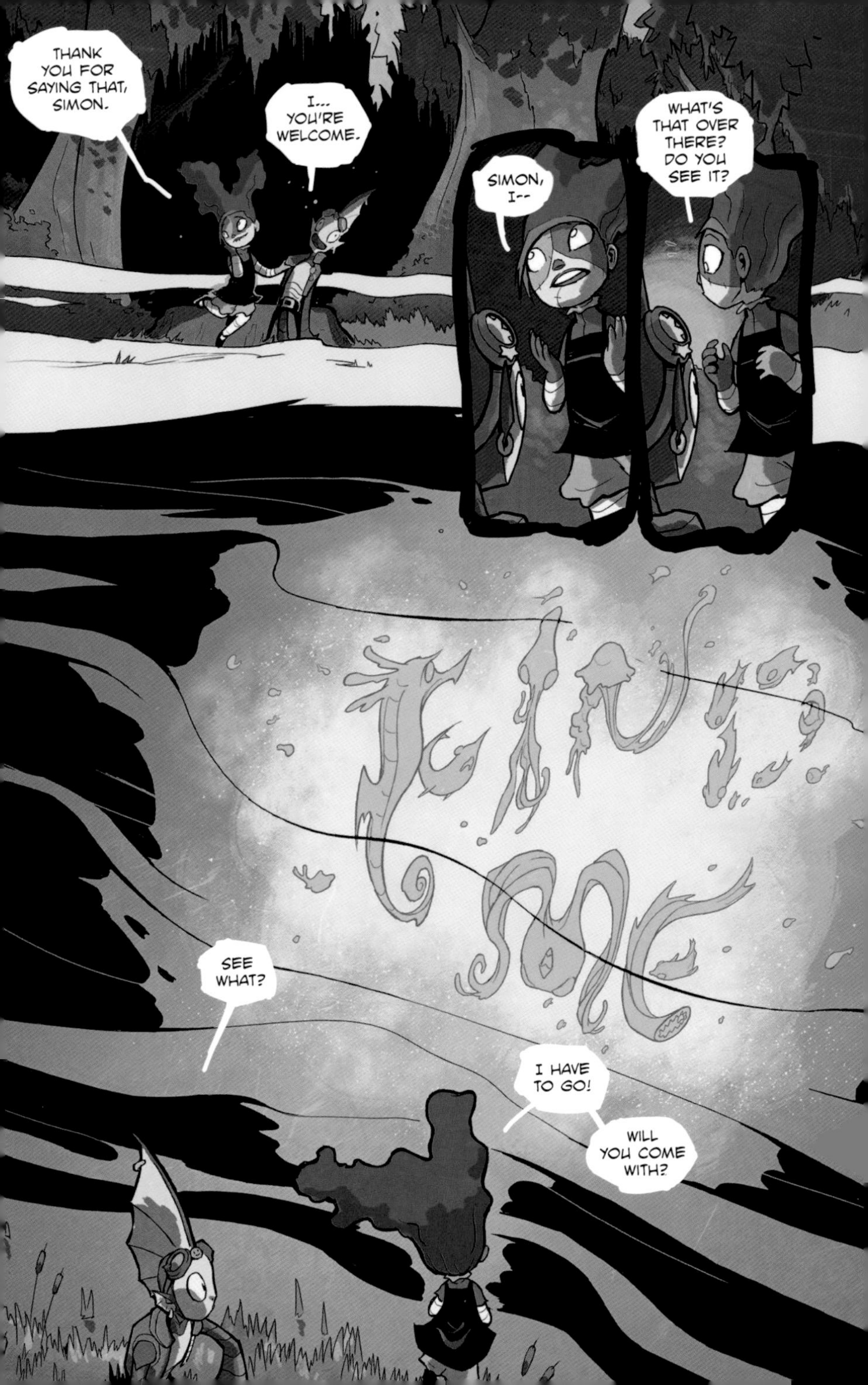

THANK YOU FOR SAYING THAT, SIMON.
I... YOU'RE WELCOME.
SIMON, I--
WHAT'S THAT OVER THERE? DO YOU SEE IT?
SEE WHAT?
I HAVE TO GO!
WILL YOU COME WITH?

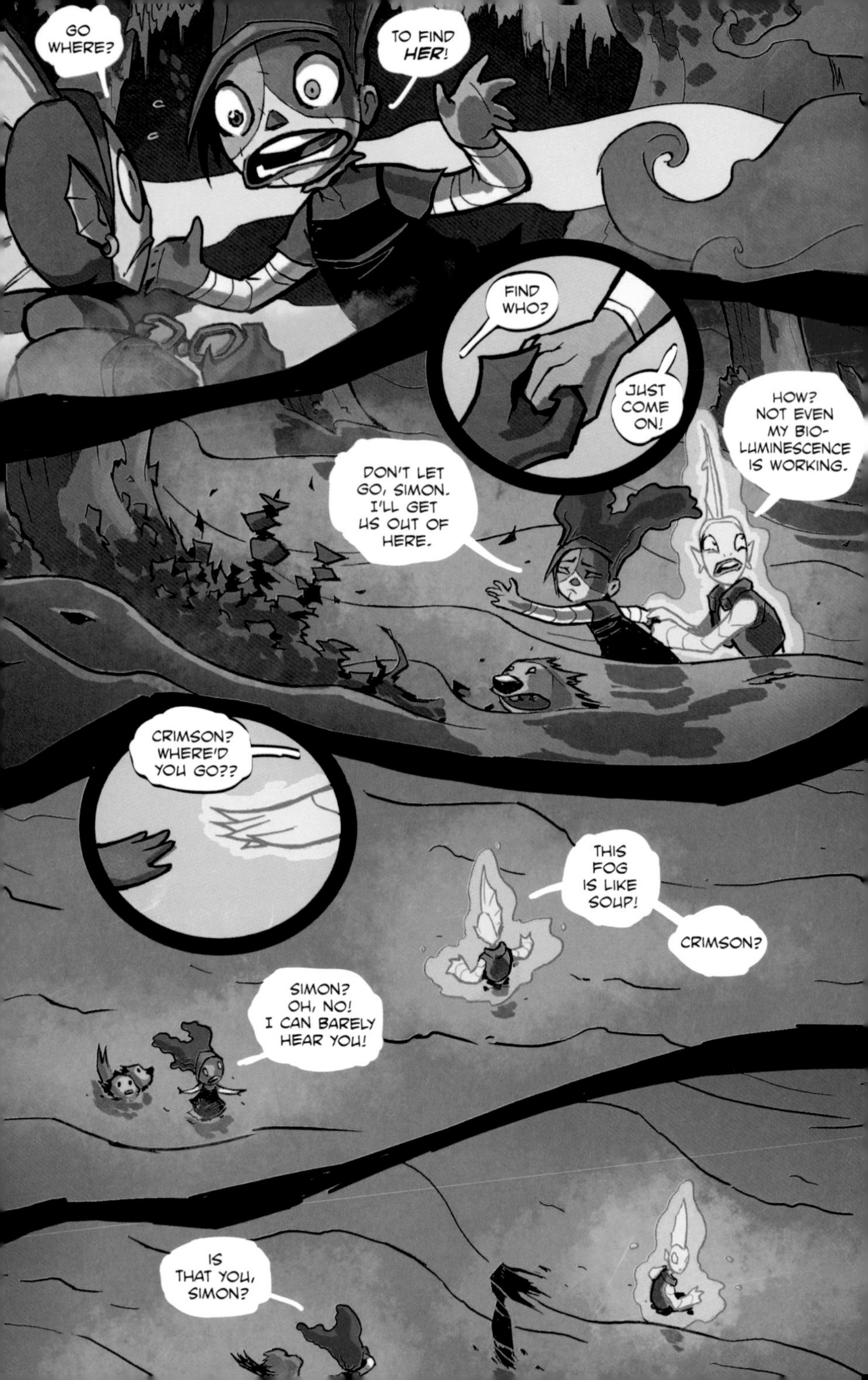
GO WHERE?
TO FIND HER!
FIND WHO?
JUST COME ON!
HOW? NOT EVEN MY BIO-LUMINESCENCE IS WORKING.
DON'T LET GO, SIMON. I'LL GET US OUT OF HERE.
CRIMSON? WHERE'D YOU GO??
THIS FOG IS LIKE SOUP!
CRIMSON?
SIMON? OH, NO! I CAN BARELY HEAR YOU!
IS THAT YOU, SIMON?

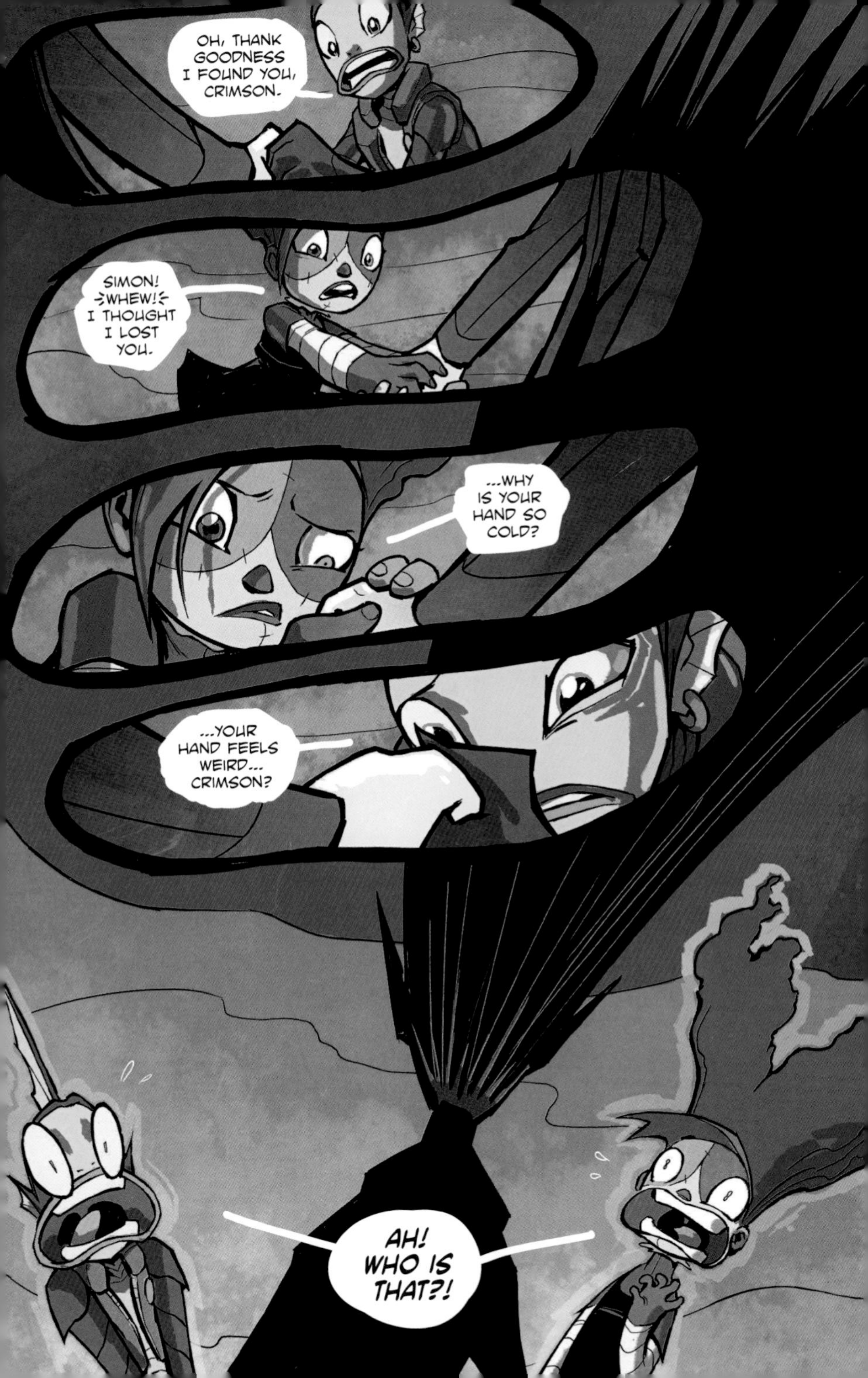
OH, THANK GOODNESS I FOUND YOU, CRIMSON.
SIMON! ⁘WHEW!⁘ I THOUGHT I LOST YOU.
...WHY IS YOUR HAND SO COLD?
...YOUR HAND FEELS WEIRD... CRIMSON?
AH! WHO IS THAT?!

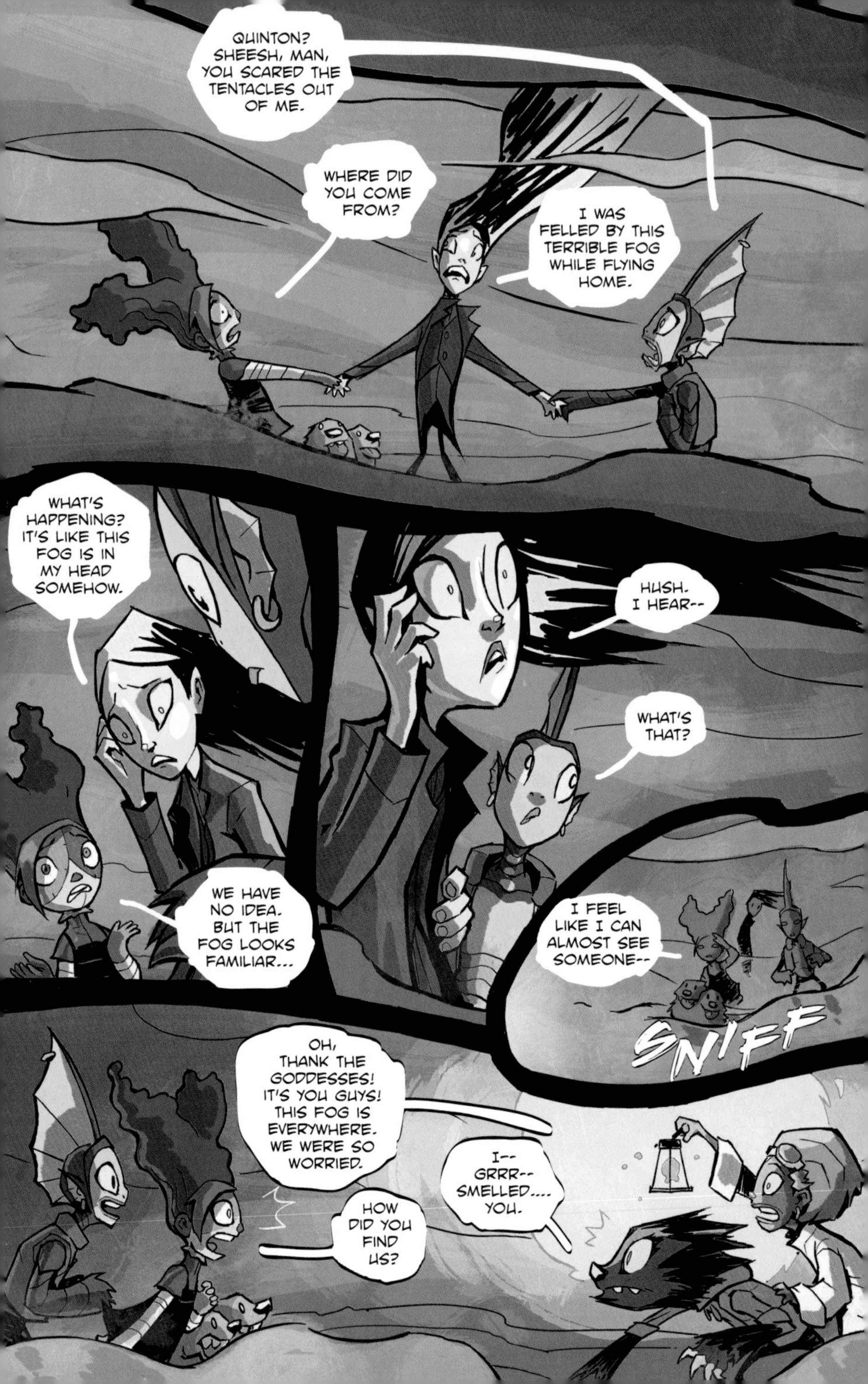
QUINTON? SHEESH, MAN, YOU SCARED THE TENTACLES OUT OF ME.
WHERE DID YOU COME FROM?
I WAS FELLED BY THIS TERRIBLE FOG WHILE FLYING HOME.
WHAT'S HAPPENING? IT'S LIKE THIS FOG IS IN MY HEAD SOMEHOW.
HUSH. I HEAR--
WHAT'S THAT?
WE HAVE NO IDEA. BUT THE FOG LOOKS FAMILIAR...
I FEEL LIKE I CAN ALMOST SEE SOMEONE--
SNIFF
OH, THANK THE GODDESSES! IT'S YOU GUYS! THIS FOG IS EVERYWHERE. WE WERE SO WORRIED.
HOW DID YOU FIND US?
I-- GRRR-- SMELLED.... YOU.

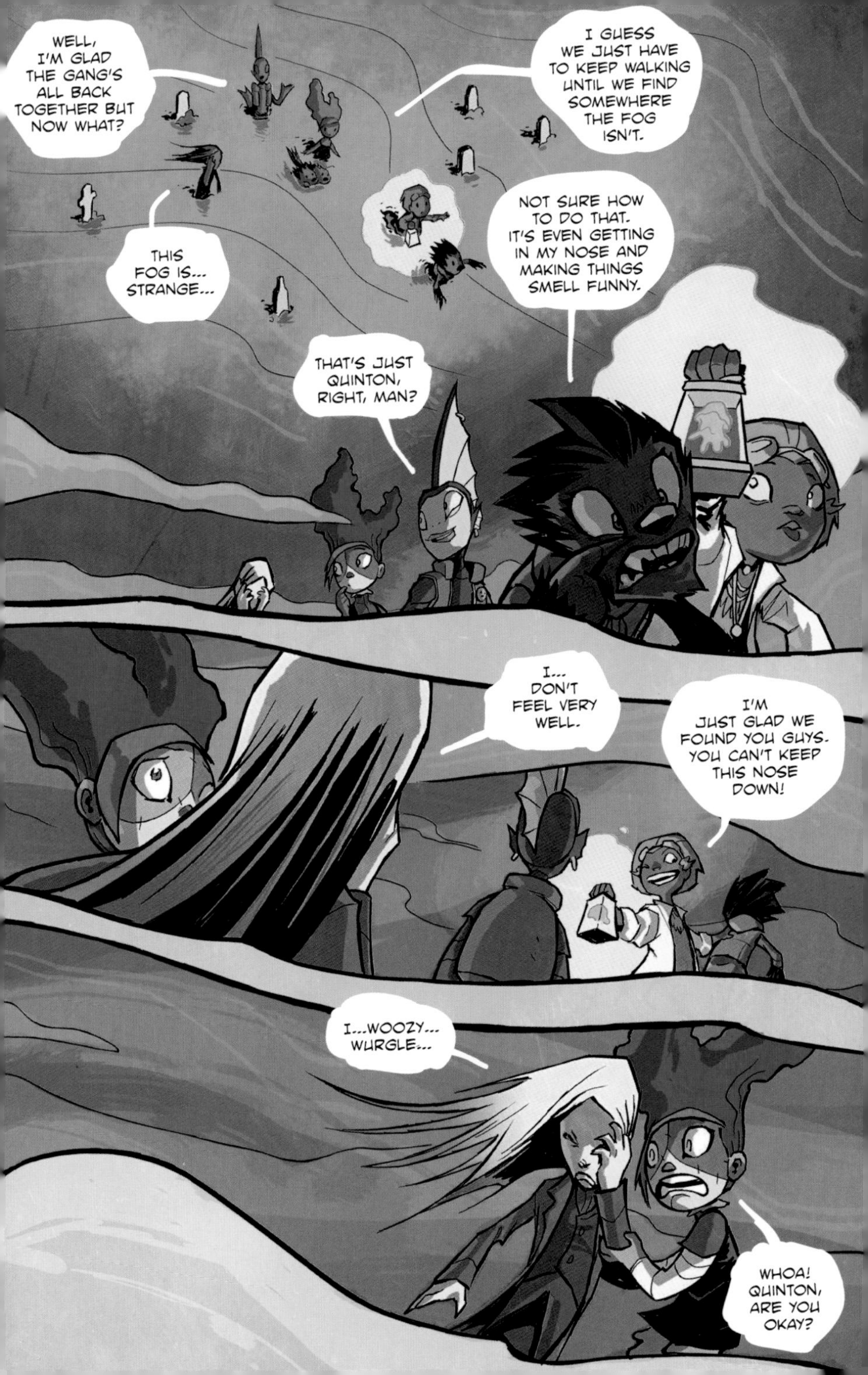
WELL, I'M GLAD THE GANG'S ALL BACK TOGETHER BUT NOW WHAT?
I GUESS WE JUST HAVE TO KEEP WALKING UNTIL WE FIND SOMEWHERE THE FOG ISN'T.
THIS FOG IS... STRANGE...
NOT SURE HOW TO DO THAT. IT'S EVEN GETTING IN MY NOSE AND MAKING THINGS SMELL FUNNY.
THAT'S JUST QUINTON, RIGHT, MAN?
I... DON'T FEEL VERY WELL.
I'M JUST GLAD WE FOUND YOU GUYS. YOU CAN'T KEEP THIS NOSE DOWN!
I...WOOZY... WURGLE...
WHOA! QUINTON, ARE YOU OKAY?

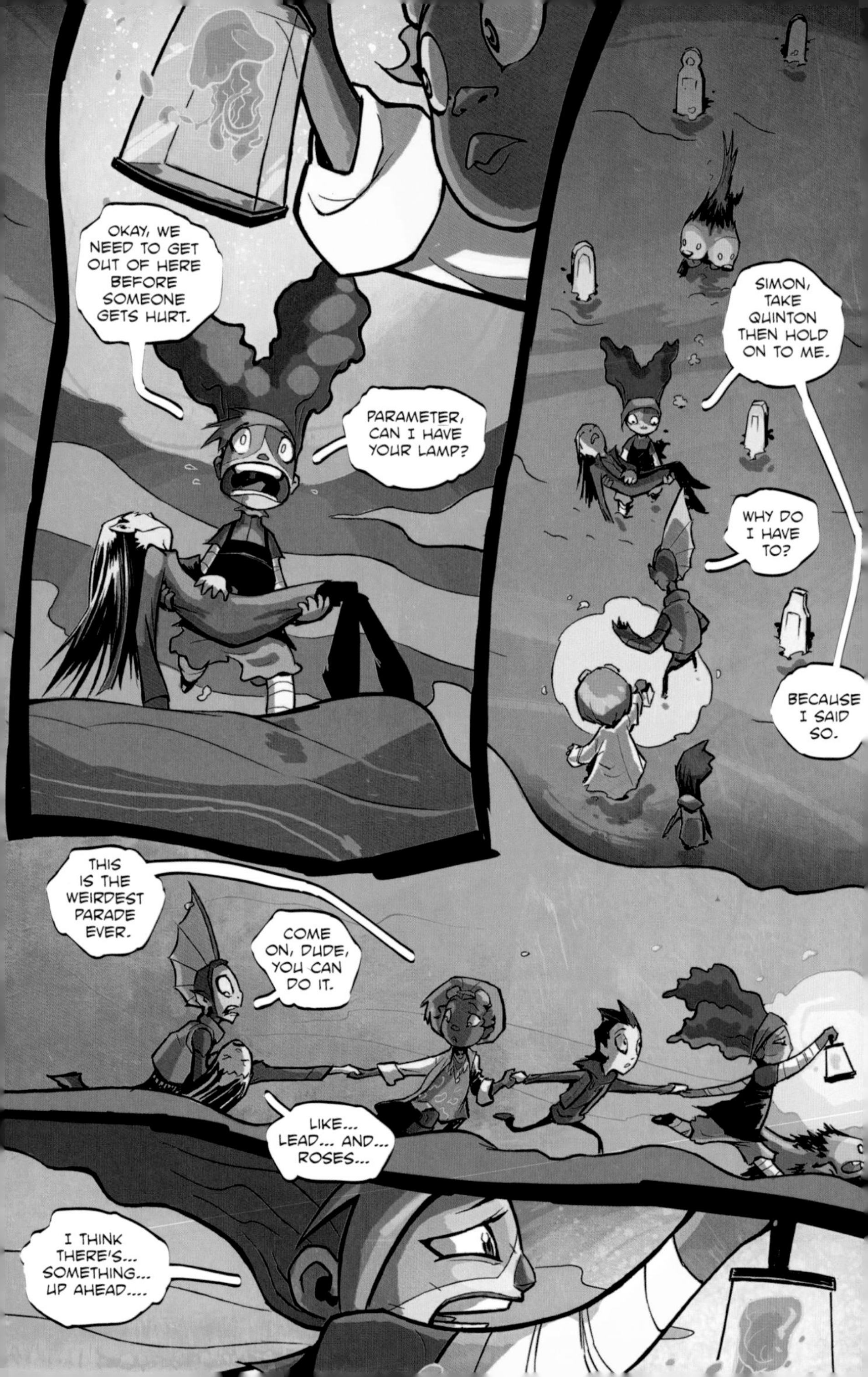
OKAY, WE NEED TO GET OUT OF HERE BEFORE SOMEONE GETS HURT.
PARAMETER, CAN I HAVE YOUR LAMP?
SIMON, TAKE QUINTON THEN HOLD ON TO ME.
WHY DO I HAVE TO?
BECAUSE I SAID SO.
THIS IS THE WEIRDEST PARADE EVER.
COME ON, DUDE, YOU CAN DO IT.
LIKE... LEAD... AND... ROSES...
I THINK THERE'S... SOMETHING... UP AHEAD....

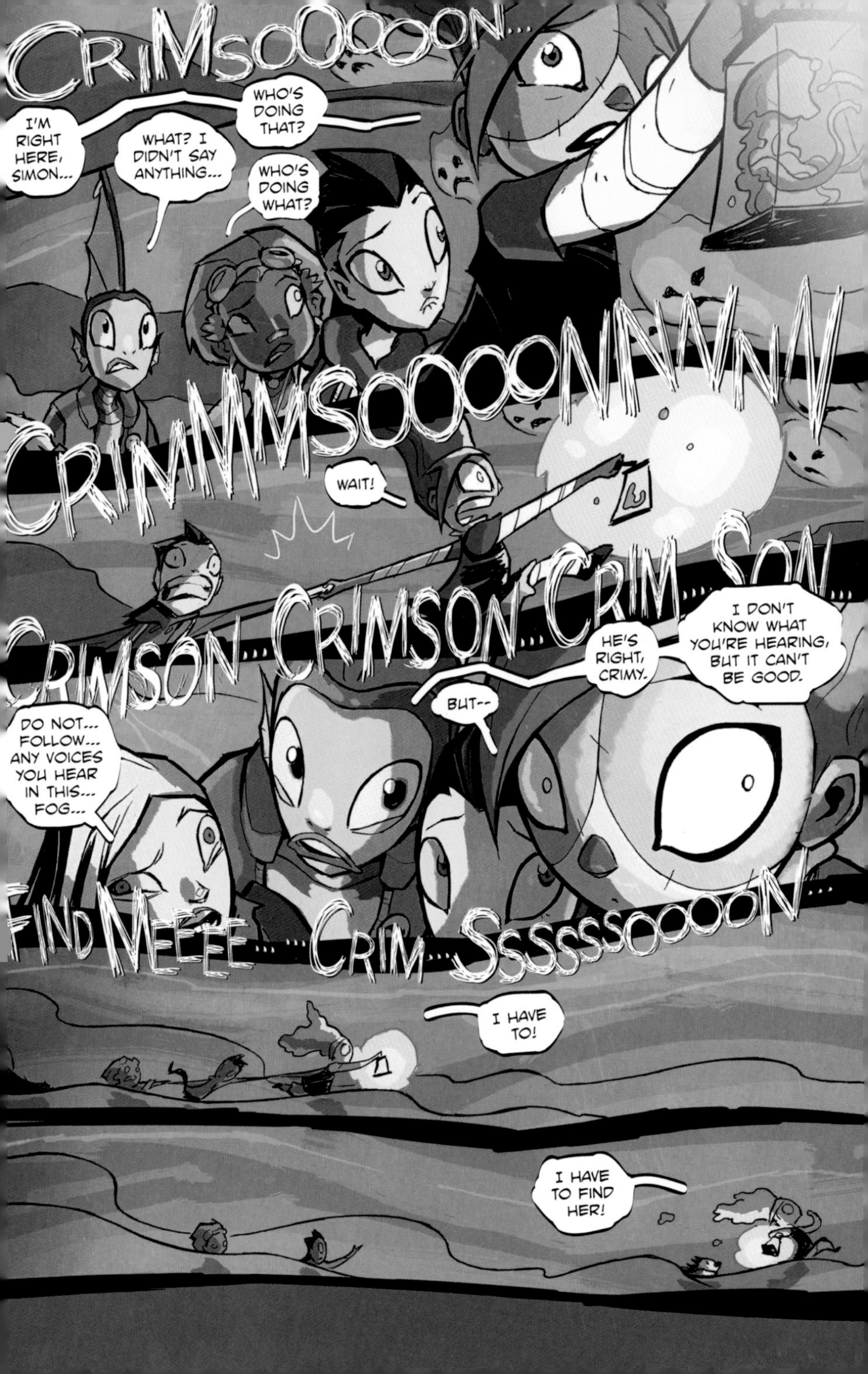
CRIMSOOOOOON...
I'M RIGHT HERE, SIMON...
WHAT? I DIDN'T SAY ANYTHING...
WHO'S DOING THAT?
WHO'S DOING WHAT?
CRIMMMSOOOOONNNNN!
WAIT!
CRIMSON... CRIMSON CRIM... SON
HE'S RIGHT, CRIMY.
I DON'T KNOW WHAT YOU'RE HEARING, BUT IT CAN'T BE GOOD.
BUT--
DO NOT... FOLLOW... ANY VOICES YOU HEAR IN THIS... FOG...
FIND MEEEE... CRIM... SSSSSSOOOOON
I HAVE TO!
I HAVE TO FIND HER!

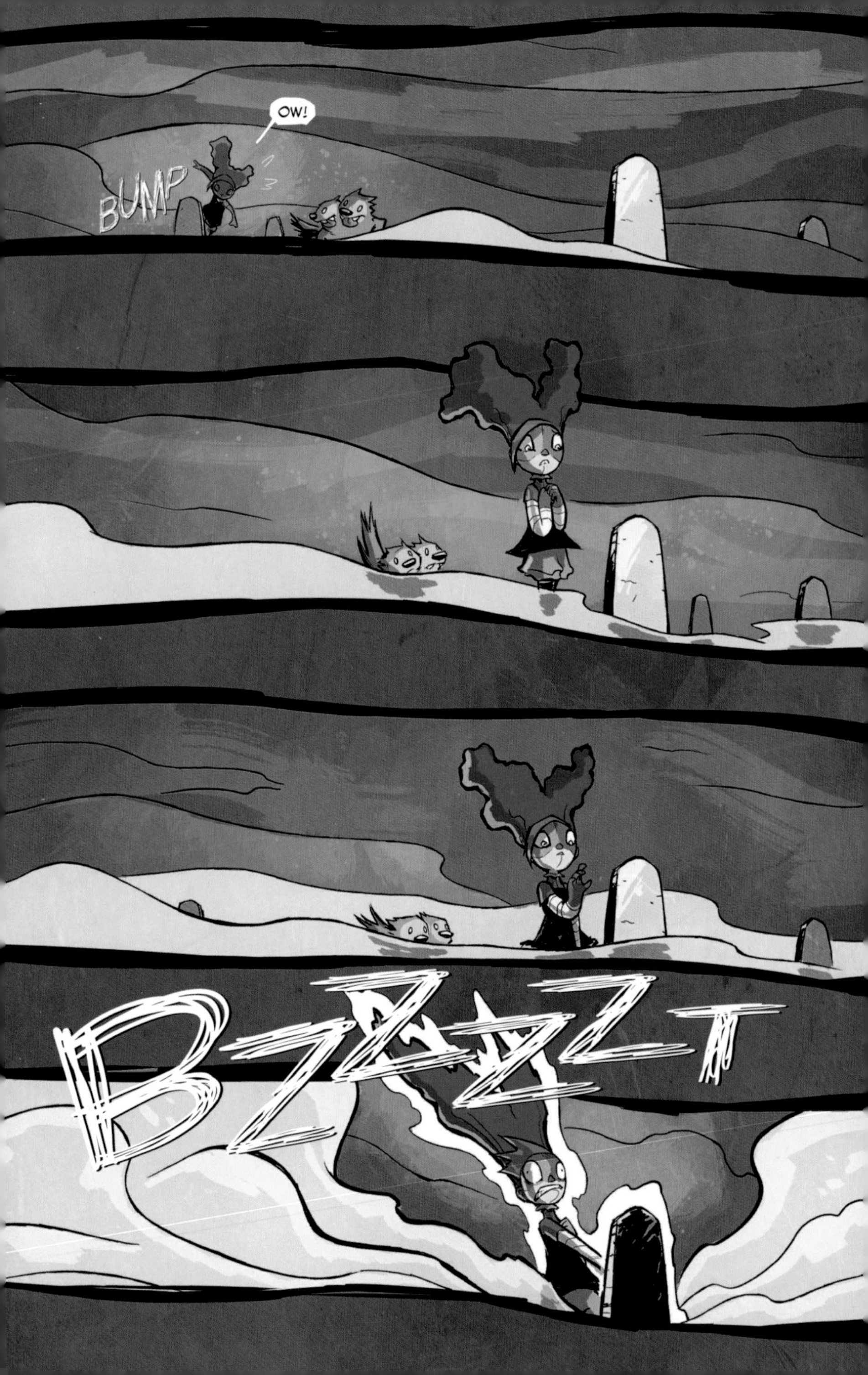
OW!
BUMP
BZZZZT

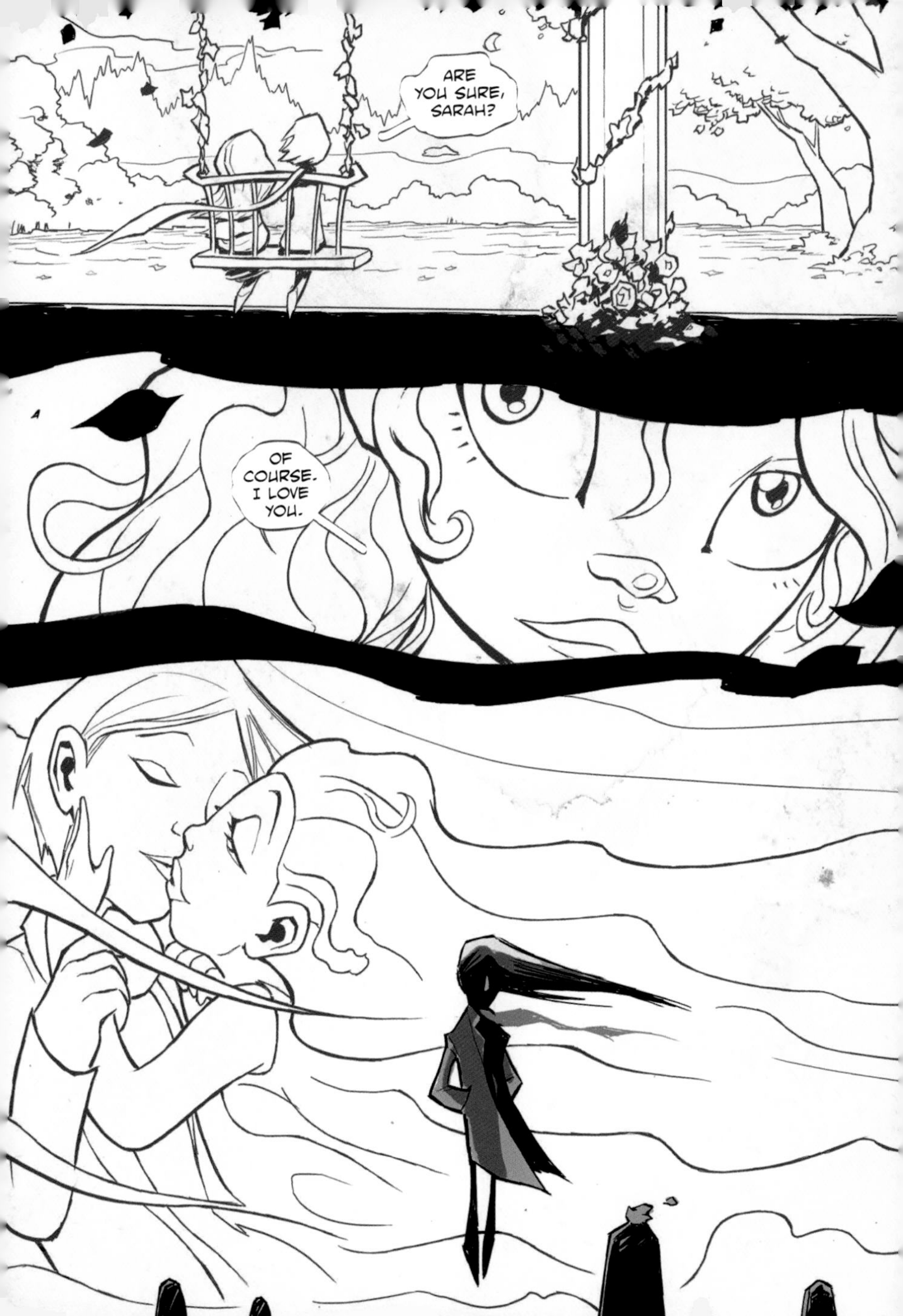
ARE YOU SURE, SARAH?
OF COURSE. I LOVE YOU.

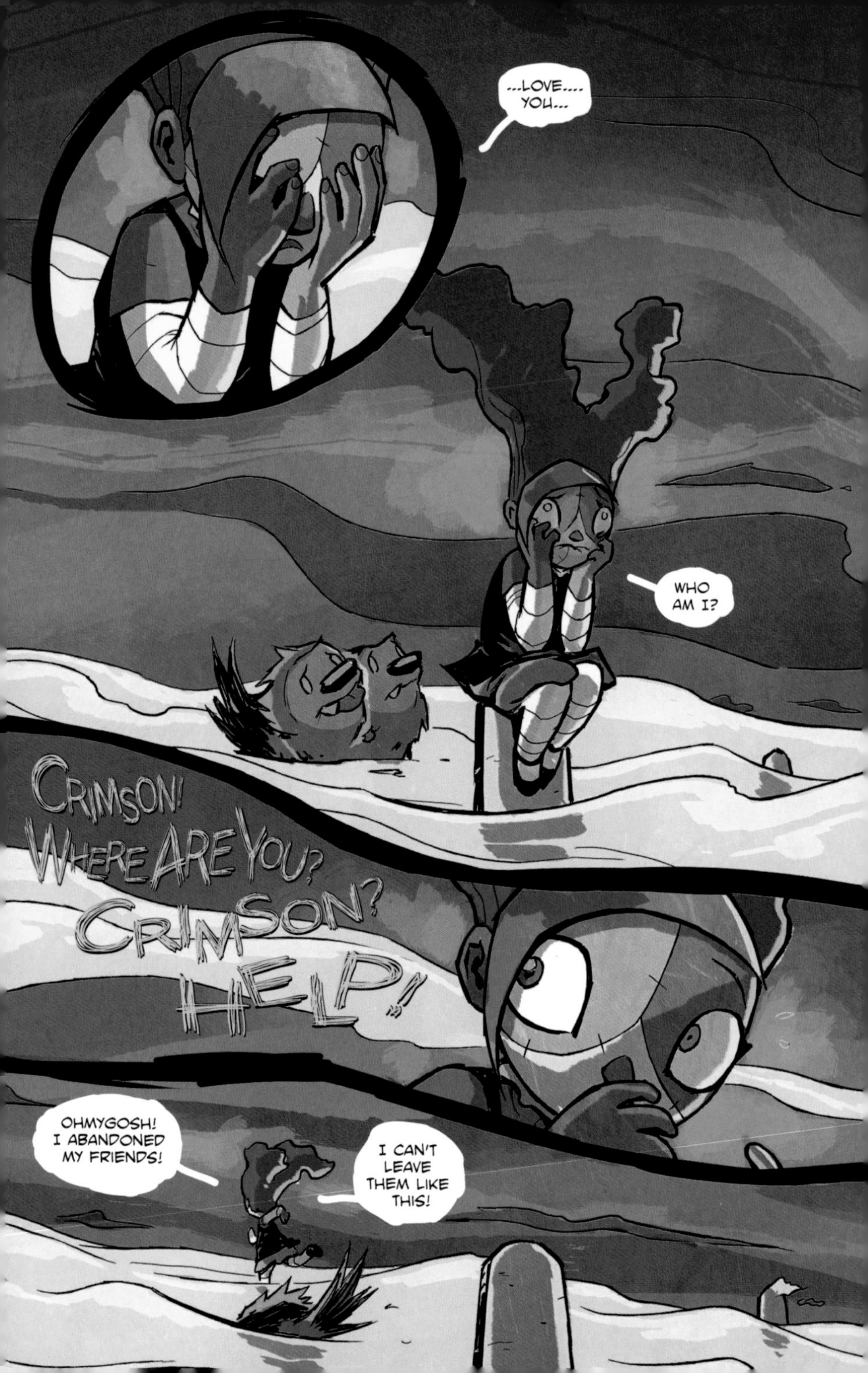
...LOVE.... YOU...
WHO AM I?
CRIMSON! WHERE ARE YOU? CRIMSON? HELP!
OHMYGOSH! I ABANDONED MY FRIENDS!
I CAN'T LEAVE THEM LIKE THIS!

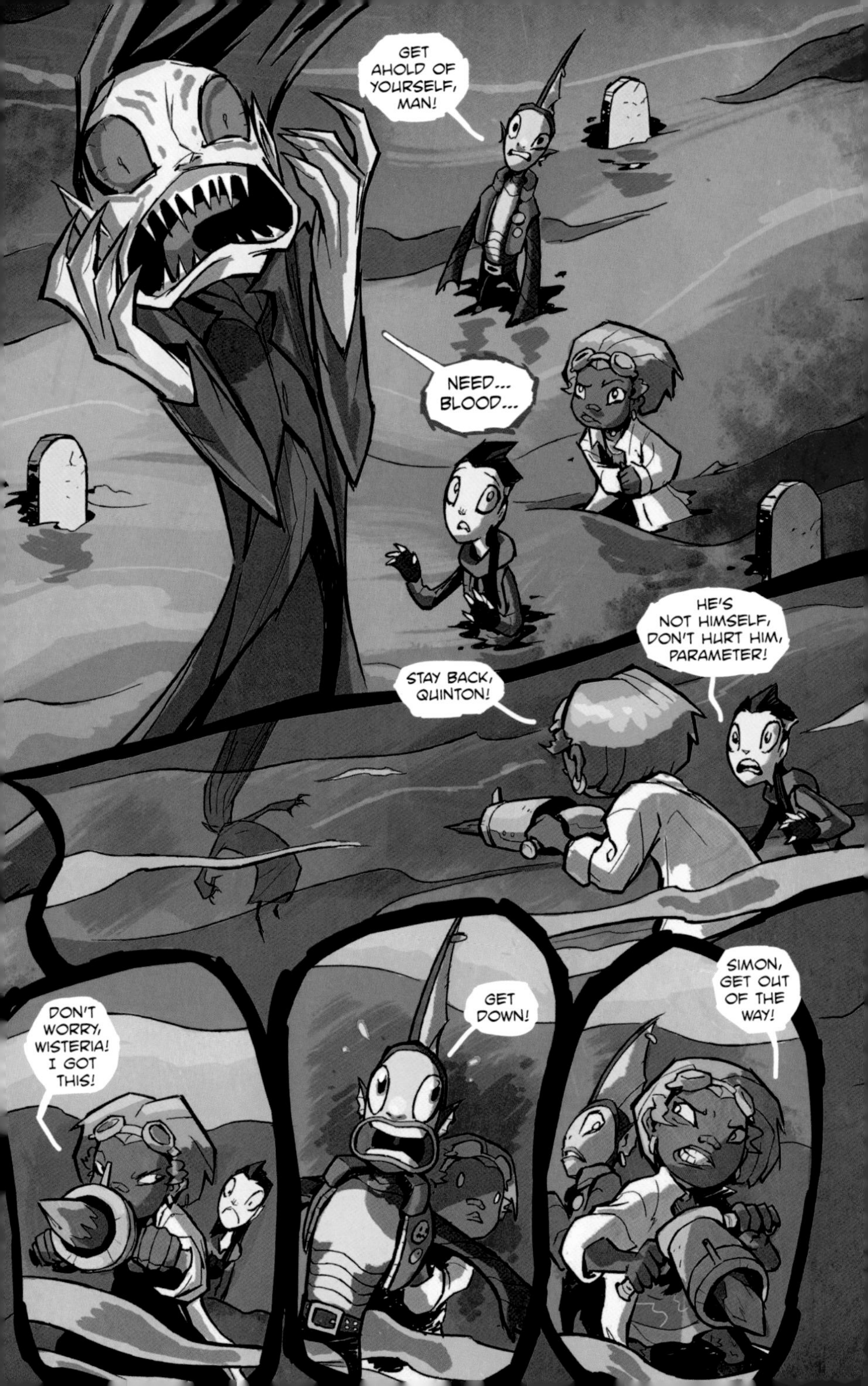
GET AHOLD OF YOURSELF, MAN!
NEED... BLOOD...
STAY BACK, QUINTON!
HE'S NOT HIMSELF, DON'T HURT HIM, PARAMETER!
DON'T WORRY, WISTERIA! I GOT THIS!
GET DOWN!
SIMON, GET OUT OF THE WAY!

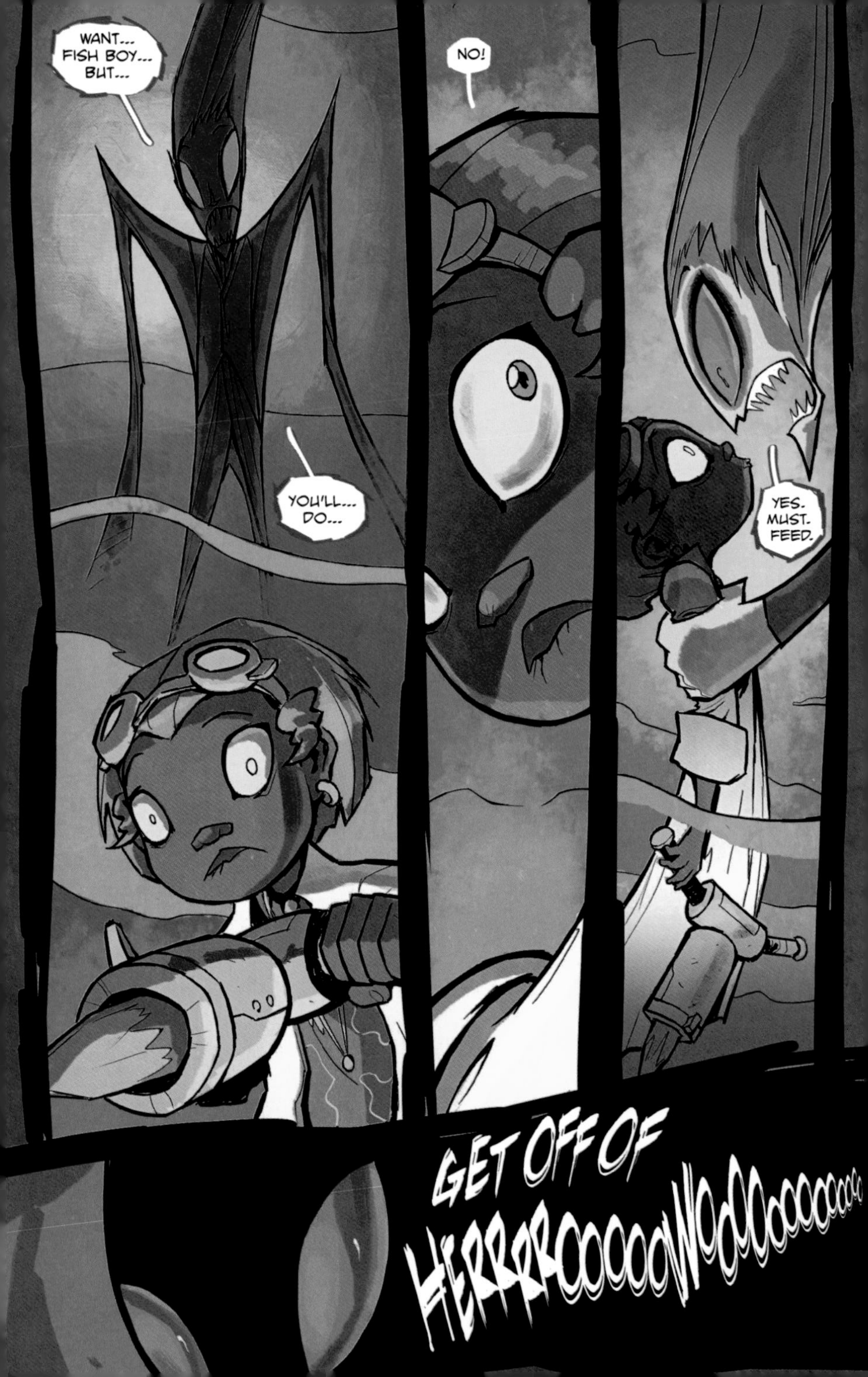
WANT... FISH BOY... BUT...
YOU'LL... DO...
NO!
YES. MUST. FEED.
GET OFF OF
HERRRROOOOOWOOOOOOOOOO

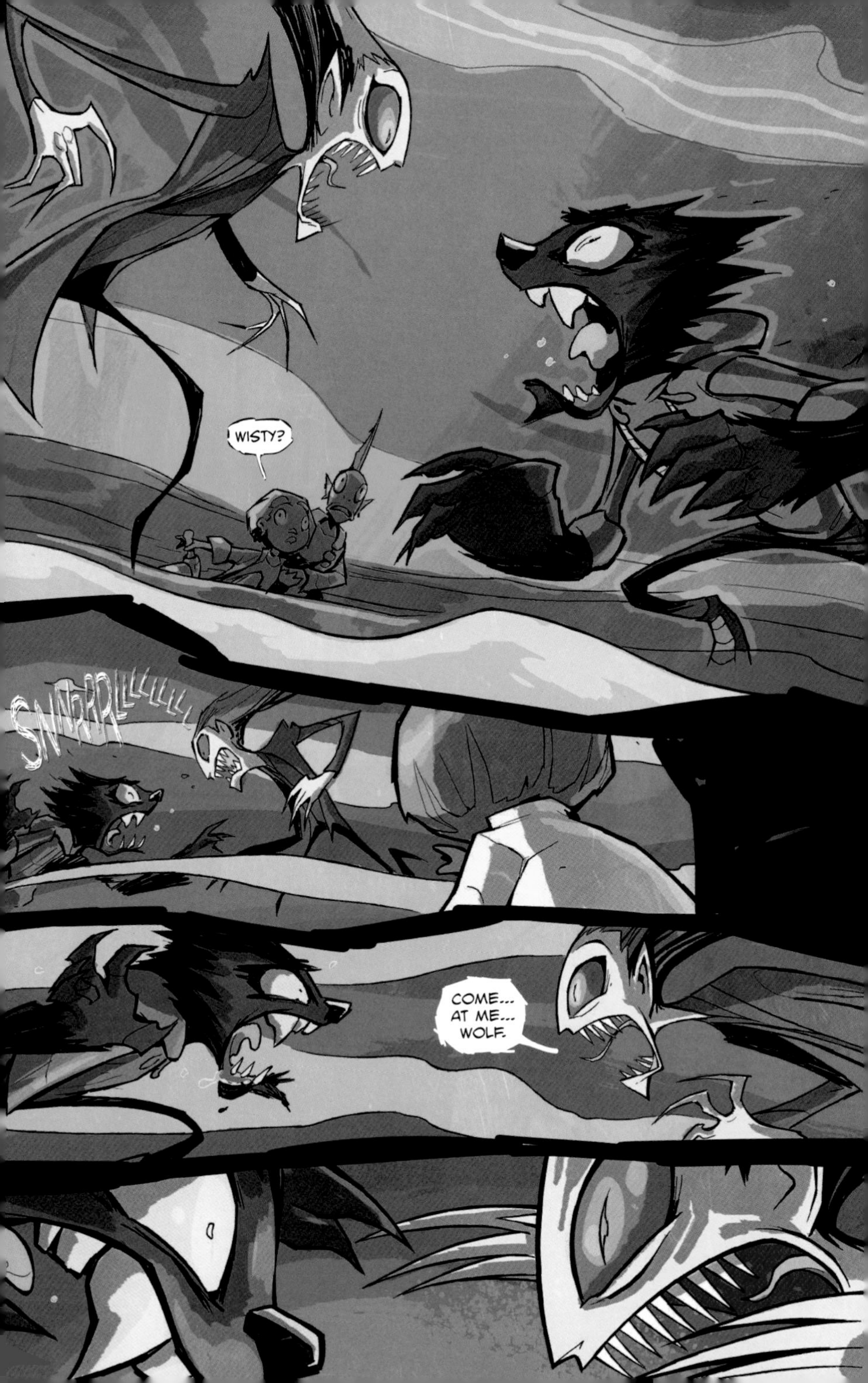
WISTY?
SNNRRRLLLLLLL
COME... AT ME... WOLF.

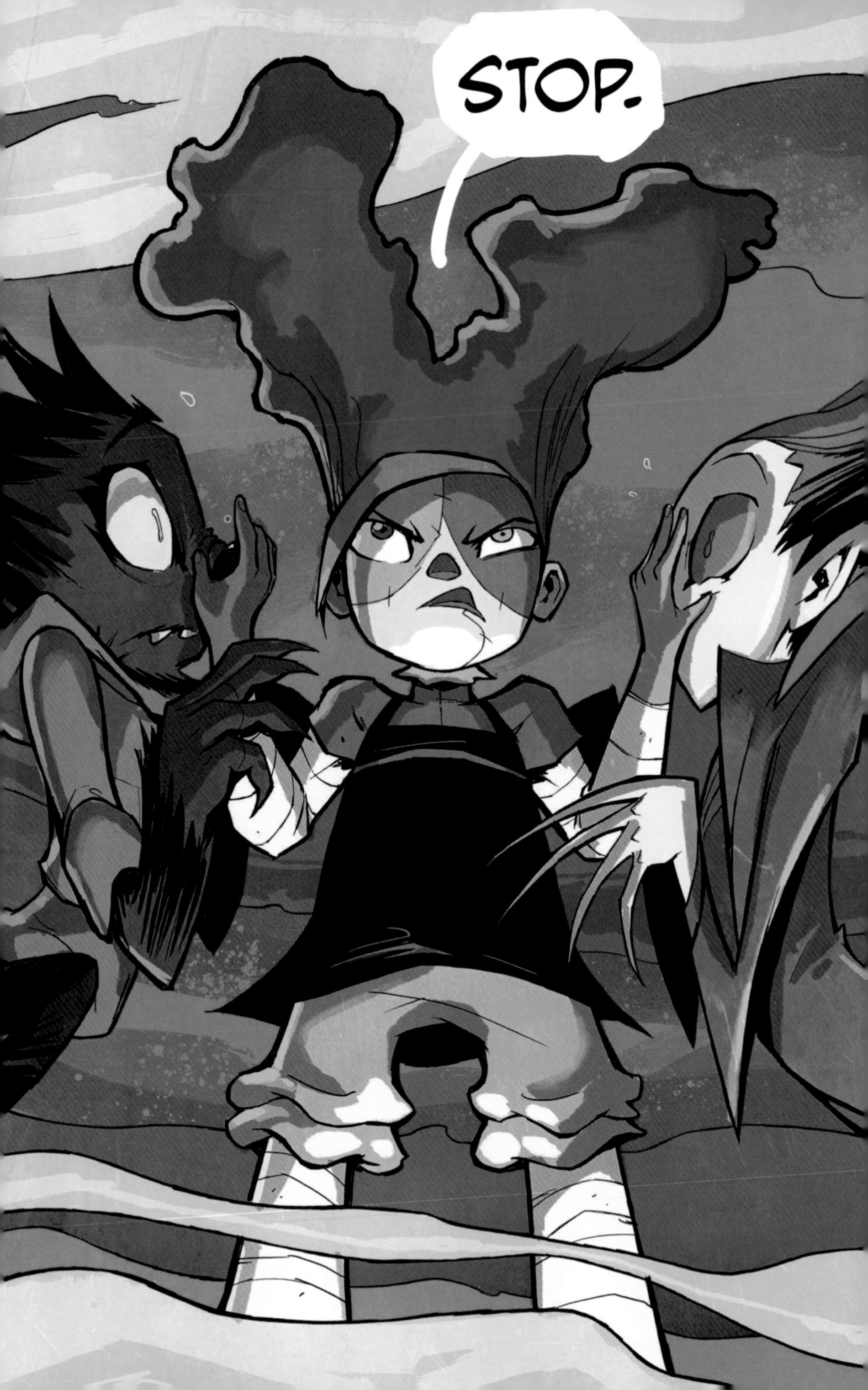
STOP.

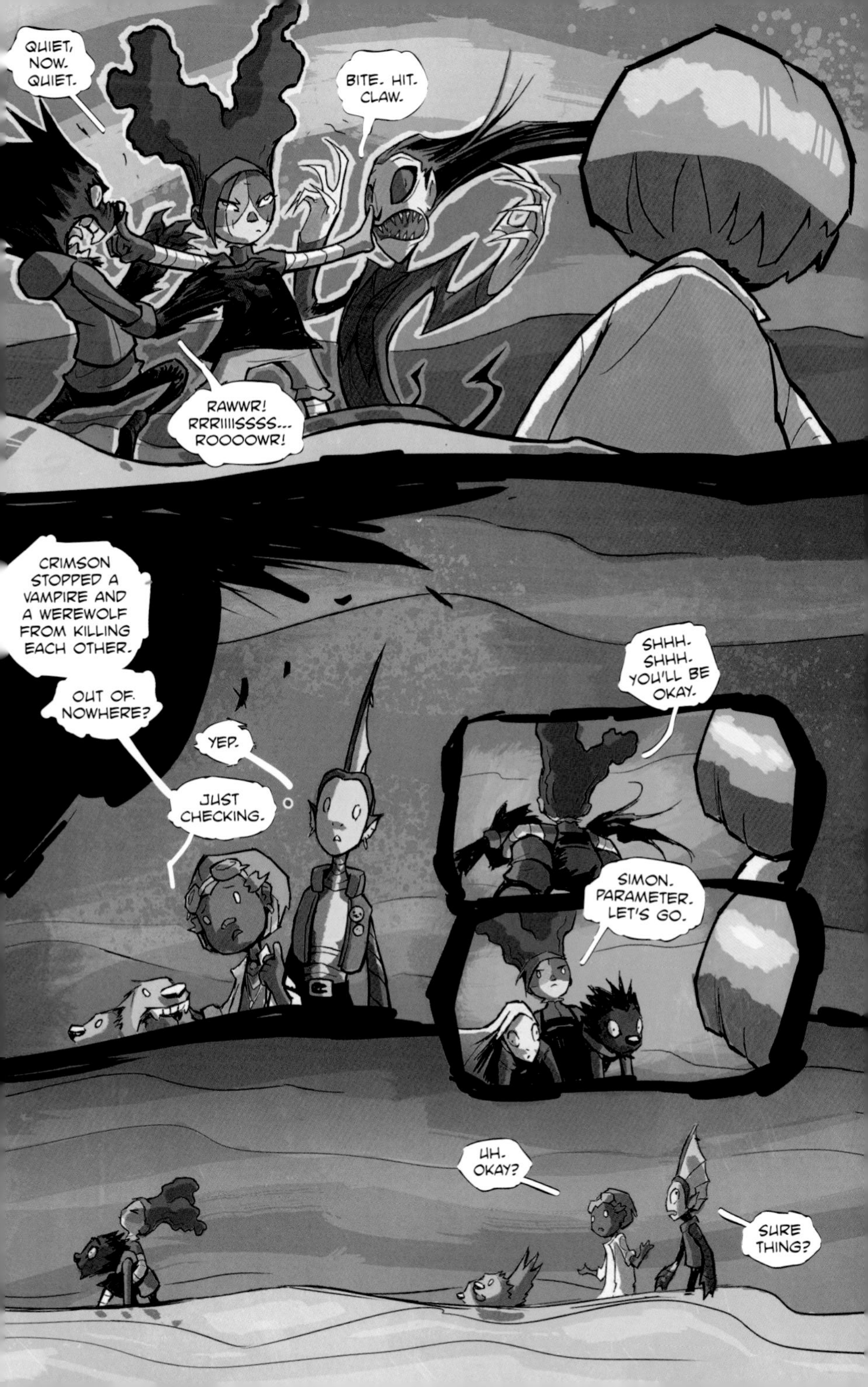
QUIET, NOW. QUIET.
BITE. HIT. CLAW.
RAWWR! RRRIIIISSSS... ROOOOWR!
CRIMSON STOPPED A VAMPIRE AND A WEREWOLF FROM KILLING EACH OTHER.
OUT OF. NOWHERE?
YEP.
JUST CHECKING.
SHHH. SHHH. YOU'LL BE OKAY.
SIMON. PARAMETER. LET'S GO.
UH. OKAY?
SURE THING?

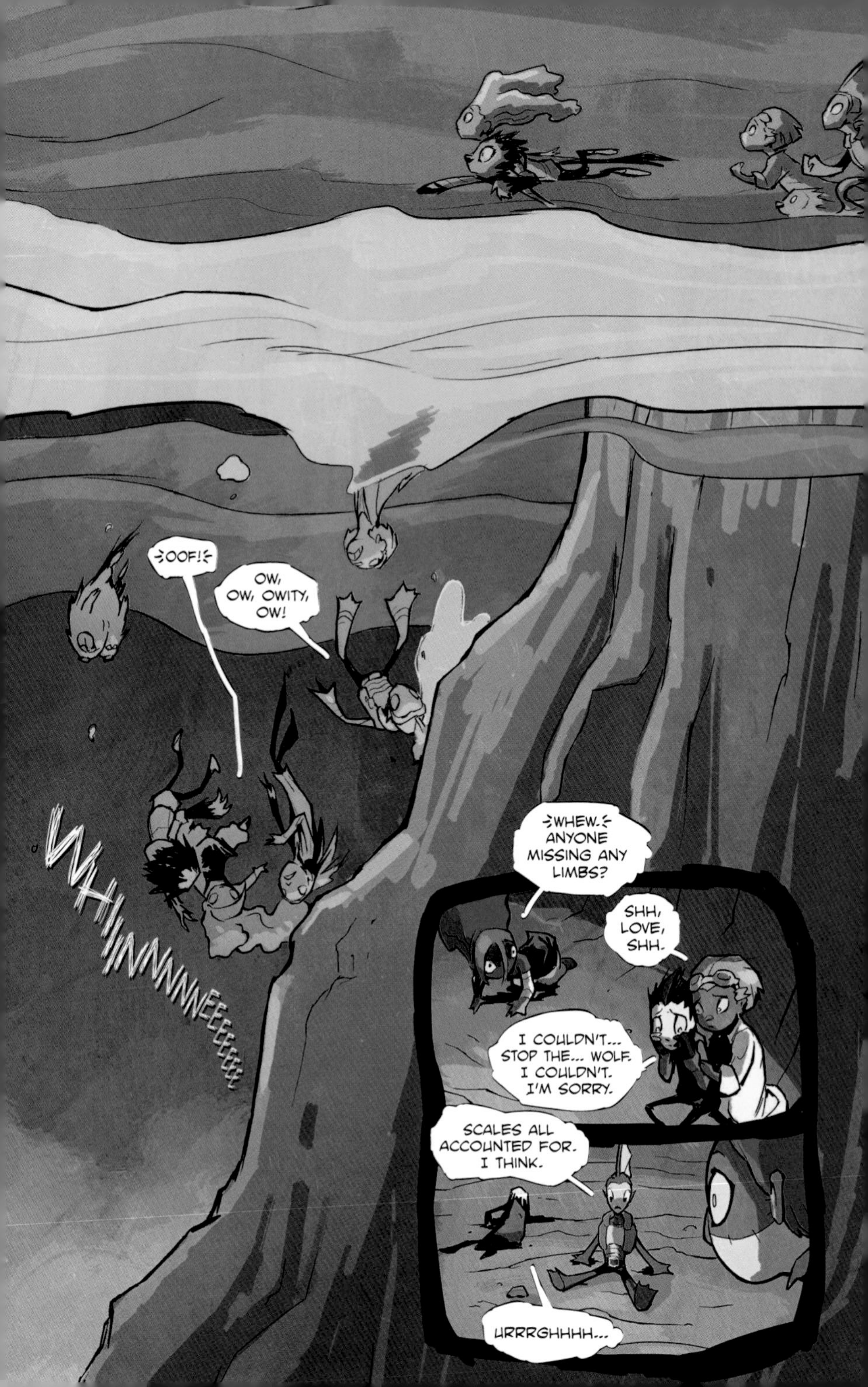
OOF!
OW, OW, OWITY, OW!
WHIIINNNNNEEEEEEE
WHEW. ANYONE MISSING ANY LIMBS?
SHH, LOVE, SHH.
I COULDN'T... STOP THE... WOLF. I COULDN'T. I'M SORRY.
SCALES ALL ACCOUNTED FOR. I THINK.
URRRGHHHH...

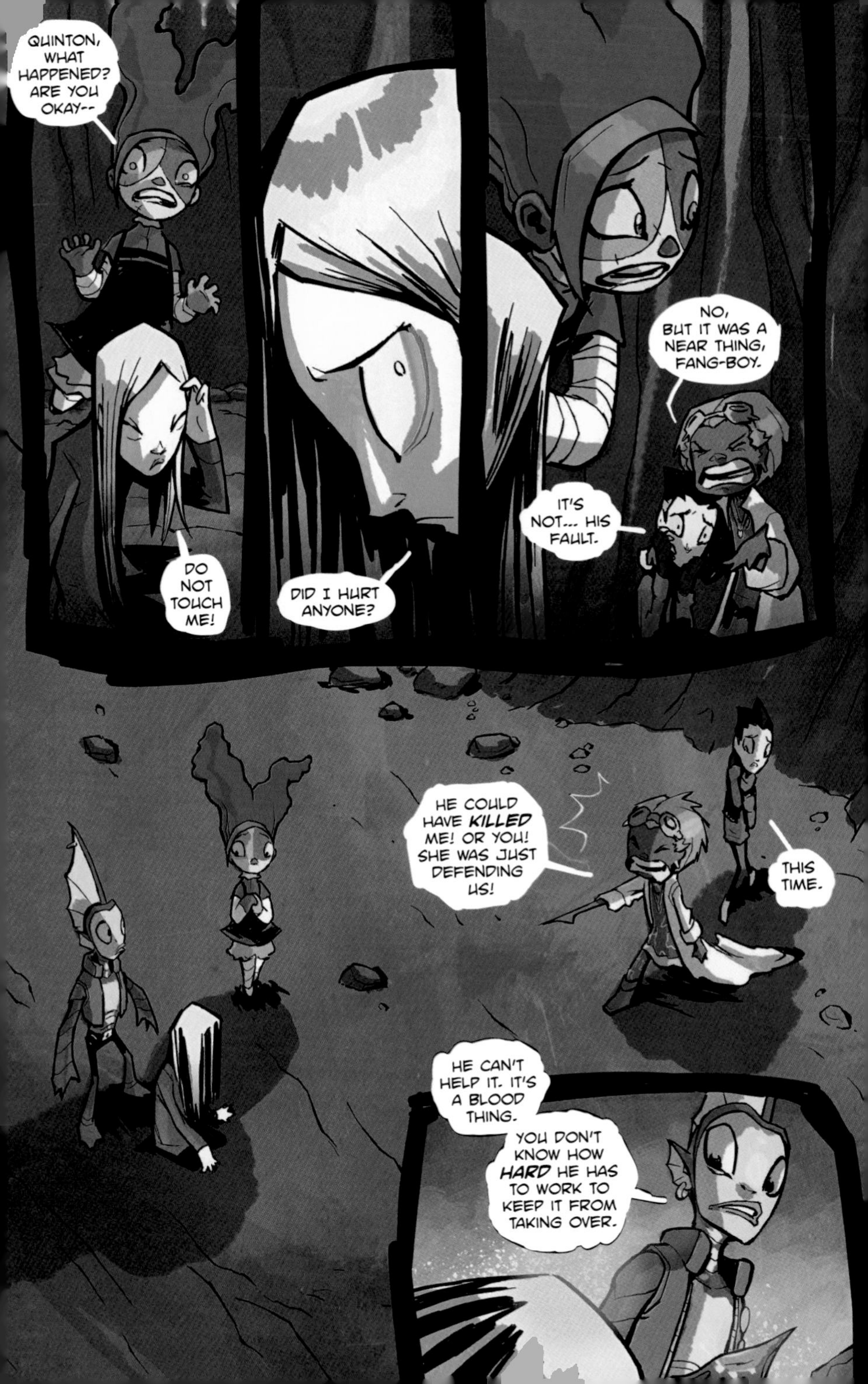
QUINTON, WHAT HAPPENED? ARE YOU OKAY--
DO NOT TOUCH ME!
DID I HURT ANYONE?
NO, BUT IT WAS A NEAR THING, FANG-BOY.
IT'S NOT... HIS FAULT.
HE COULD HAVE KILLED ME! OR YOU! SHE WAS JUST DEFENDING US!
THIS TIME.
HE CAN'T HELP IT. IT'S A BLOOD THING.
YOU DON'T KNOW HOW HARD HE HAS TO WORK TO KEEP IT FROM TAKING OVER.

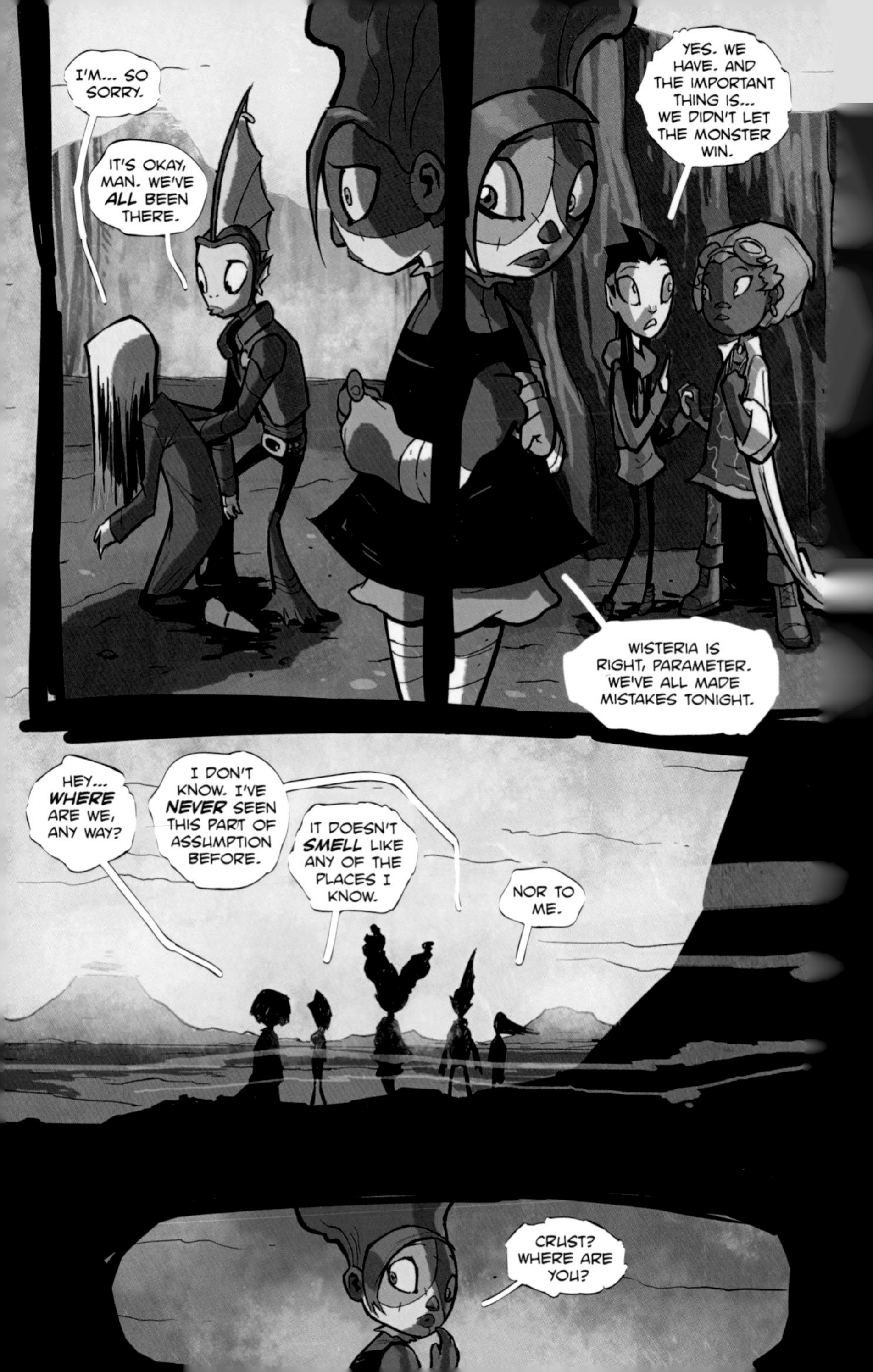
I'M... SO SORRY.
IT'S OKAY, MAN. WE'VE ALL BEEN THERE.
YES. WE HAVE. AND THE IMPORTANT THING IS... WE DIDN'T LET THE MONSTER WIN.
WISTERIA IS RIGHT, PARAMETER. WE'VE ALL MADE MISTAKES TONIGHT.
HEY... WHERE ARE WE, ANY WAY?
I DON'T KNOW. I'VE NEVER SEEN THIS PART OF ASSUMPTION BEFORE.
IT DOESN'T SMELL LIKE ANY OF THE PLACES I KNOW.
NOR TO ME.
CRUST? WHERE ARE YOU?

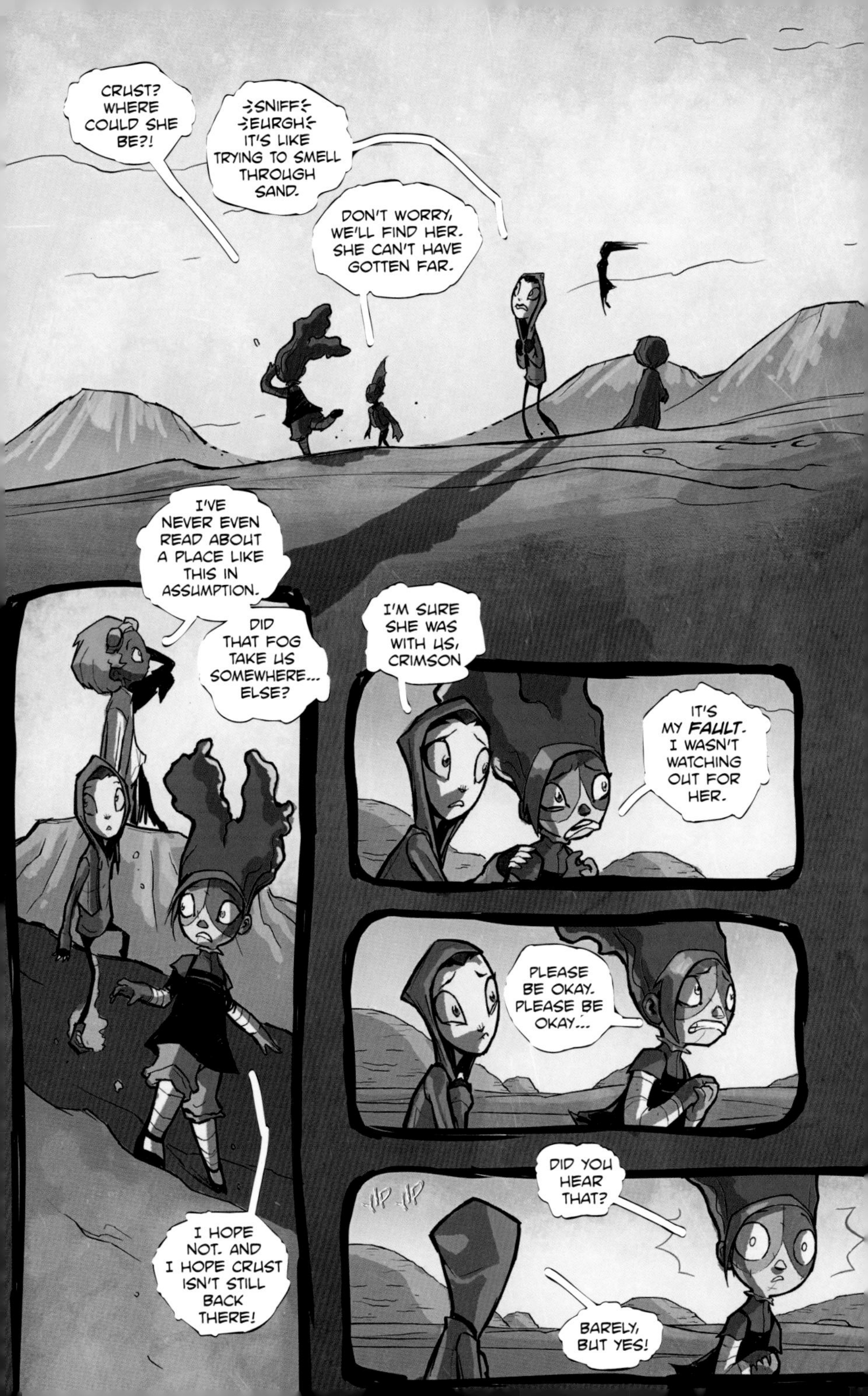
CRUST? WHERE COULD SHE BE?!
SNIFF EURGH IT'S LIKE TRYING TO SMELL THROUGH SAND.
DON'T WORRY, WE'LL FIND HER. SHE CAN'T HAVE GOTTEN FAR.
I'VE NEVER EVEN READ ABOUT A PLACE LIKE THIS IN ASSUMPTION.
DID THAT FOG TAKE US SOMEWHERE... ELSE?
I HOPE NOT. AND I HOPE CRUST ISN'T STILL BACK THERE!
I'M SURE SHE WAS WITH US, CRIMSON
IT'S MY FAULT. I WASN'T WATCHING OUT FOR HER.
PLEASE BE OKAY. PLEASE BE OKAY...
YIP YIP
DID YOU HEAR THAT?
BARELY, BUT YES!

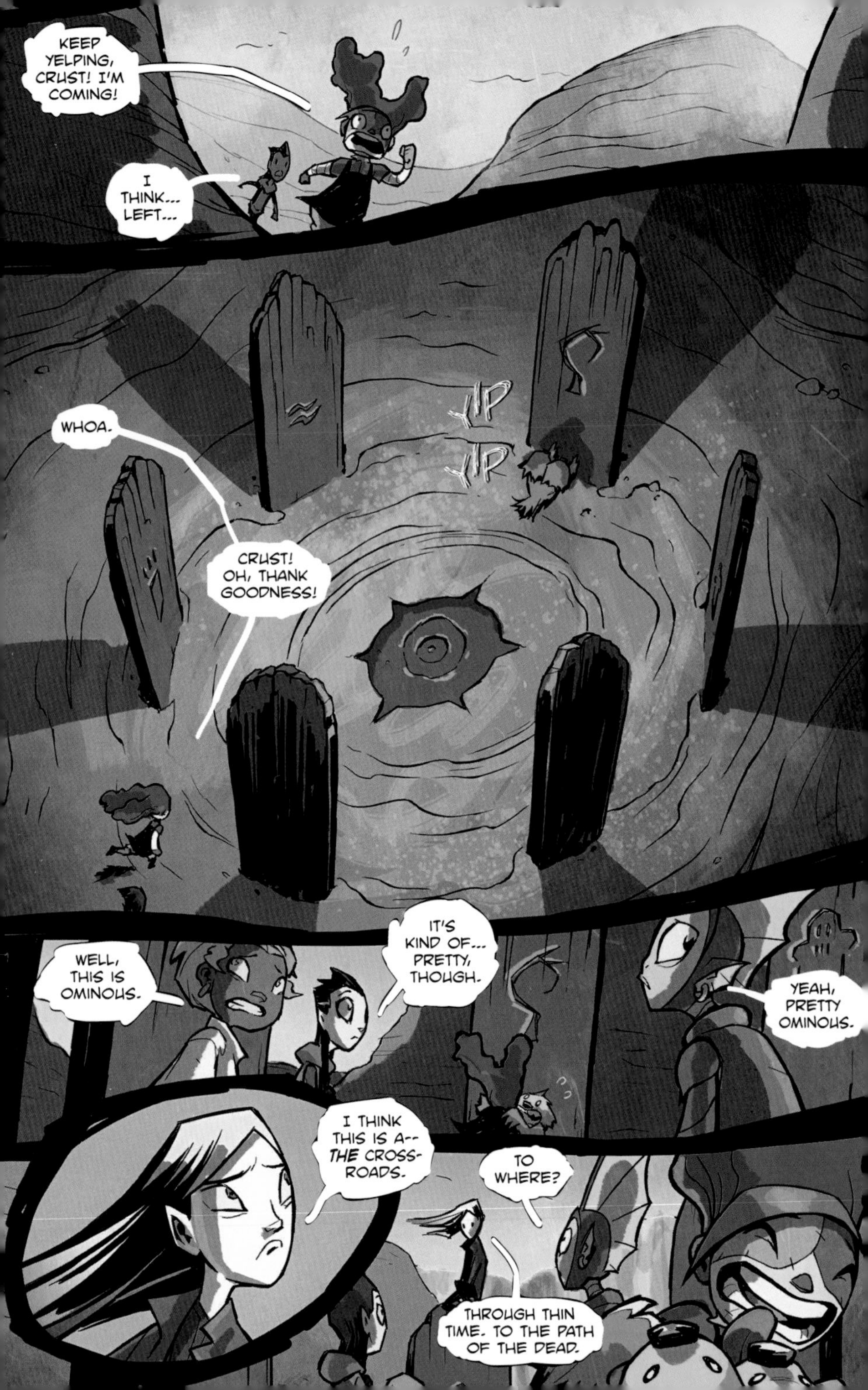
KEEP YELPING, CRUST! I'M COMING!
I THINK... LEFT...
WHOA.
YIP YIP
CRUST! OH, THANK GOODNESS!
WELL, THIS IS OMINOUS.
IT'S KIND OF... PRETTY, THOUGH.
YEAH, PRETTY OMINOUS.
I THINK THIS IS A-- *THE* CROSS-ROADS.
TO WHERE?
THROUGH THIN TIME. TO THE PATH OF THE DEAD.

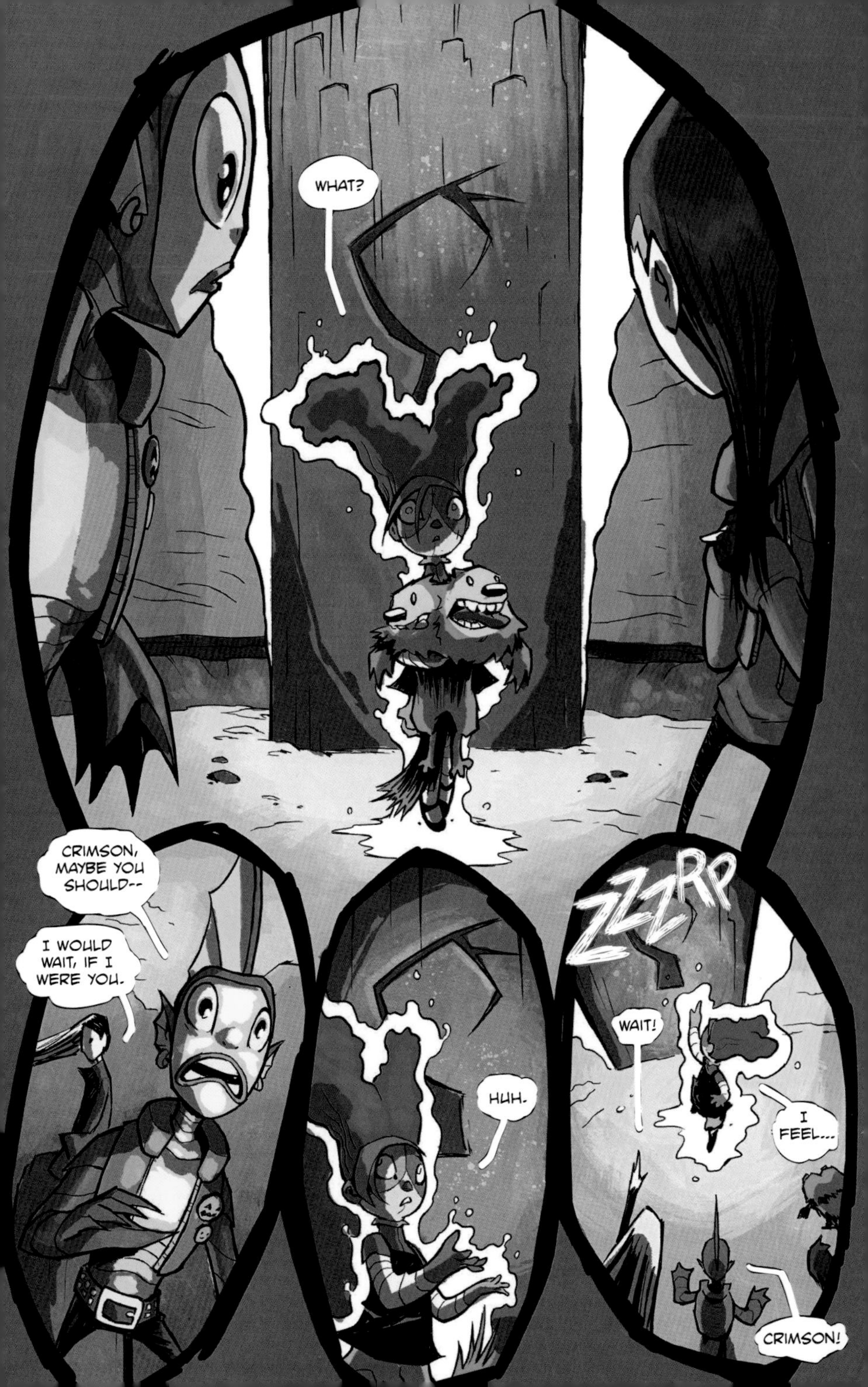
WHAT?
CRIMSON, MAYBE YOU SHOULD--
I WOULD WAIT, IF I WERE YOU.
HUH.
ZZZRP
WAIT!
I FEEL...
CRIMSON!

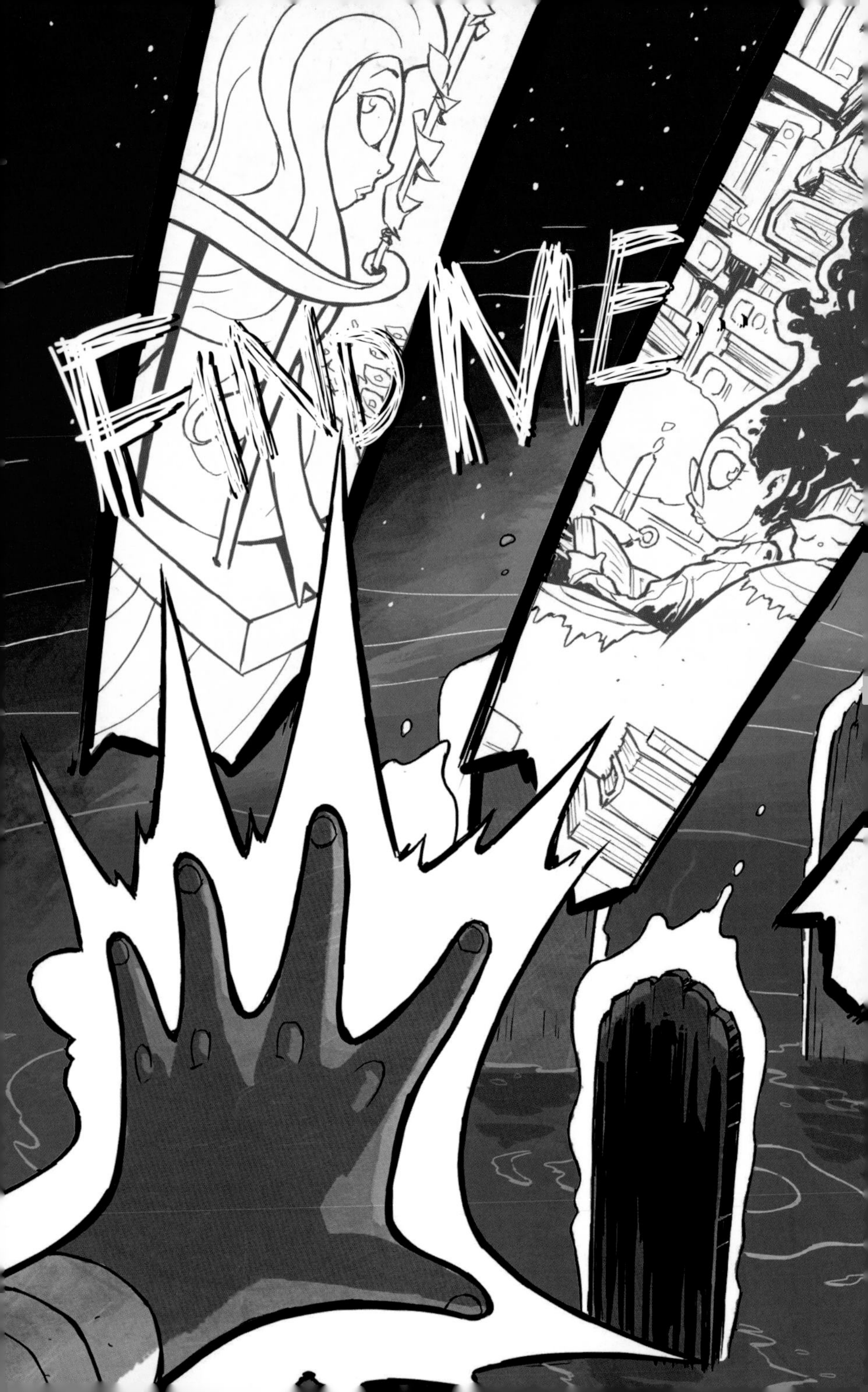
FIND ME

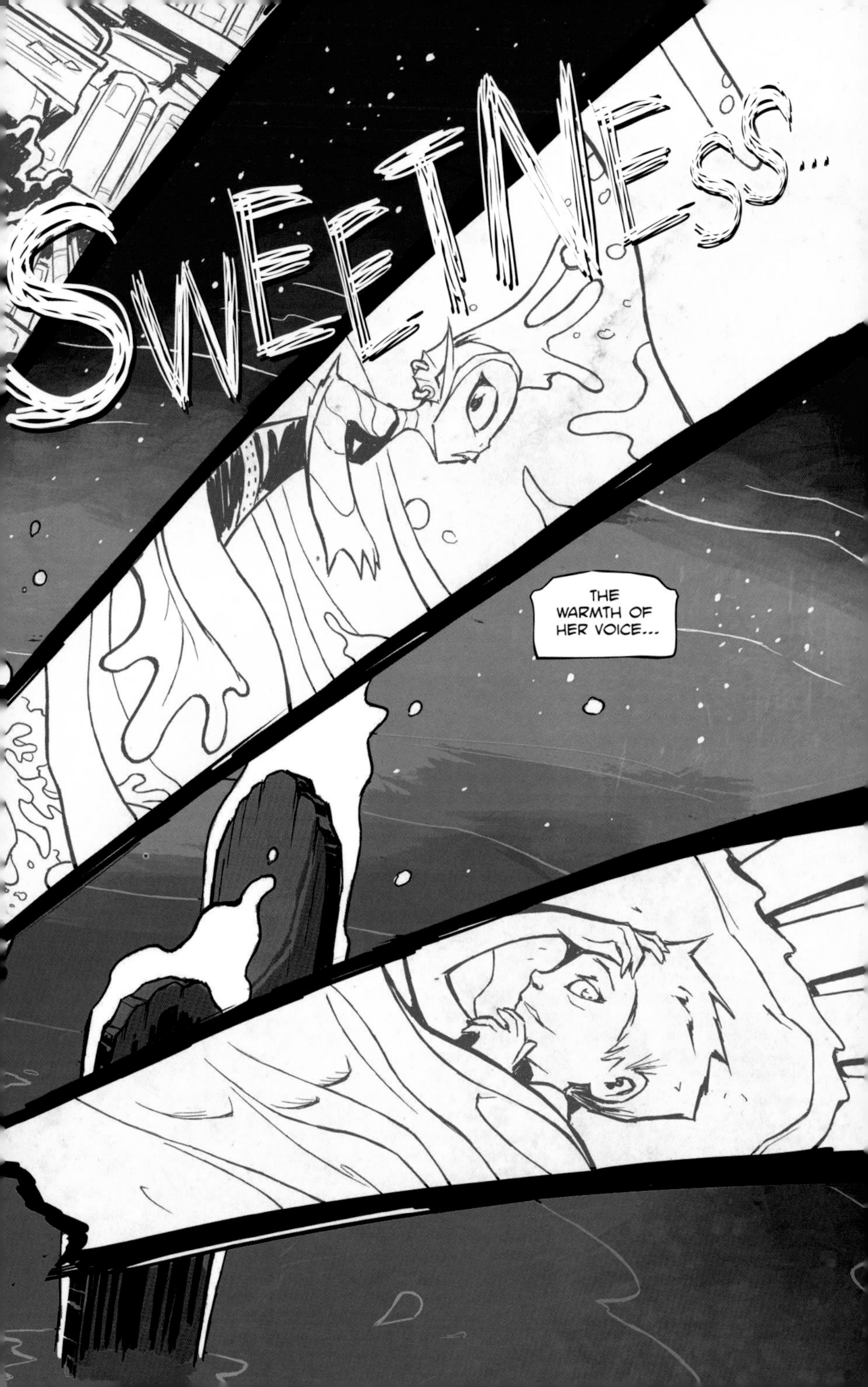
SWEETNESS...
THE WARMTH OF HER VOICE...

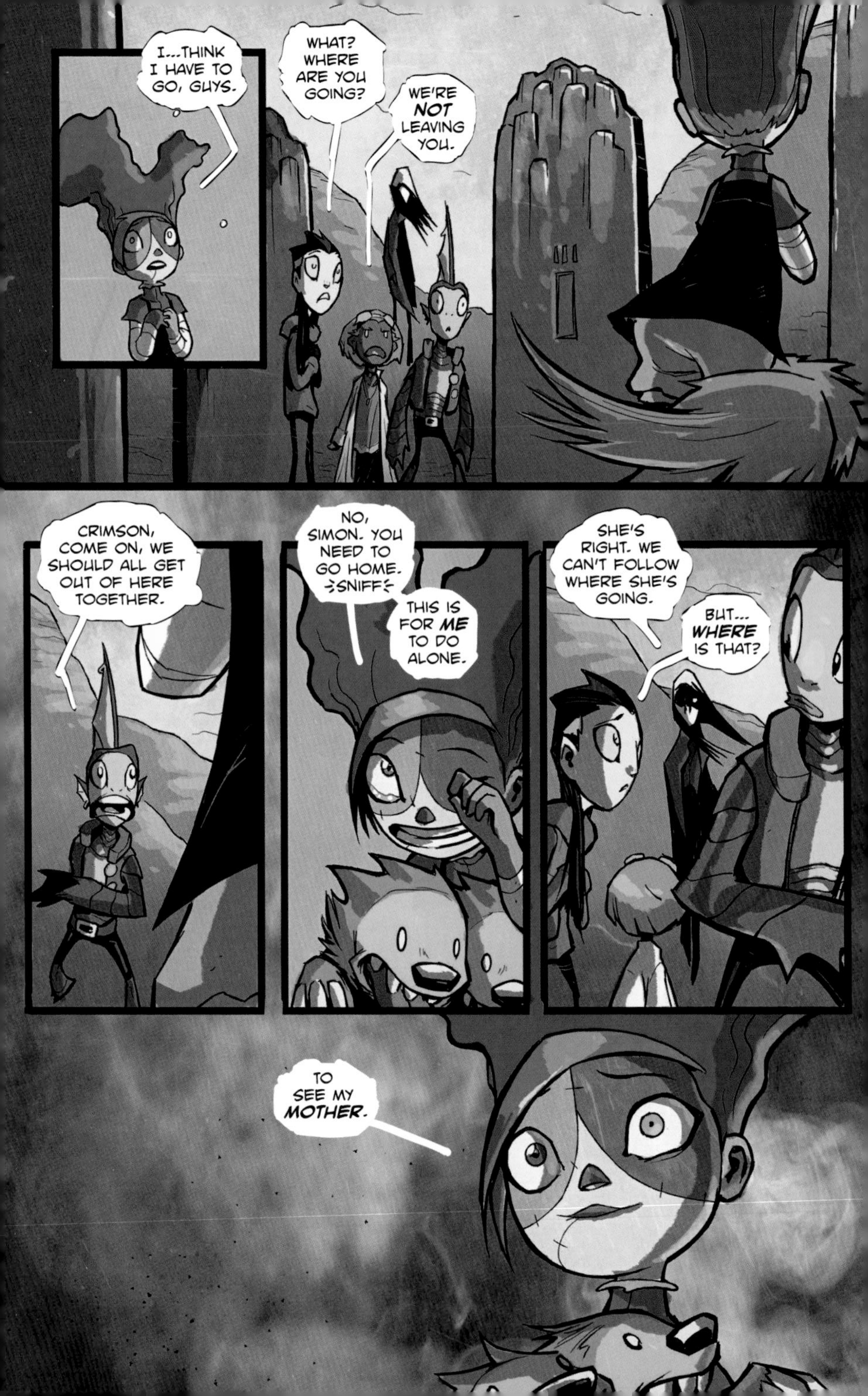
I...THINK I HAVE TO GO, GUYS.
WHAT? WHERE ARE YOU GOING?
WE'RE NOT LEAVING YOU.
CRIMSON, COME ON, WE SHOULD ALL GET OUT OF HERE TOGETHER.
NO, SIMON. YOU NEED TO GO HOME. *SNIFF*
THIS IS FOR ME TO DO ALONE.
SHE'S RIGHT. WE CAN'T FOLLOW WHERE SHE'S GOING.
BUT... WHERE IS THAT?
TO SEE MY MOTHER.

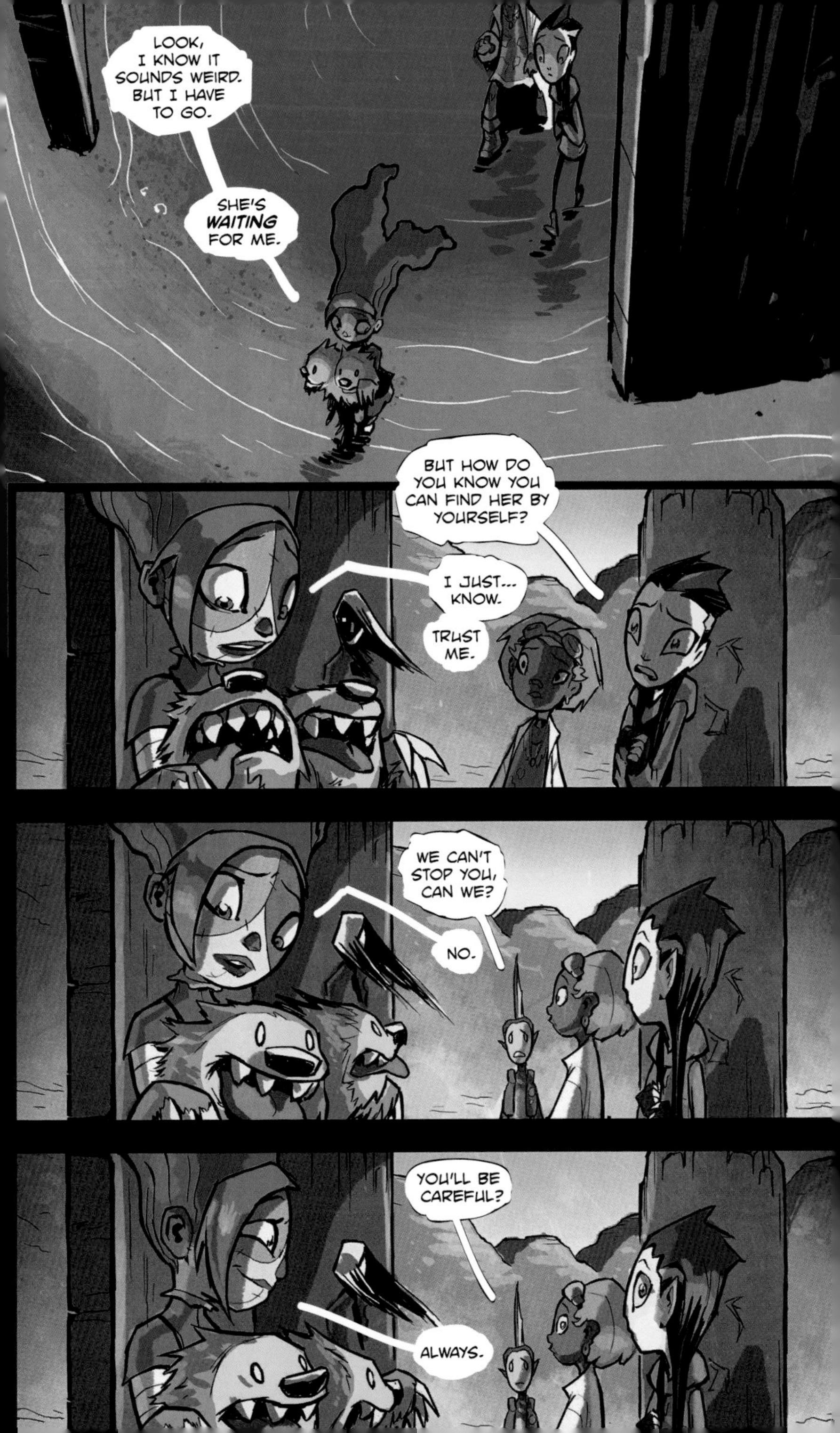
LOOK, I KNOW IT SOUNDS WEIRD. BUT I HAVE TO GO.
SHE'S *WAITING* FOR ME.
BUT HOW DO YOU KNOW YOU CAN FIND HER BY YOURSELF?
I JUST... KNOW.
TRUST ME.
WE CAN'T STOP YOU, CAN WE?
NO.
YOU'LL BE CAREFUL?
ALWAYS.

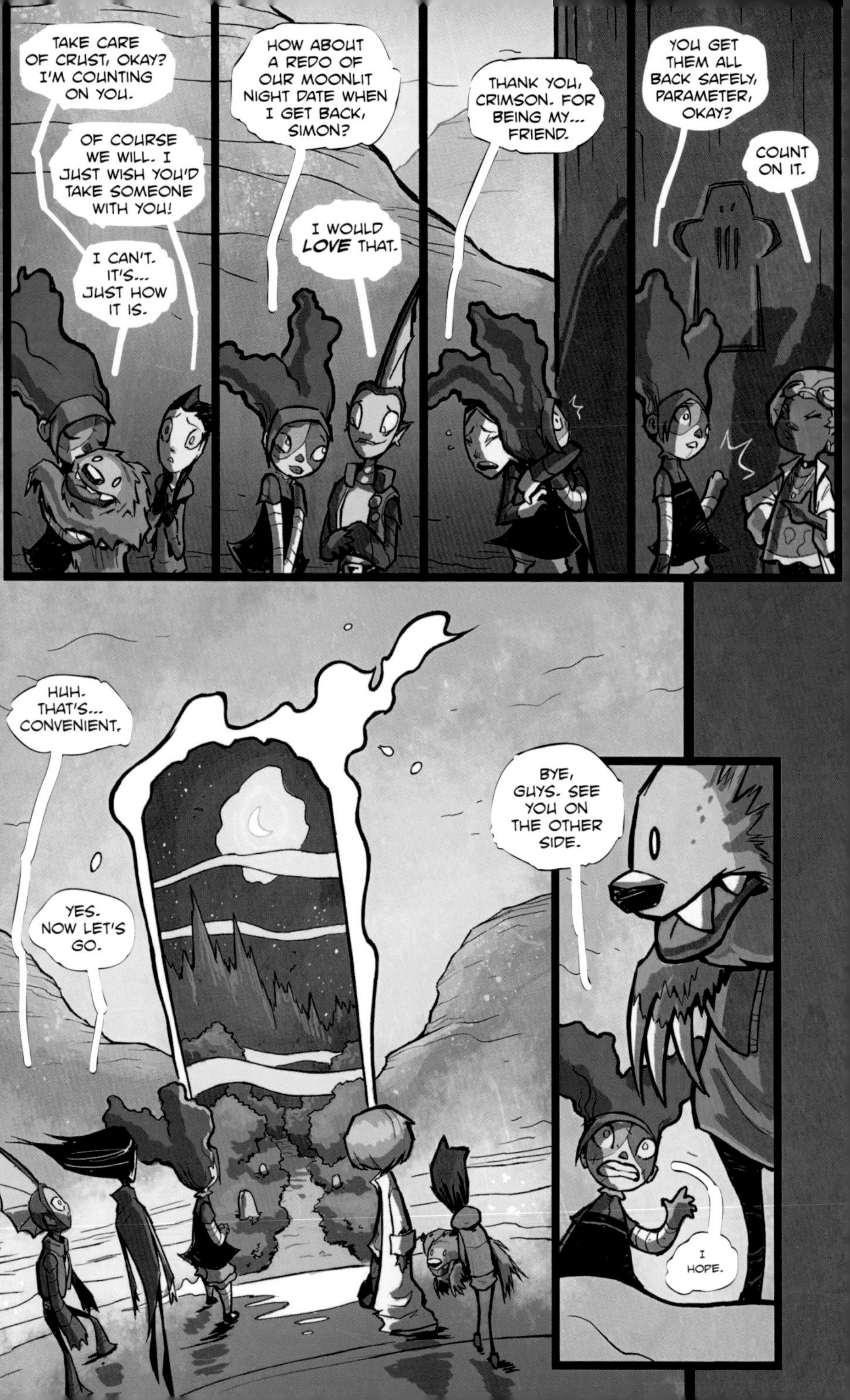
TAKE CARE OF CRUST, OKAY? I'M COUNTING ON YOU.
OF COURSE WE WILL. I JUST WISH YOU'D TAKE SOMEONE WITH YOU!
I CAN'T. IT'S... JUST HOW IT IS.
HOW ABOUT A REDO OF OUR MOONLIT NIGHT DATE WHEN I GET BACK, SIMON?
I WOULD LOVE THAT.
THANK YOU, CRIMSON. FOR BEING MY... FRIEND.
YOU GET THEM ALL BACK SAFELY, PARAMETER, OKAY?
COUNT ON IT.
HUH. THAT'S... CONVENIENT.
YES. NOW LET'S GO.
BYE, GUYS. SEE YOU ON THE OTHER SIDE.
I HOPE.

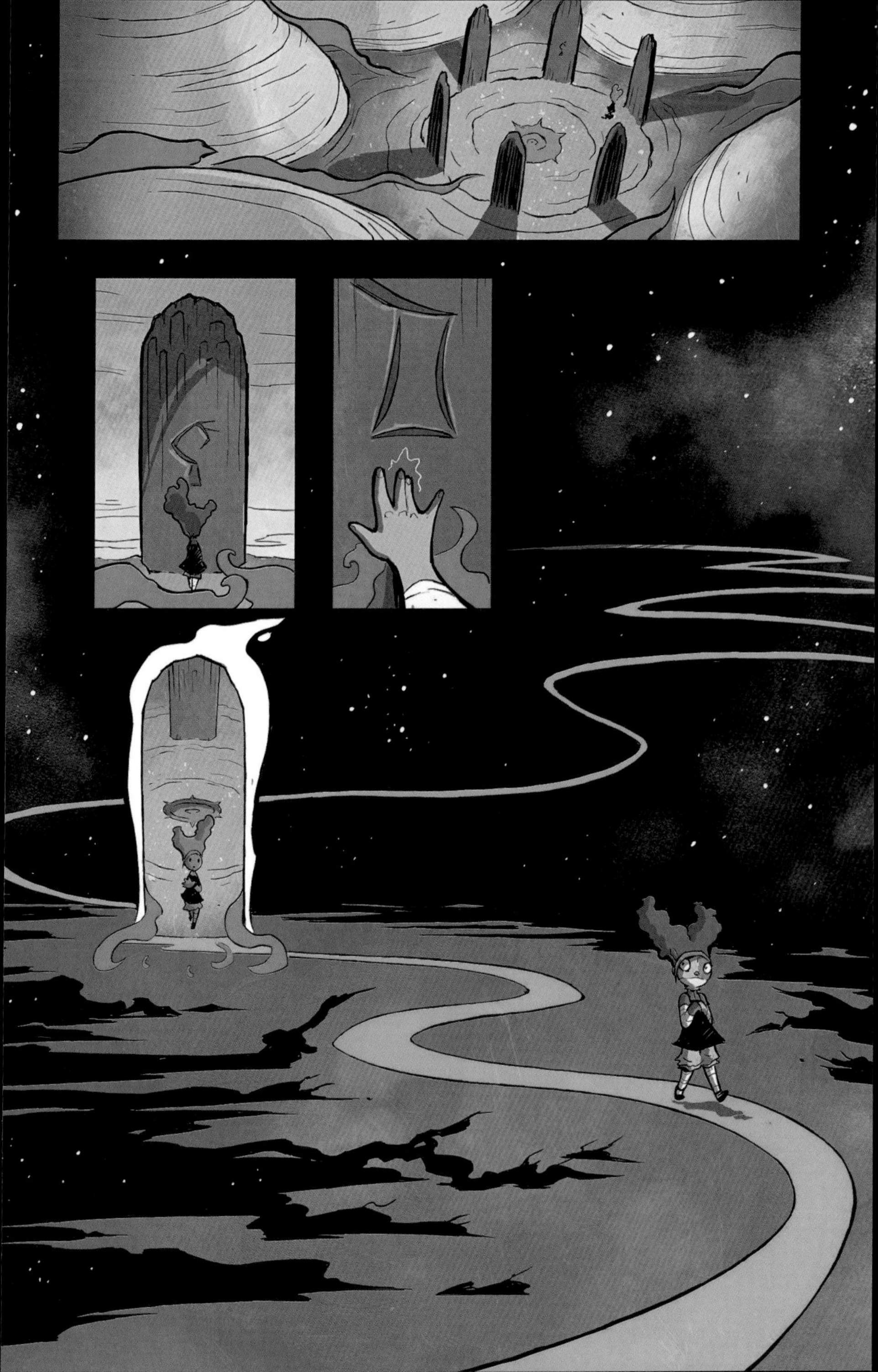

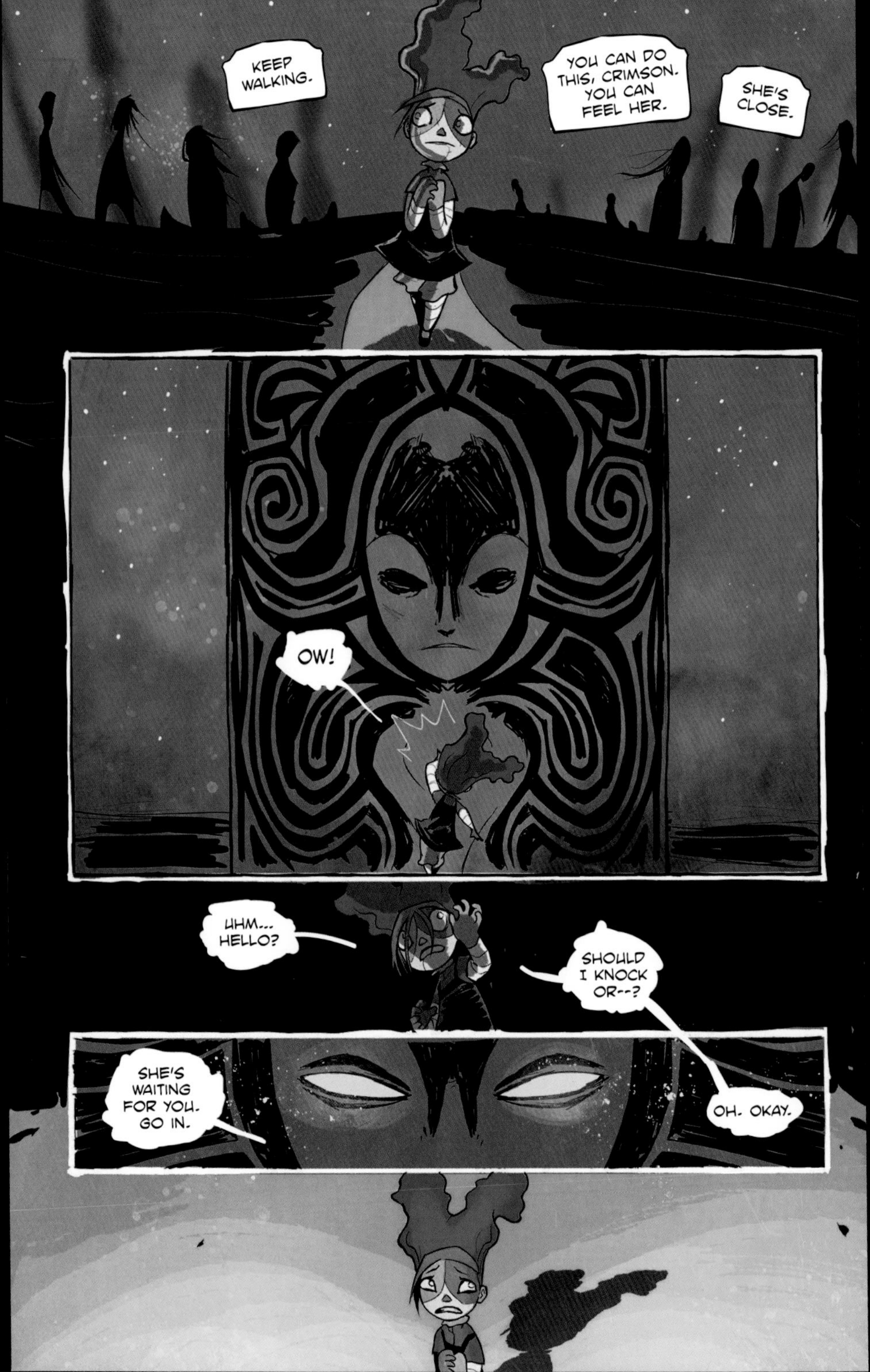
KEEP WALKING.
YOU CAN DO THIS, CRIMSON. YOU CAN FEEL HER.
SHE'S CLOSE.
OW!
UHM... HELLO?
SHOULD I KNOCK OR--?
SHE'S WAITING FOR YOU. GO IN.
OH. OKAY.

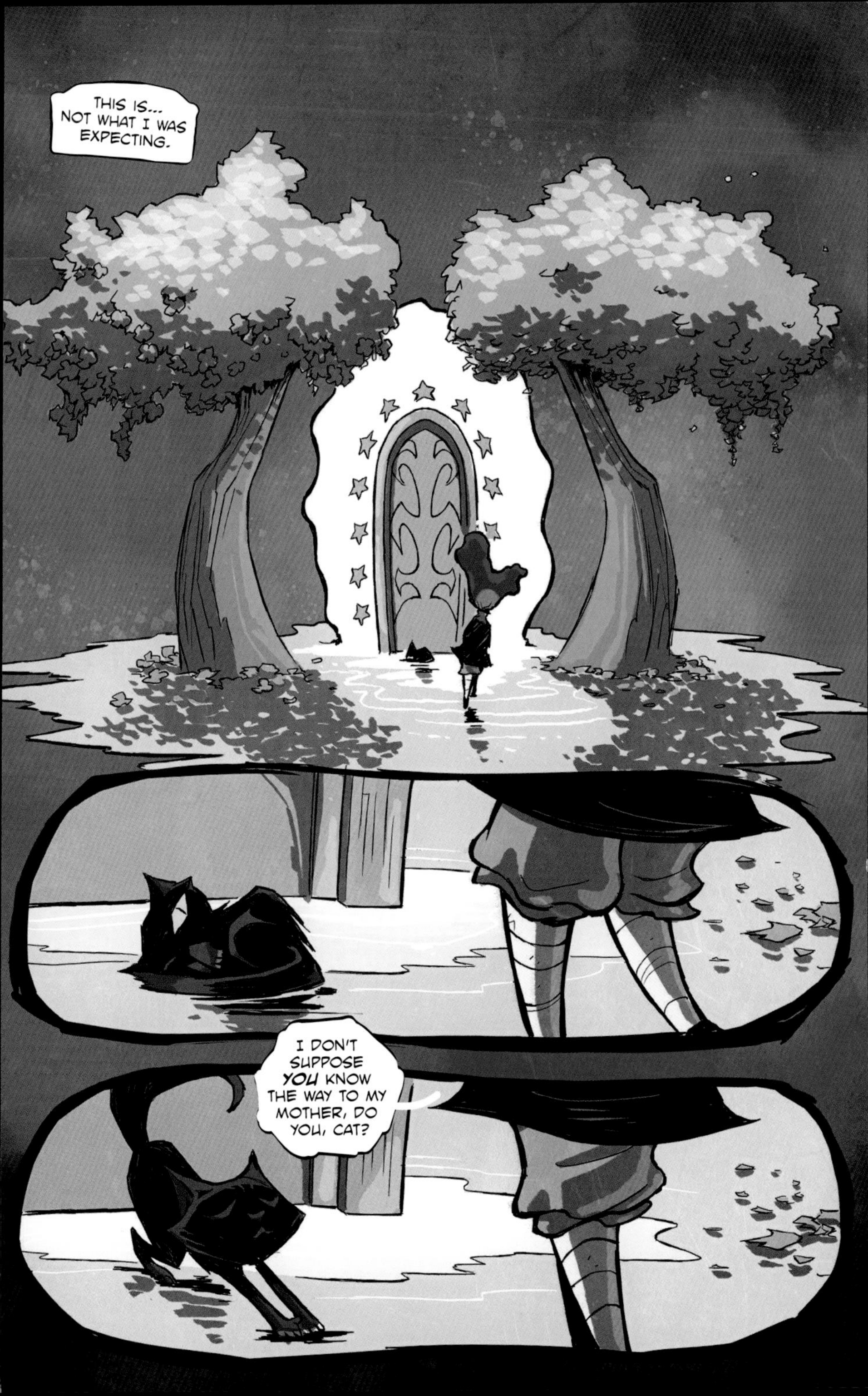
THIS IS... NOT WHAT I WAS EXPECTING.
I DON'T SUPPOSE *YOU* KNOW THE WAY TO MY MOTHER, DO YOU, CAT?

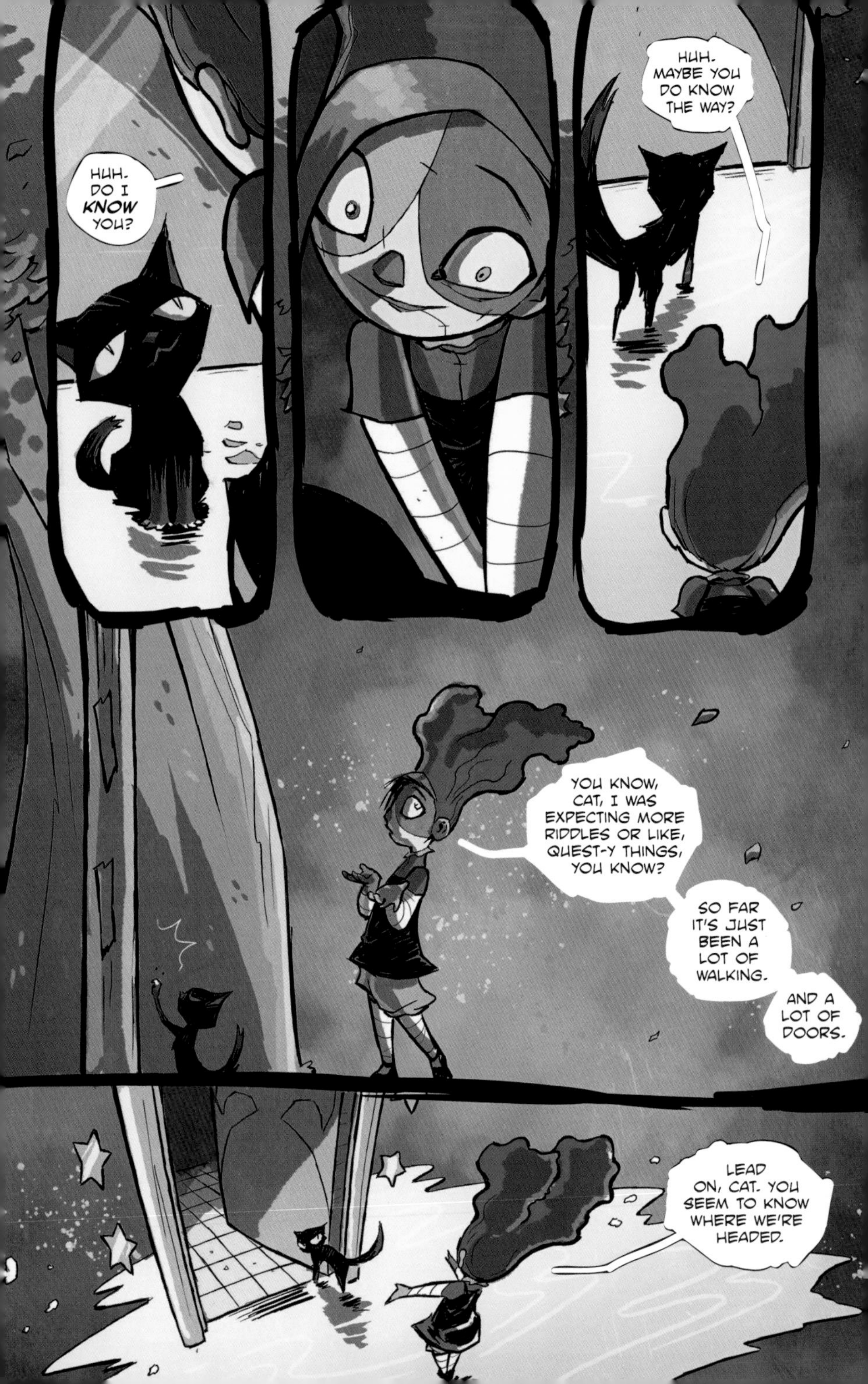
HUH. DO I **KNOW** YOU?
HUH. MAYBE YOU DO KNOW THE WAY?
YOU KNOW, CAT, I WAS EXPECTING MORE RIDDLES OR LIKE, QUEST-Y THINGS, YOU KNOW?
SO FAR IT'S JUST BEEN A LOT OF WALKING.
AND A LOT OF DOORS.
LEAD ON, CAT. YOU SEEM TO KNOW WHERE WE'RE HEADED.

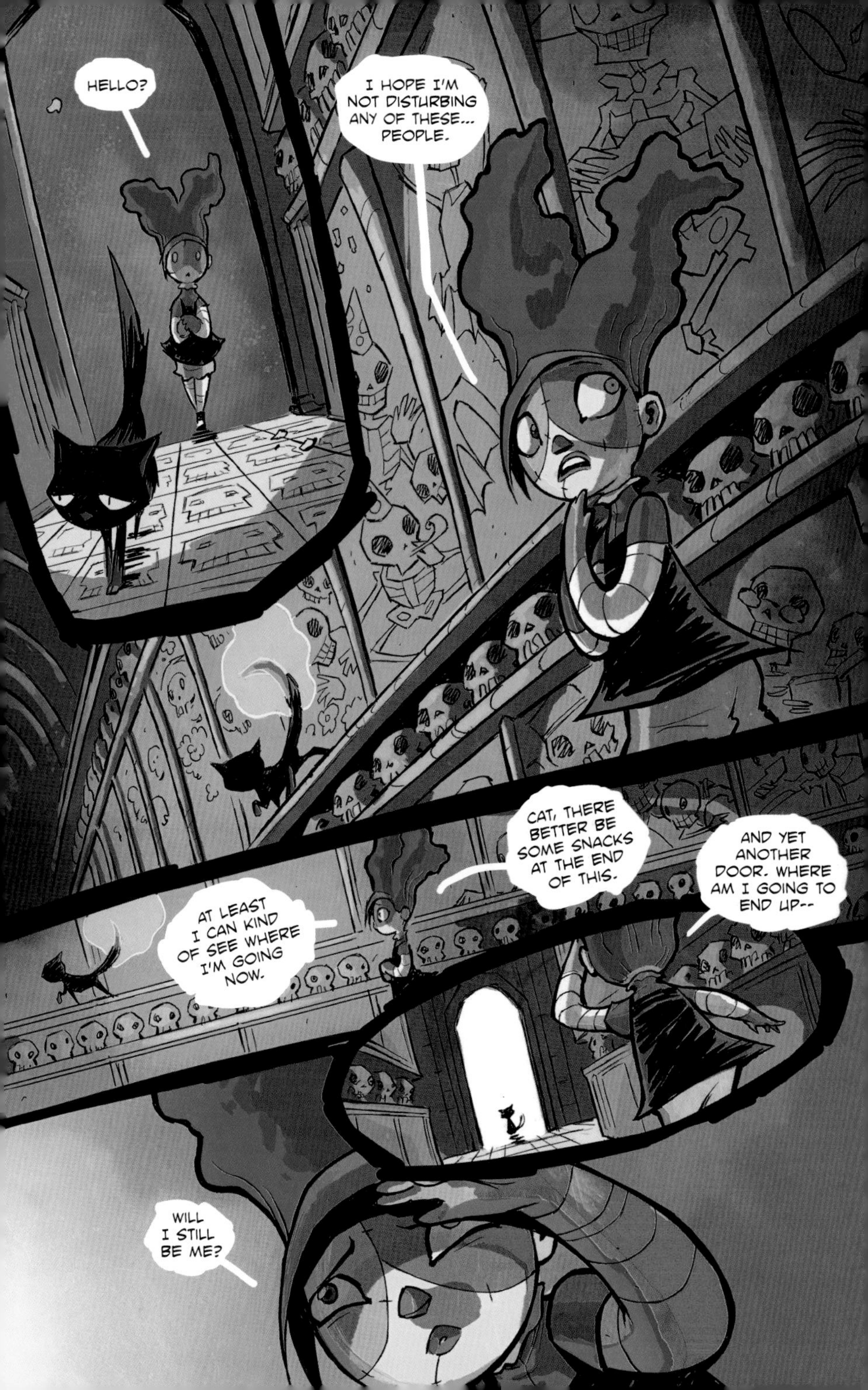
HELLO?
I HOPE I'M NOT DISTURBING ANY OF THESE... PEOPLE.
AT LEAST I CAN KIND OF SEE WHERE I'M GOING NOW.
CAT, THERE BETTER BE SOME SNACKS AT THE END OF THIS.
AND YET ANOTHER DOOR. WHERE AM I GOING TO END UP--
WILL I STILL BE ME?

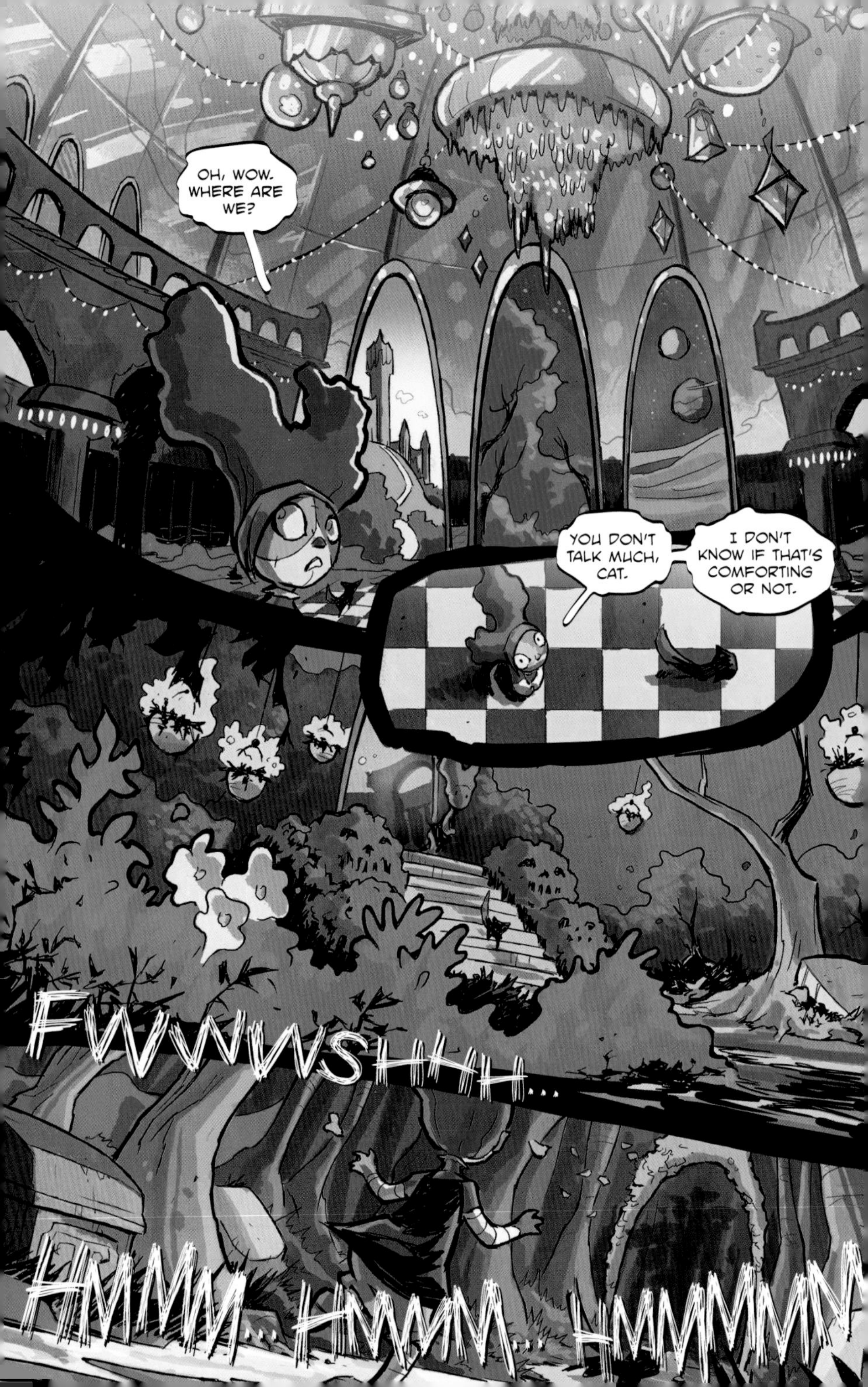
OH, WOW. WHERE ARE WE?
YOU DON'T TALK MUCH, CAT.
I DON'T KNOW IF THAT'S COMFORTING OR NOT.
FWWWSHHH...
HMMM... HMMM... HMMMMM

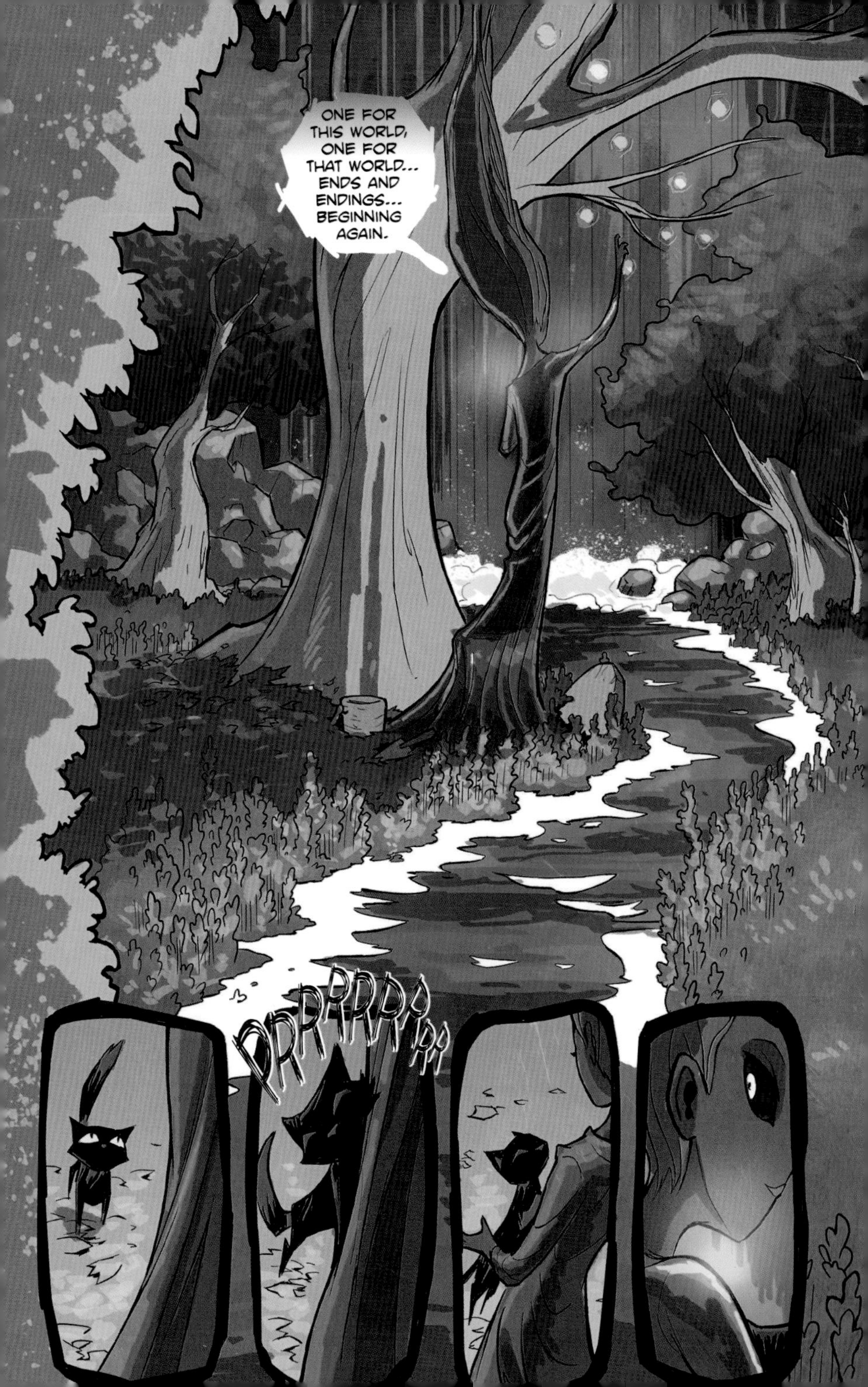
ONE FOR THIS WORLD, ONE FOR THAT WORLD... ENDS AND ENDINGS... BEGINNING AGAIN.
PRRRRRRRRR

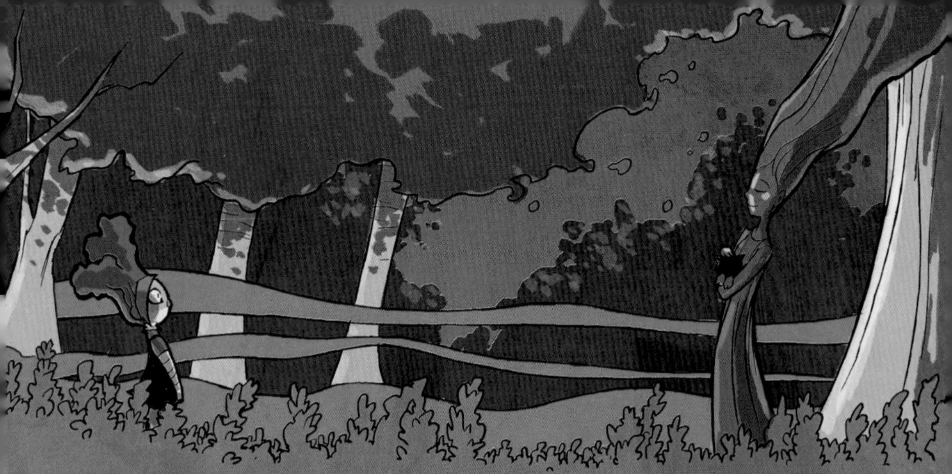

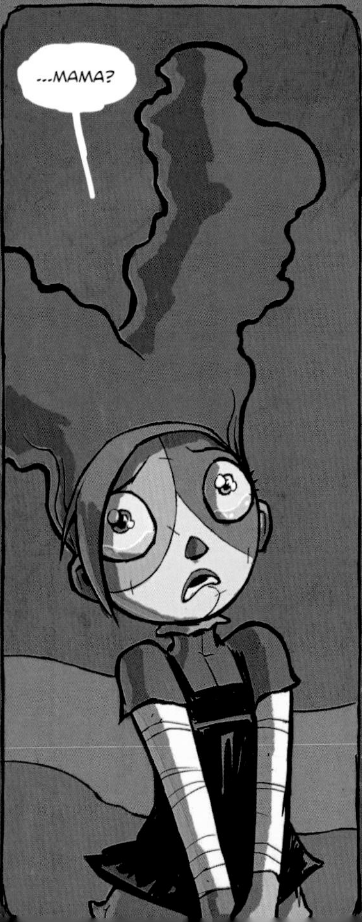
...MAMA?

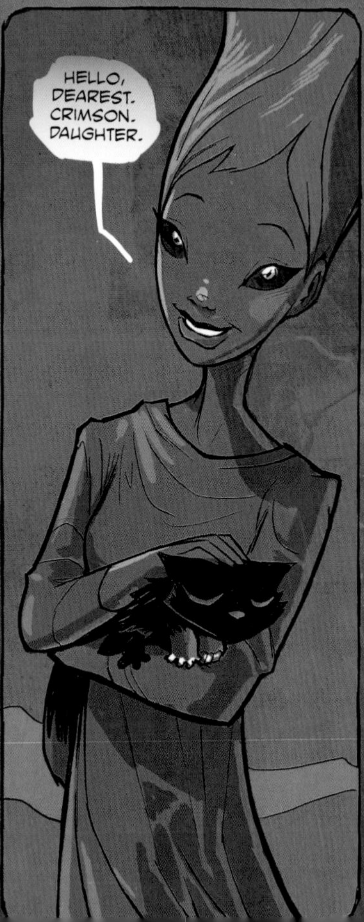
HELLO, DEAREST. CRIMSON. DAUGHTER.

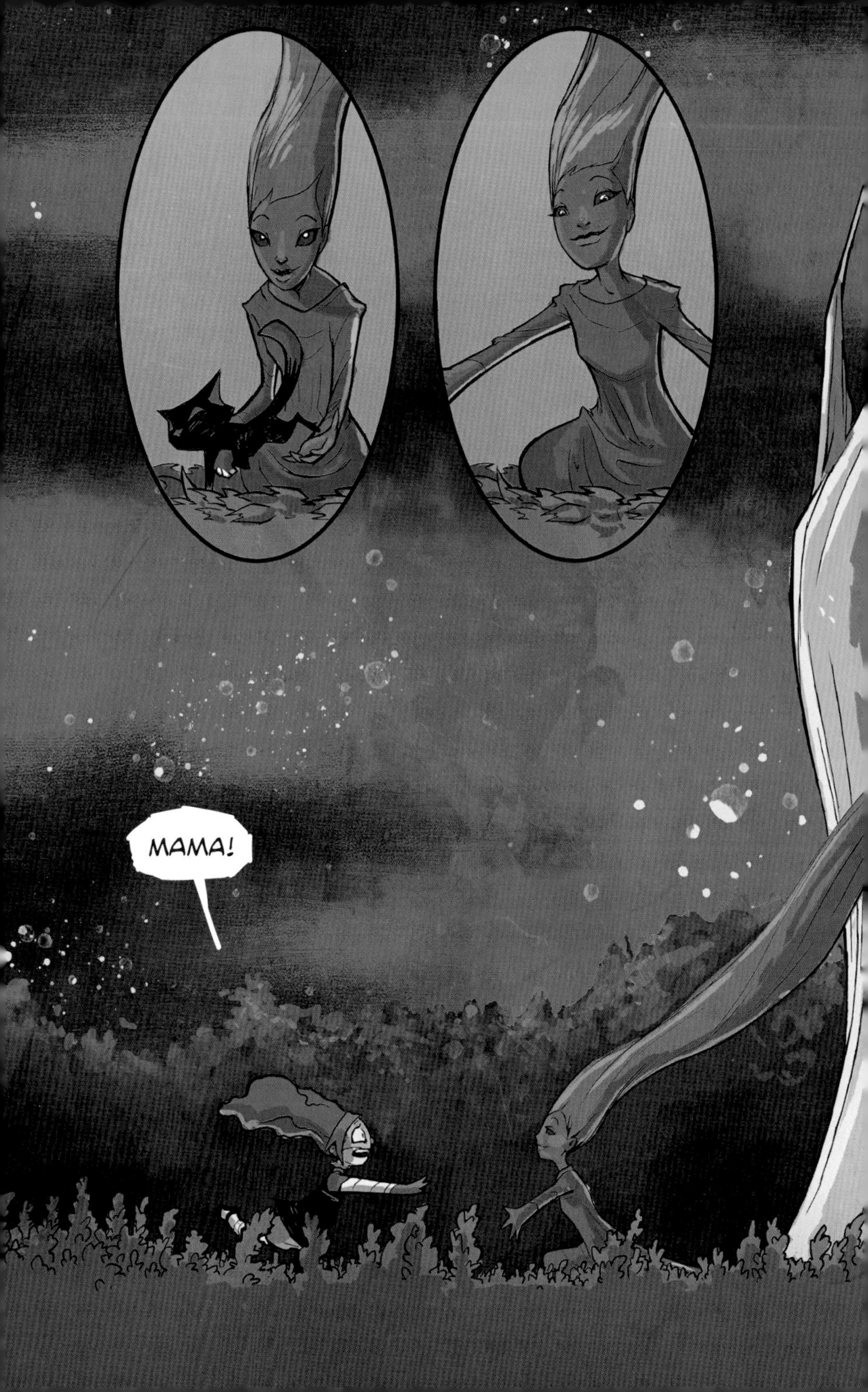
MAMA!

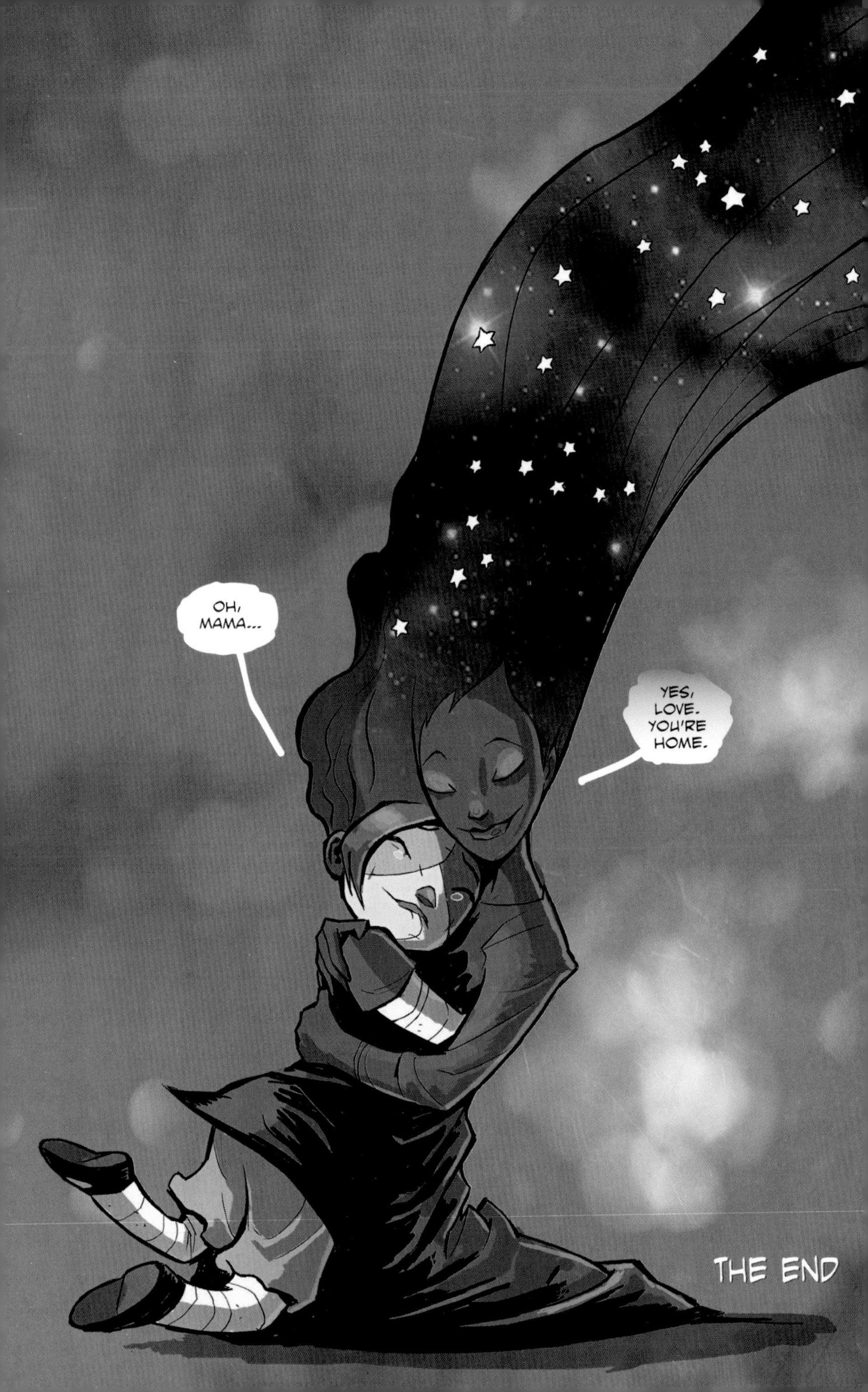
OH, MAMA...
YES, LOVE. YOU'RE HOME.
THE END

STITCHED
CHARACTER BIOGRAPHIES

CRIMSON VOLANIA MULCH
Brand-new and brimming with curiosity, Crimson is a mystery even to herself. Made up of different girls, she doesn't know who she was, so how can she decide who she should be? Waking up in Assumption Cemetery is only the beginning, but she knows at least four things already: she has great hair, she loves animals, vampire boys are seriously pretty, and she definitely needs to find her selves. Whoever they were.

WISTERIA SMIALS
A shy werewolf who paints, Wisteria is a loyal friend with a soft, kind heart...but watch out. If you threaten those close to her or waste time bickering, Wisteria's inner wolf will come out. And it is not to be messed with. No one knows where she lives, which is a bit curious, even for Assumption.

SIMON
A swamp boy with a bioluminescent personality, Simon likes snacks, swimming, and Crimson. A lot. He lives in Assumption's swampy bayou and has no trouble saying what he thinks. He's determined and a bit overly confident, but he'll always be there for a friend.

QUINTON
Assumption's resident vampire boy, he's pretty, he's properly brooding, and he's more than a little stuck up. He's older than even he can remember and doesn't let much touch his undead heart. Until he meets Crimson and has to face a past he's not quite ready to deal with.

PARAMETER JONES
A "magical technician" with a prickly personality and more power than skills, Parameter is Assumption's only human resident. Well, only *living* human resident. Parameter is there to learn and practice magic and become the best. Just don't call her a witch.

CRUST
Half badger, half hedgehog, all cute. Crust is the perfect pet for Crimson and the most adorable undead companion ever made. Was she a gift from Crimson's mom? Does she like cupcakes? All she knows is that she loves Crimson and will follow her anywhere.

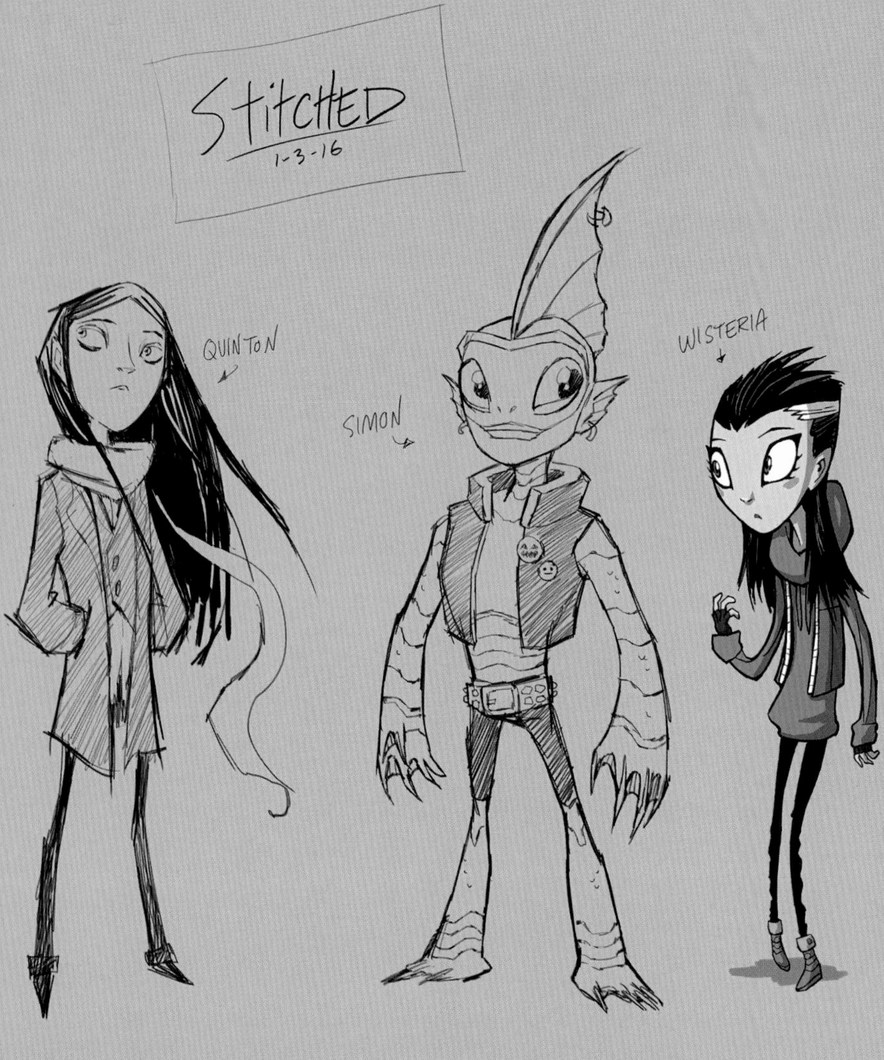

Stitched
1-3-16
QUINTON
SIMON
WISTERIA

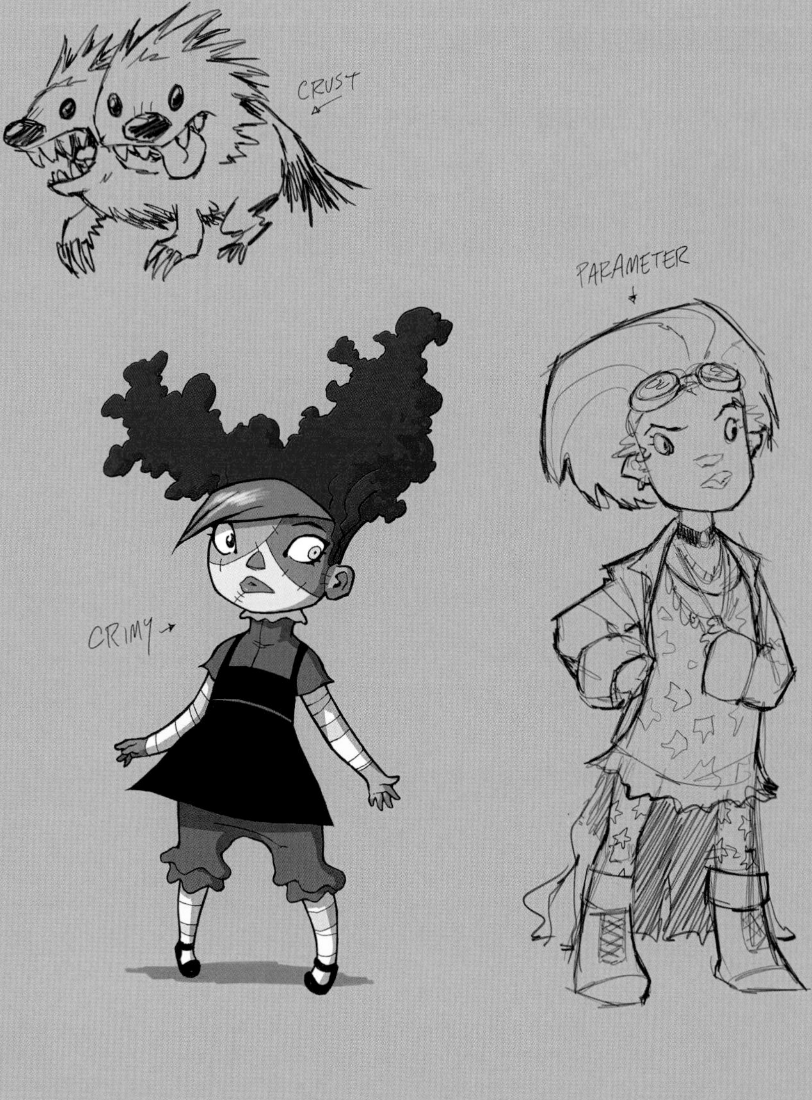
CRUST
PARAMETER
CRIMY

Welcome to Charmz

IN STITCHES

Crimson Volania Mulch might be my favorite character to write. She's a lot like me, sometimes, and also not like me at all. She's a lot braver than I am, for instance. And her hair is way cooler.

When I started writing STITCHED I wanted Crimson to be the kind of girl that anyone would want to be like, or be friends with. Even when she messes up (and she messes up A LOT) you know she's trying to be a good person. We all make mistakes, it's how we learn from them and help other people we've hurt that ultimately defines what kind of person we are. You can't go through life never trying anything because you're afraid you'll fail. You might, and that's okay!

I've failed at all kinds of things. Sometimes a story I'm writing doesn't go well, or a drawing just doesn't work out. I've made painting mistakes and editing mistakes. I'm really good at tripping UP stairs and I can't dance at all. But I still love to do it!

Something else I have in common with Crimson: scars. I have some on my face and my hand from when my kitty, Monkey, accidentally scratched me. It's not that noticeable anymore but when I first got it, it was kind of scary and long and angry. But it faded, like scars tend to do (even the ones on the inside), and they become part of who you are and who you'll be.

You may have noticed that Crimson really loves animals. So do I! Especially cats. Monkey was the best kitty I've ever had; he was so sweet and cuddly. He passed away last year and I miss him, all the time. I wanted him to have a special place in one of my stories and I thought that Assumption and being a little part of Crimson's quest was the best way to see him again. He was what you would call "polydactyl." He had extra toes that looked like thumbs! He used to stretch them out when he slept and touch my face gently. When my daughter was little he would sleep above her, like he was watching over her.

Crimson's love for animals is one of my favorite things about her. It's something she has in common with her mother, who you just met.

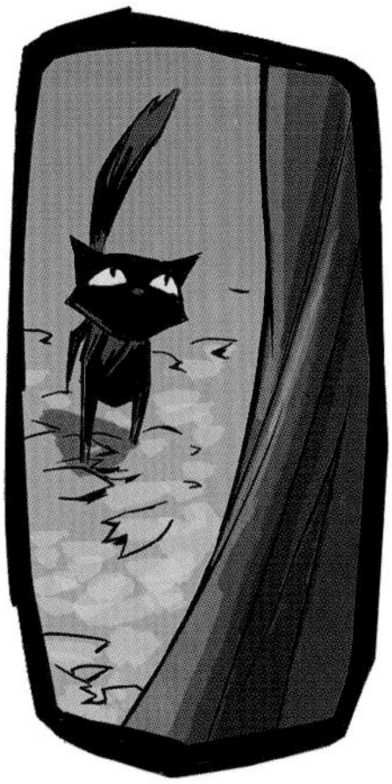

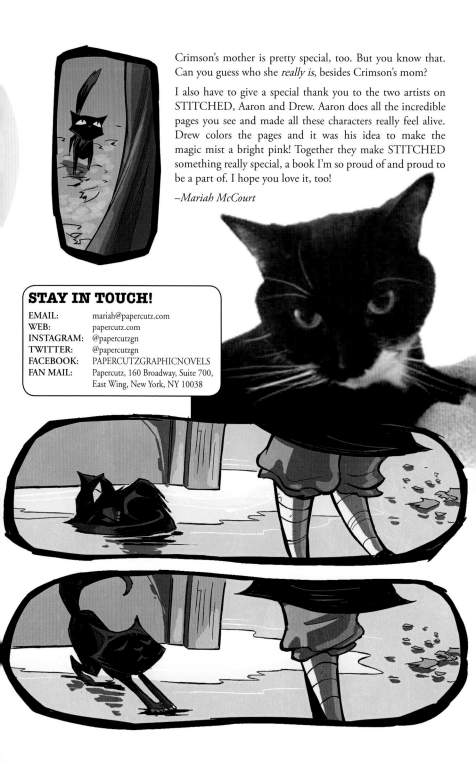

Crimson's mother is pretty special, too. But you know that. Can you guess who she *really is*, besides Crimson's mom?

I also have to give a special thank you to the two artists on STITCHED, Aaron and Drew. Aaron does all the incredible pages you see and made all these characters really feel alive. Drew colors the pages and it was his idea to make the magic mist a bright pink! Together they make STITCHED something really special, a book I'm so proud of and proud to be a part of. I hope you love it, too!

–Mariah McCourt

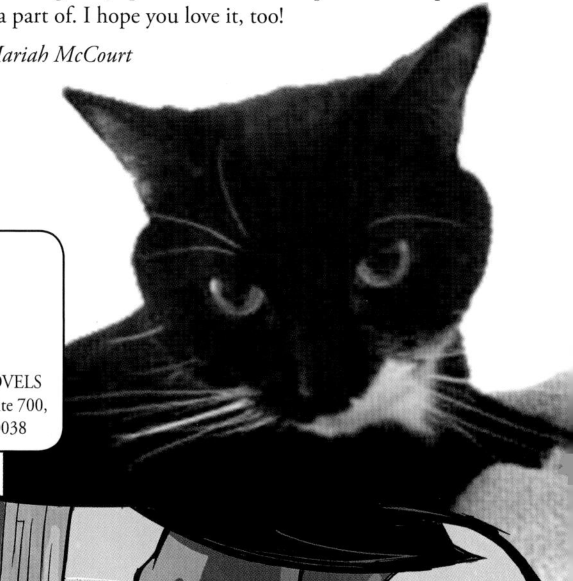

STAY IN TOUCH!

EMAIL: mariah@papercutz.com
WEB: papercutz.com
INSTAGRAM: @papercutzgn
TWITTER: @papercutzgn
FACEBOOK: PAPERCUTZGRAPHICNOVELS
FAN MAIL: Papercutz, 160 Broadway, Suite 700, East Wing, New York, NY 10038

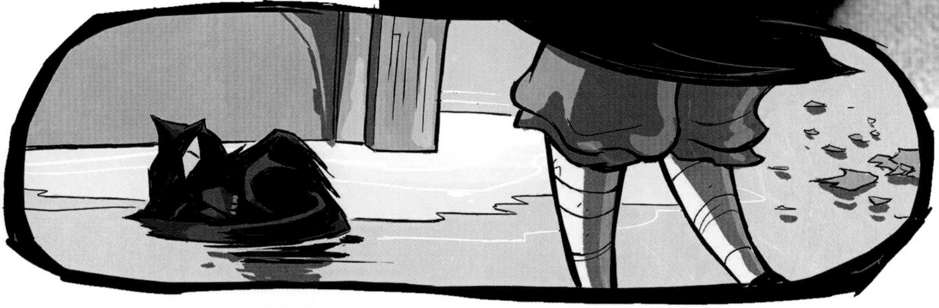

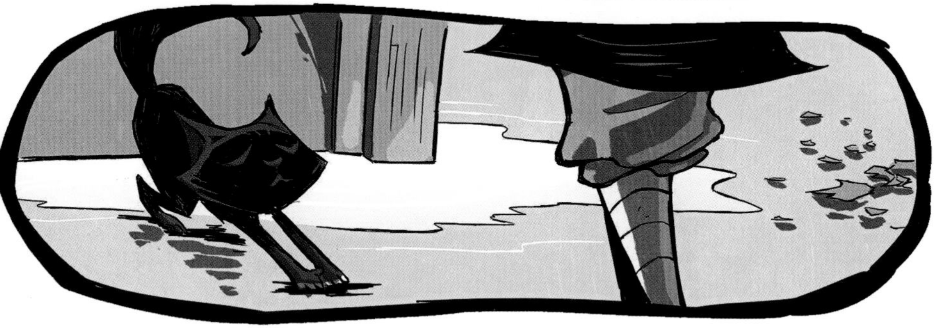

Enjoy this preview of CHLOE #4, another Charmz title!

Chloe

RAINY DAY

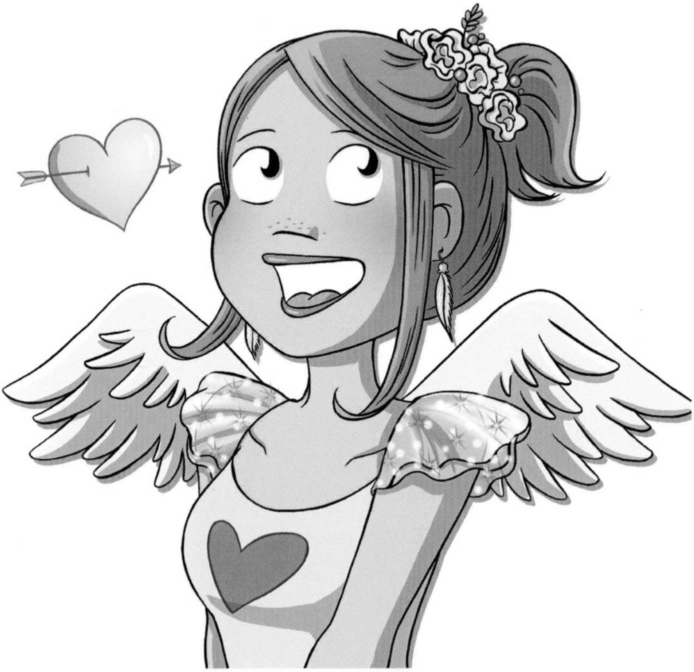

Story by Greg Tessier
Art by Amandine

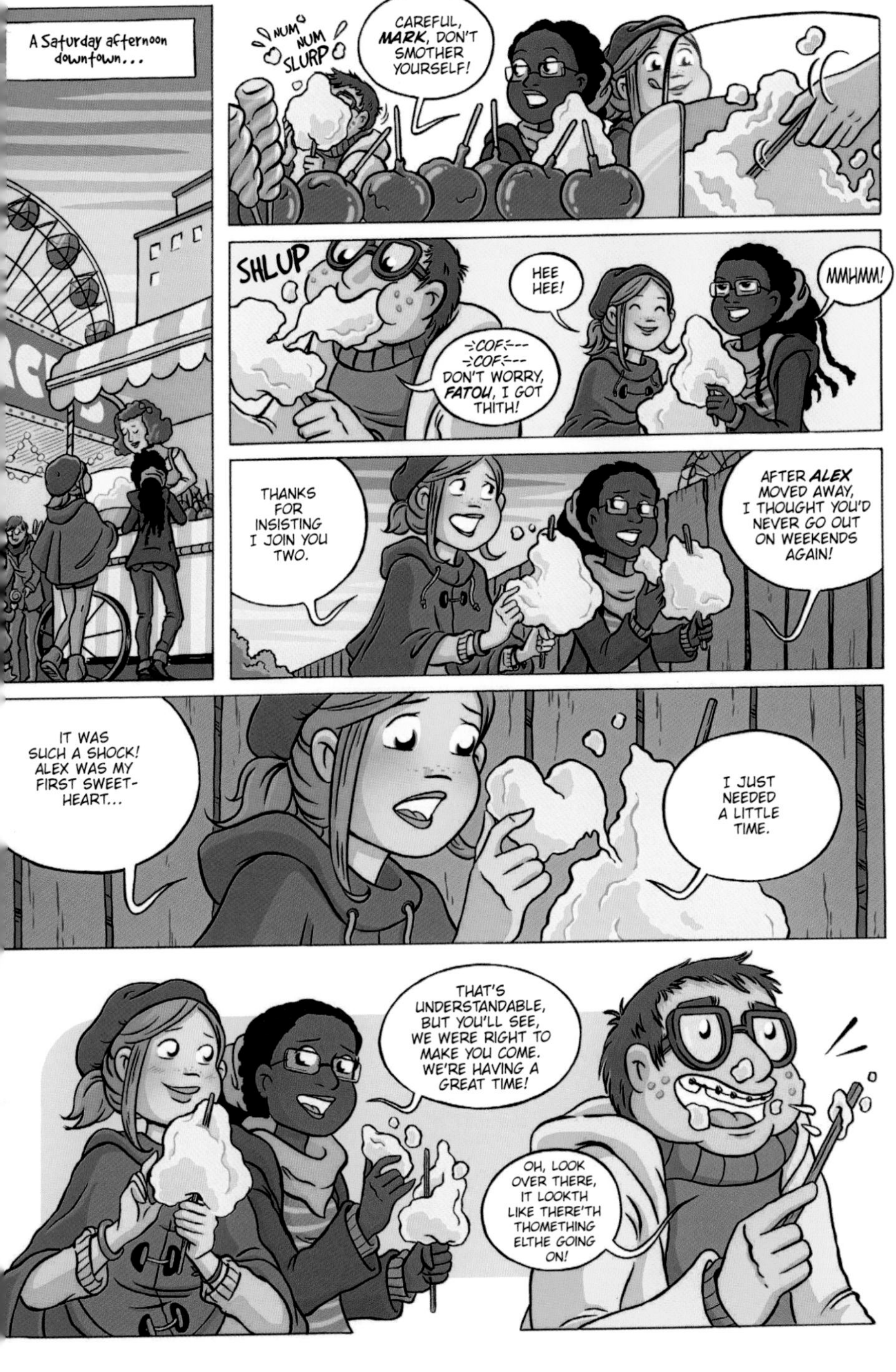
A Saturday afternoon downtown...
NUM NUM SLURP
CAREFUL, MARK, DON'T SMOTHER YOURSELF!
SHLUP
HEE HEE!
MMHMM!
-COF- -COF- DON'T WORRY, FATOU, I GOT THITH!
THANKS FOR INSISTING I JOIN YOU TWO.
AFTER ALEX MOVED AWAY, I THOUGHT YOU'D NEVER GO OUT ON WEEKENDS AGAIN!
IT WAS SUCH A SHOCK! ALEX WAS MY FIRST SWEET-HEART...
I JUST NEEDED A LITTLE TIME.
THAT'S UNDERSTANDABLE, BUT YOU'LL SEE, WE WERE RIGHT TO MAKE YOU COME. WE'RE HAVING A GREAT TIME!
OH, LOOK OVER THERE, IT LOOKTH LIKE THERE'TH THOMETHING ELTHE GOING ON!

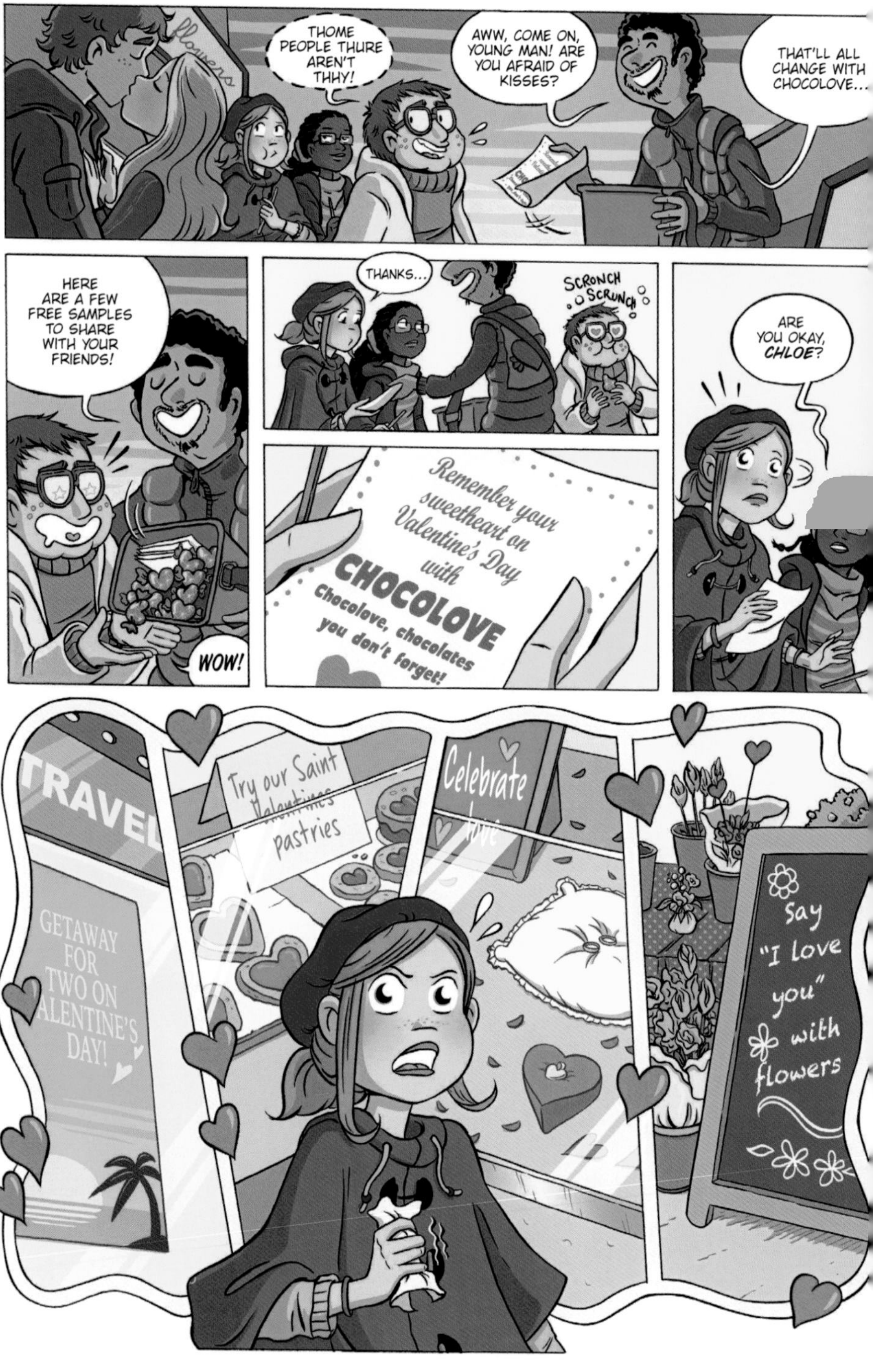
THOME PEOPLE THURE AREN'T THHY!
AWW, COME ON, YOUNG MAN! ARE YOU AFRAID OF KISSES?
THAT'LL ALL CHANGE WITH CHOCOLOVE...
HERE ARE A FEW FREE SAMPLES TO SHARE WITH YOUR FRIENDS!
WOW!
THANKS...
SCRONCH SCRUNCH
Remember your sweetheart on Valentine's Day with
CHOCOLOVE
Chocolove, chocolates you don't forget!
ARE YOU OKAY, CHLOE?
TRAVEL
GETAWAY FOR TWO ON VALENTINE'S DAY!
Try our Saint Valentine's pastries
Celebrate love
Say "I love you" with flowers

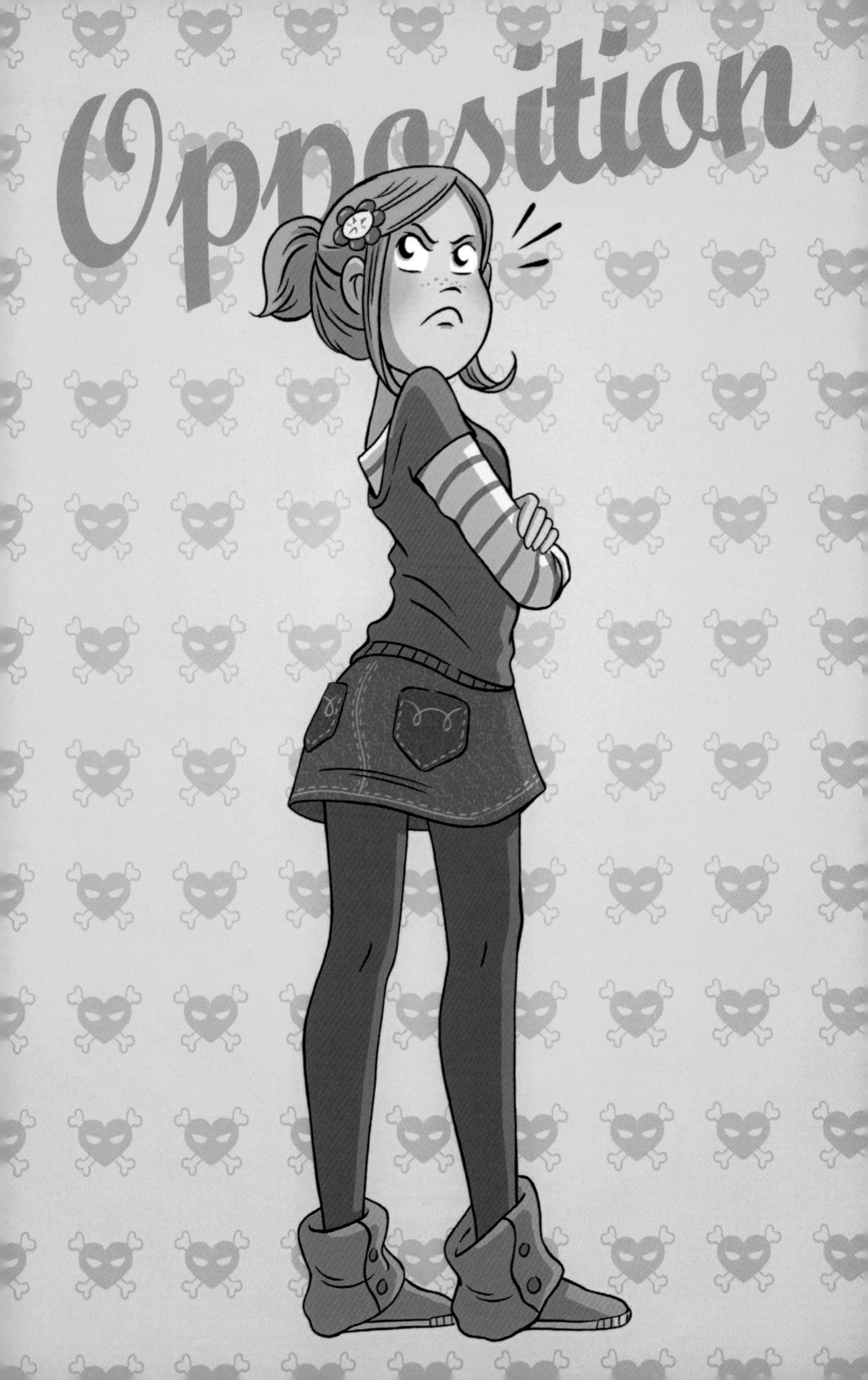
Opposition

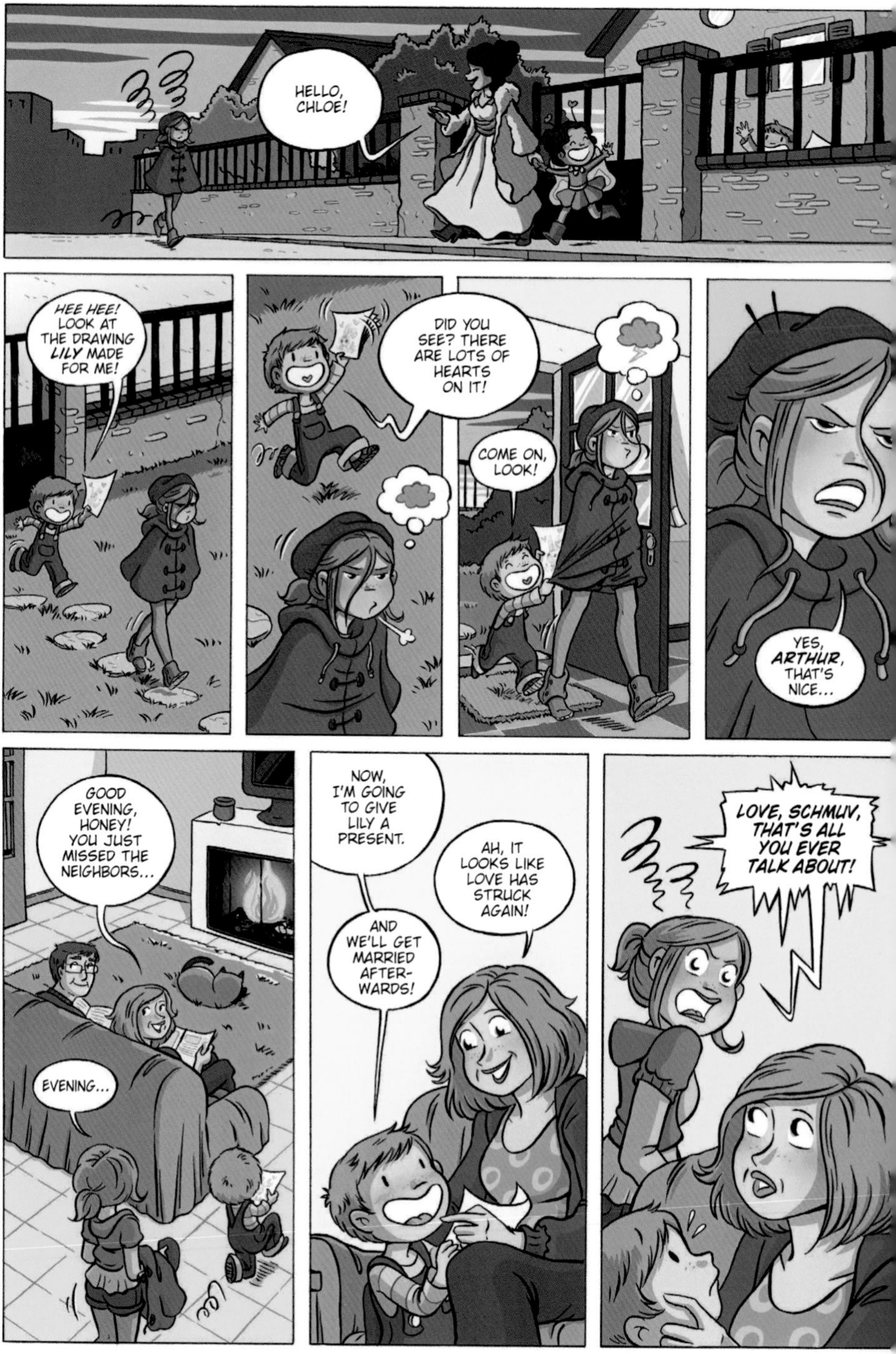
HELLO, CHLOE!
HEE HEE! LOOK AT THE DRAWING LILY MADE FOR ME!
DID YOU SEE? THERE ARE LOTS OF HEARTS ON IT!
COME ON, LOOK!
YES, ARTHUR, THAT'S NICE...
GOOD EVENING, HONEY! YOU JUST MISSED THE NEIGHBORS...
EVENING...
NOW, I'M GOING TO GIVE LILY A PRESENT.
AND WE'LL GET MARRIED AFTER-WARDS!
AH, IT LOOKS LIKE LOVE HAS STRUCK AGAIN!
LOVE, SCHMUV, THAT'S ALL YOU EVER TALK ABOUT!

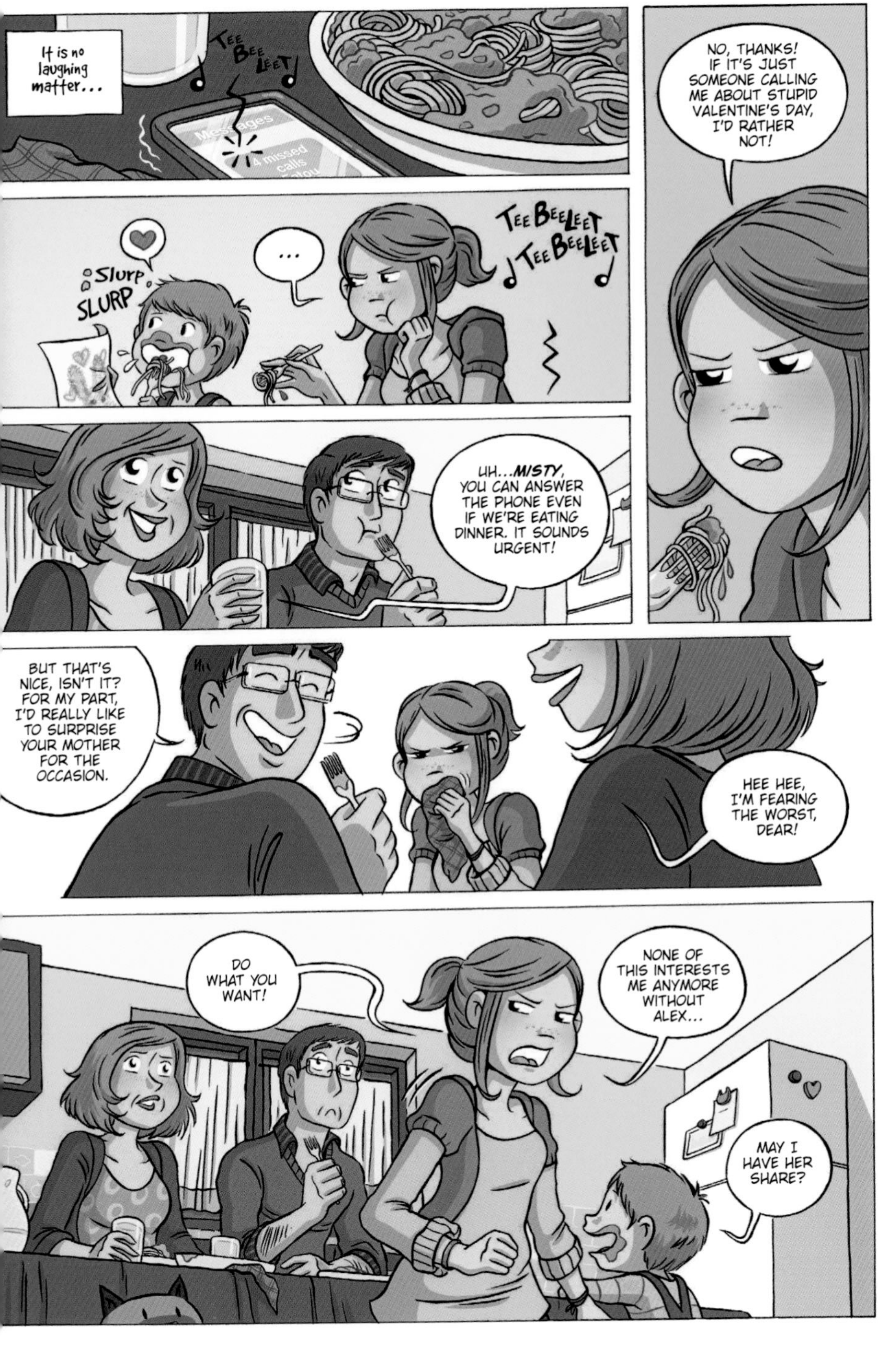

It is no laughing matter...
TEE BEE LEET
Messages
4 missed calls
SLURP
SLURP
...
TEE BEELEET TEE BEELEET
NO, THANKS! IF IT'S JUST SOMEONE CALLING ME ABOUT STUPID VALENTINE'S DAY, I'D RATHER NOT!
UH...MISTY, YOU CAN ANSWER THE PHONE EVEN IF WE'RE EATING DINNER. IT SOUNDS URGENT!
BUT THAT'S NICE, ISN'T IT? FOR MY PART, I'D REALLY LIKE TO SURPRISE YOUR MOTHER FOR THE OCCASION.
HEE HEE, I'M FEARING THE WORST, DEAR!
DO WHAT YOU WANT!
NONE OF THIS INTERESTS ME ANYMORE WITHOUT ALEX...
MAY I HAVE HER SHARE?

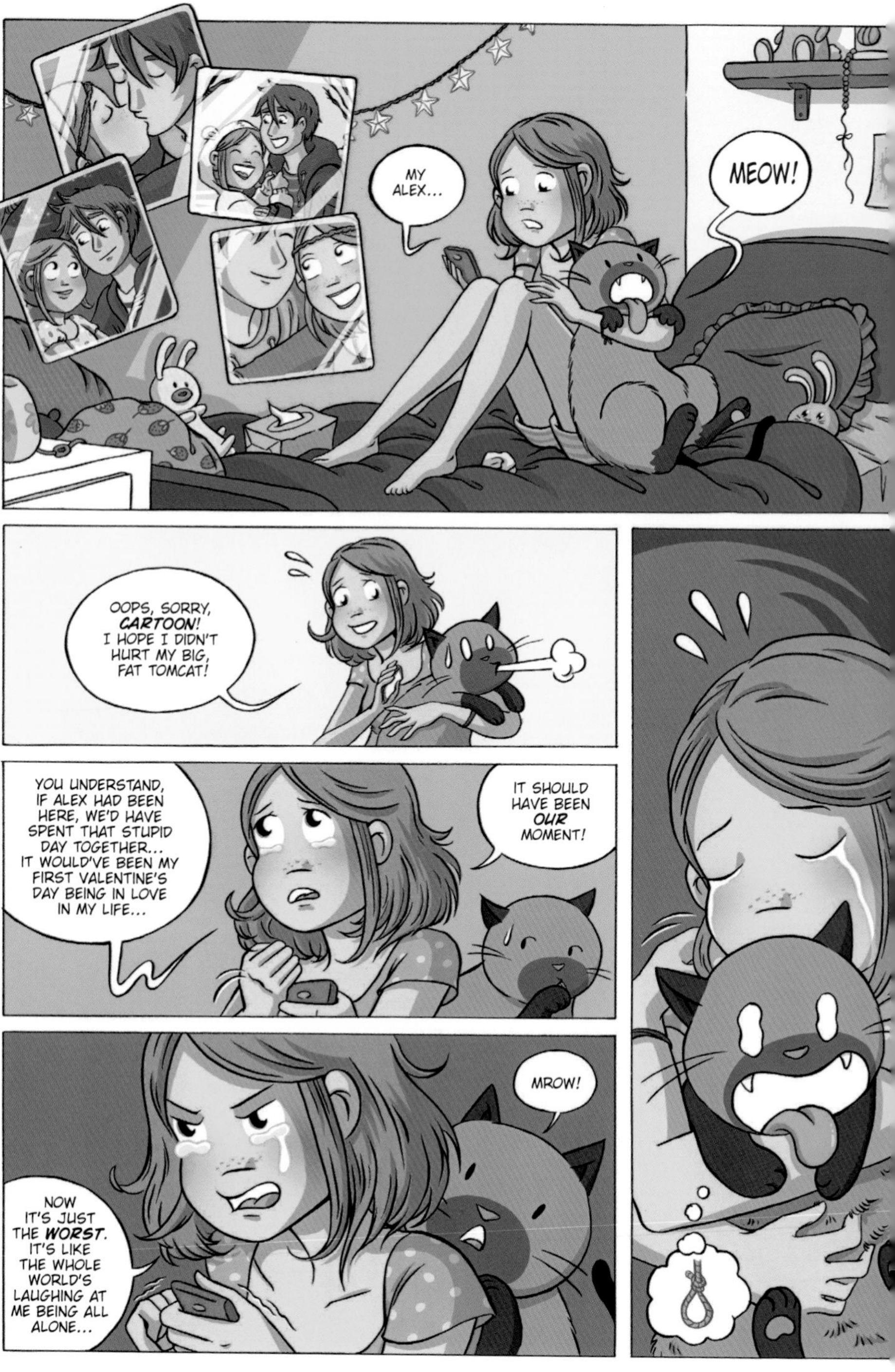
MY ALEX...
MEOW!
OOPS, SORRY, CARTOON! I HOPE I DIDN'T HURT MY BIG, FAT TOMCAT!
YOU UNDERSTAND, IF ALEX HAD BEEN HERE, WE'D HAVE SPENT THAT STUPID DAY TOGETHER... IT WOULD'VE BEEN MY FIRST VALENTINE'S DAY BEING IN LOVE IN MY LIFE...
IT SHOULD HAVE BEEN OUR MOMENT!
MROW!
NOW IT'S JUST THE WORST. IT'S LIKE THE WHOLE WORLD'S LAUGHING AT ME BEING ALL ALONE...

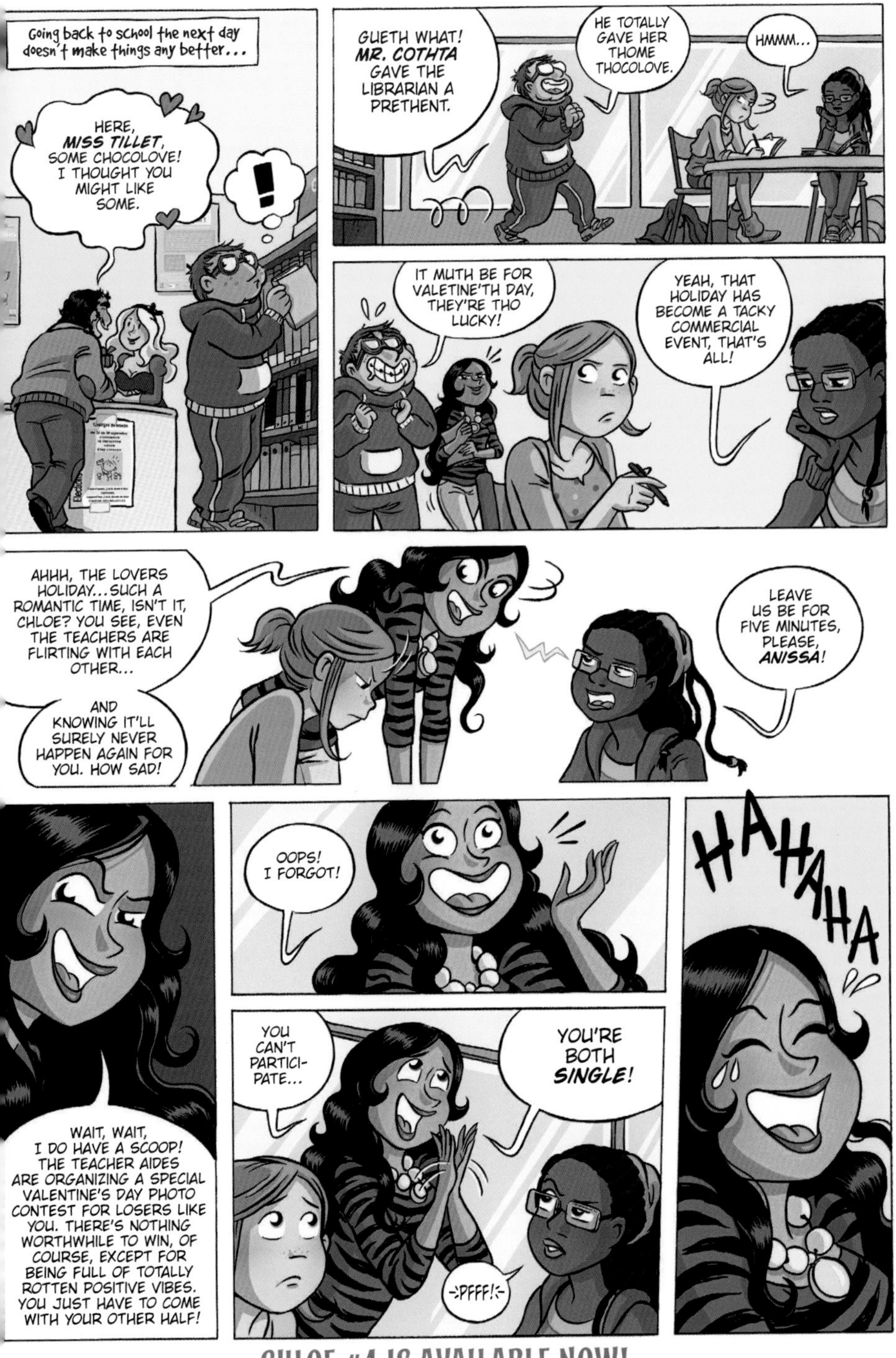
Going back to school the next day doesn't make things any better...
HERE, MISS TILLET, SOME CHOCOLOVE! I THOUGHT YOU MIGHT LIKE SOME.
!
GUETH WHAT! MR. COTHTA GAVE THE LIBRARIAN A PRETHENT.
HE TOTALLY GAVE HER THOME THOCOLOVE.
HMMM...
IT MUTH BE FOR VALETINE'TH DAY, THEY'RE THO LUCKY!
YEAH, THAT HOLIDAY HAS BECOME A TACKY COMMERCIAL EVENT, THAT'S ALL!
AHHH, THE LOVERS HOLIDAY...SUCH A ROMANTIC TIME, ISN'T IT, CHLOE? YOU SEE, EVEN THE TEACHERS ARE FLIRTING WITH EACH OTHER...
AND KNOWING IT'LL SURELY NEVER HAPPEN AGAIN FOR YOU. HOW SAD!
LEAVE US BE FOR FIVE MINUTES, PLEASE, ANISSA!
WAIT, WAIT, I DO HAVE A SCOOP! THE TEACHER AIDES ARE ORGANIZING A SPECIAL VALENTINE'S DAY PHOTO CONTEST FOR LOSERS LIKE YOU. THERE'S NOTHING WORTHWHILE TO WIN, OF COURSE, EXCEPT FOR BEING FULL OF TOTALLY ROTTEN POSITIVE VIBES. YOU JUST HAVE TO COME WITH YOUR OTHER HALF!
OOPS! I FORGOT!
YOU CAN'T PARTICI-PATE...
YOU'RE BOTH SINGLE!
PFFF!
HAHAHAHA

CHLOE #4 IS AVAILABLE NOW!

ENJOY THIS PREVIEW OF GHOST FRIENDS FOREVER #1
ANOTHER CHARMZ TITLE!

GFFs
GHOST FRIENDS FOREVER

MY HEART LIES IN THE 90s

STORY BY MONICA GALLAGHER
ART BY KATA KANE

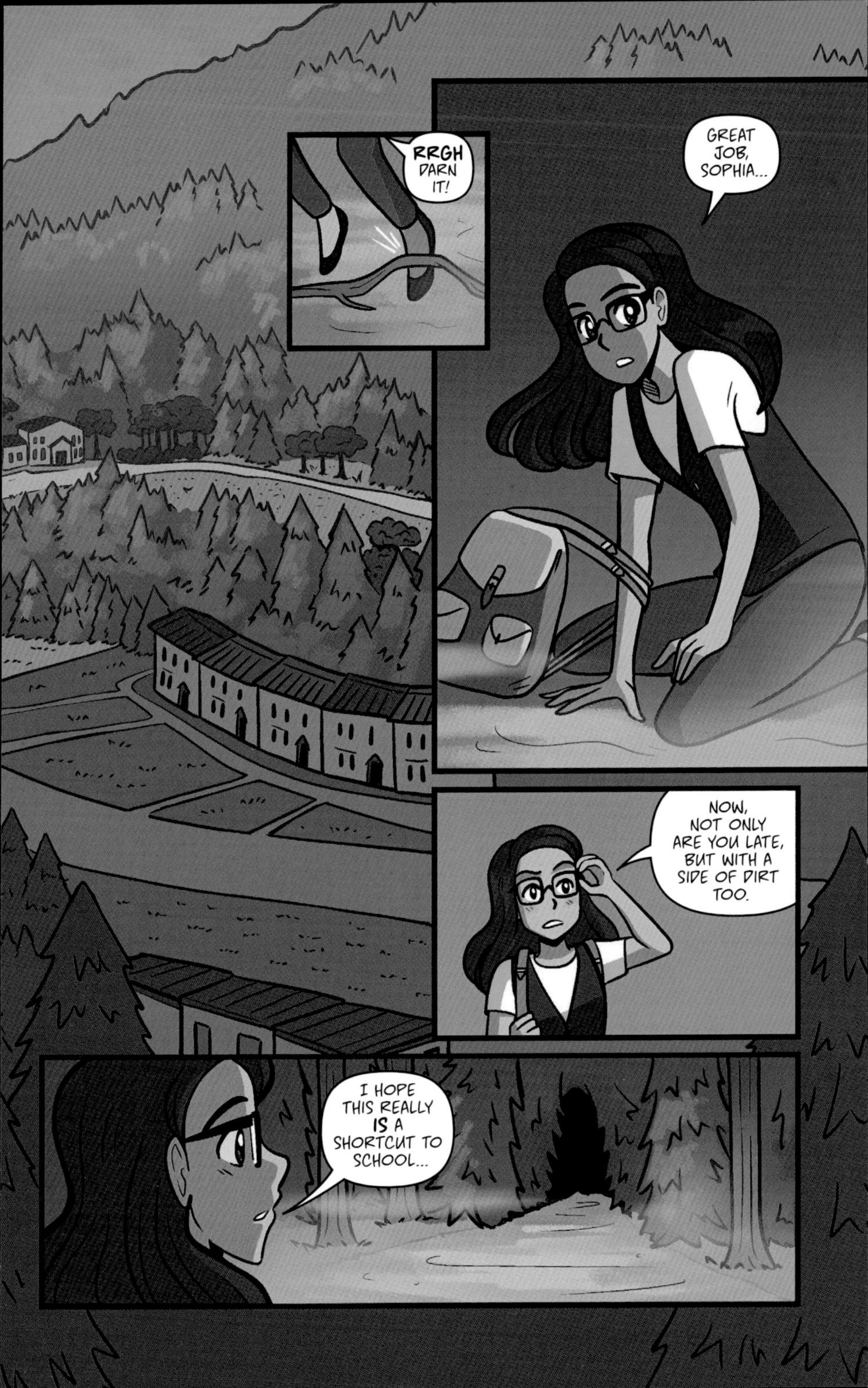
RRGH DARN IT!
GREAT JOB, SOPHIA...
NOW, NOT ONLY ARE YOU LATE, BUT WITH A SIDE OF DIRT TOO.
I HOPE THIS REALLY **IS** A SHORTCUT TO SCHOOL...

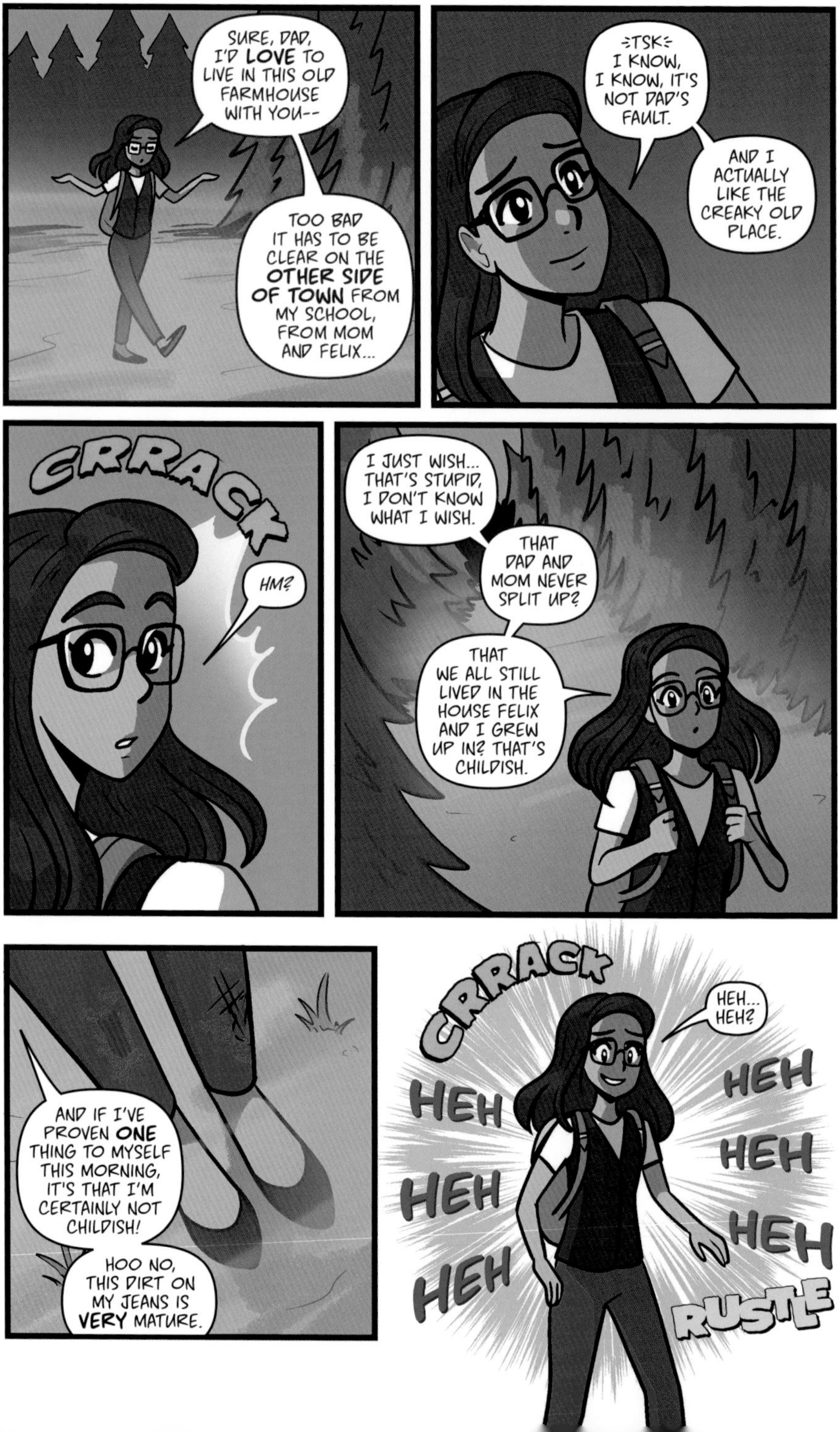
SURE, DAD, I'D **LOVE** TO LIVE IN THIS OLD FARMHOUSE WITH YOU--
TOO BAD IT HAS TO BE CLEAR ON THE **OTHER SIDE OF TOWN** FROM MY SCHOOL, FROM MOM AND FELIX...
TSK
I KNOW, I KNOW, IT'S NOT DAD'S FAULT.
AND I ACTUALLY LIKE THE CREAKY OLD PLACE.
CRRACK
HM?
I JUST WISH... THAT'S STUPID, I DON'T KNOW WHAT I WISH.
THAT DAD AND MOM NEVER SPLIT UP?
THAT WE ALL STILL LIVED IN THE HOUSE FELIX AND I GREW UP IN? THAT'S CHILDISH.
AND IF I'VE PROVEN **ONE** THING TO MYSELF THIS MORNING, IT'S THAT I'M CERTAINLY NOT CHILDISH!
HOO NO, THIS DIRT ON MY JEANS IS **VERY** MATURE.
CRRACK
HEH... HEH?
HEH
HEH
HEH
HEH
HEH
HEH
RUSTLE

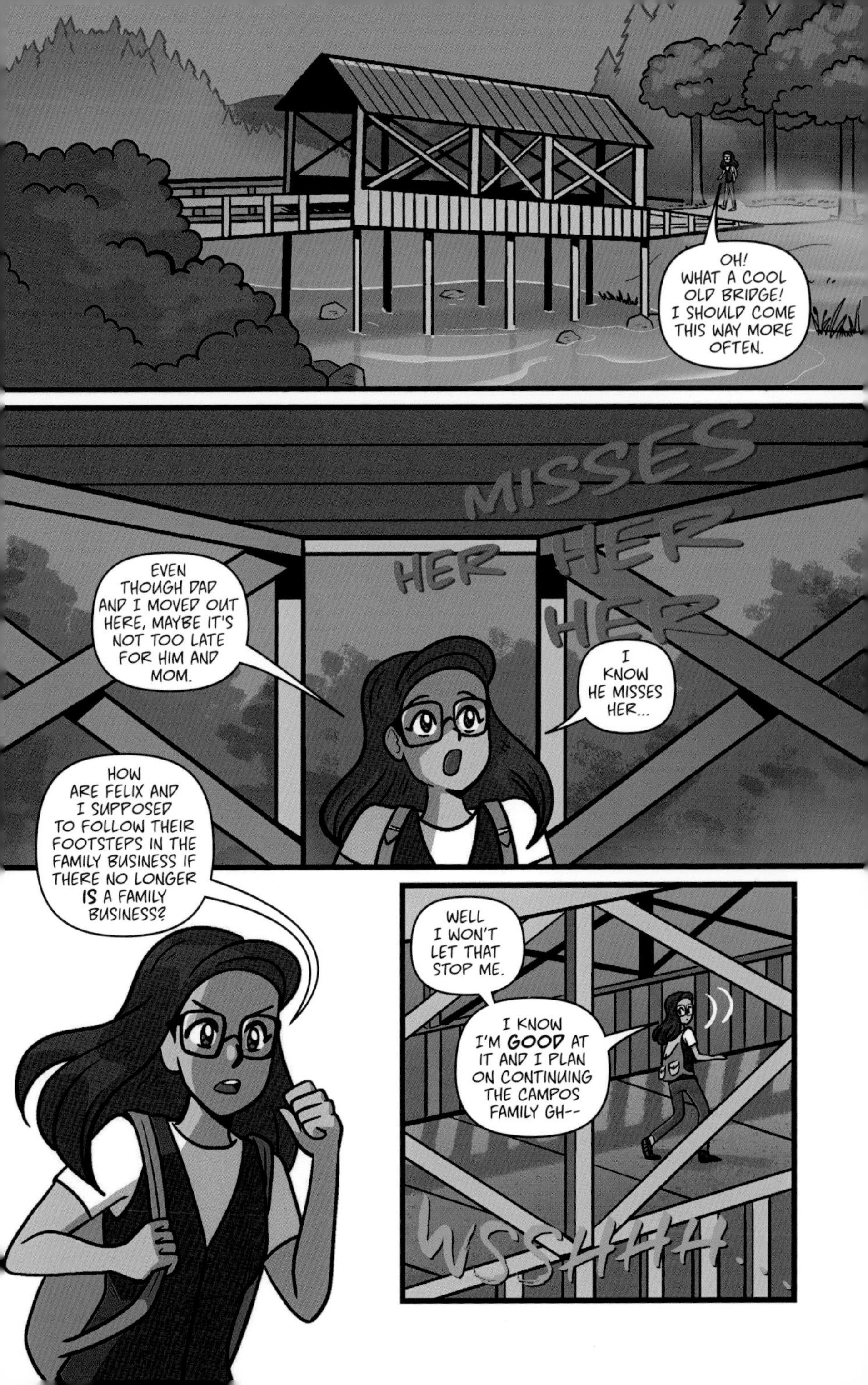
OH! WHAT A COOL OLD BRIDGE! I SHOULD COME THIS WAY MORE OFTEN.
MISSES
HER HER
HER
EVEN THOUGH DAD AND I MOVED OUT HERE, MAYBE IT'S NOT TOO LATE FOR HIM AND MOM.
I KNOW HE MISSES HER...
HOW ARE FELIX AND I SUPPOSED TO FOLLOW THEIR FOOTSTEPS IN THE FAMILY BUSINESS IF THERE NO LONGER **IS** A FAMILY BUSINESS?
WELL I WON'T LET THAT STOP ME.
I KNOW I'M **GOOD** AT IT AND I PLAN ON CONTINUING THE CAMPOS FAMILY GH--
WSSHHH

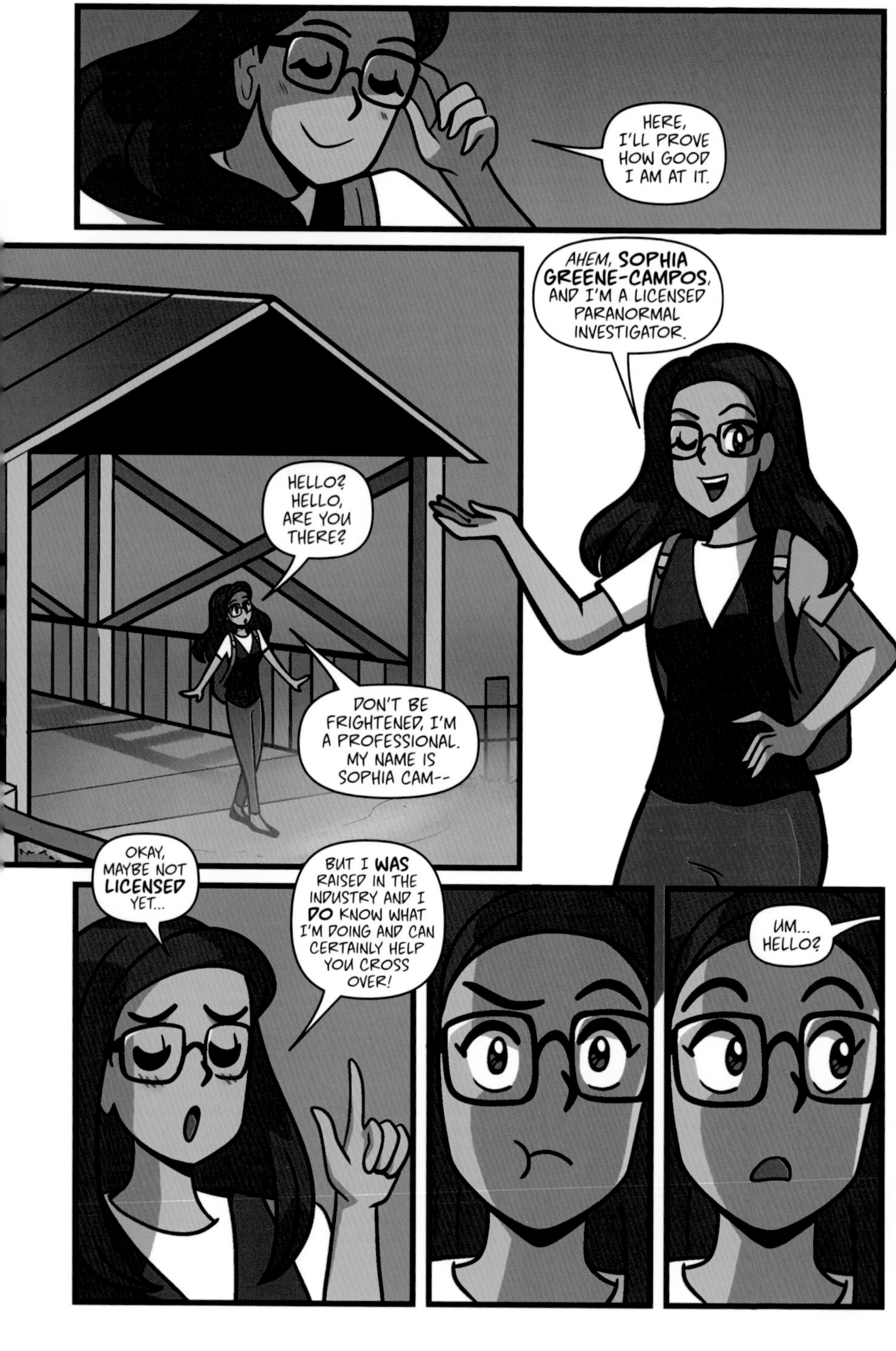
HERE, I'LL PROVE HOW GOOD I AM AT IT.
AHEM, SOPHIA GREENE-CAMPOS, AND I'M A LICENSED PARANORMAL INVESTIGATOR.
HELLO? HELLO, ARE YOU THERE?
DON'T BE FRIGHTENED, I'M A PROFESSIONAL. MY NAME IS SOPHIA CAM--
OKAY, MAYBE NOT LICENSED YET...
BUT I WAS RAISED IN THE INDUSTRY AND I DO KNOW WHAT I'M DOING AND CAN CERTAINLY HELP YOU CROSS OVER!
UM... HELLO?

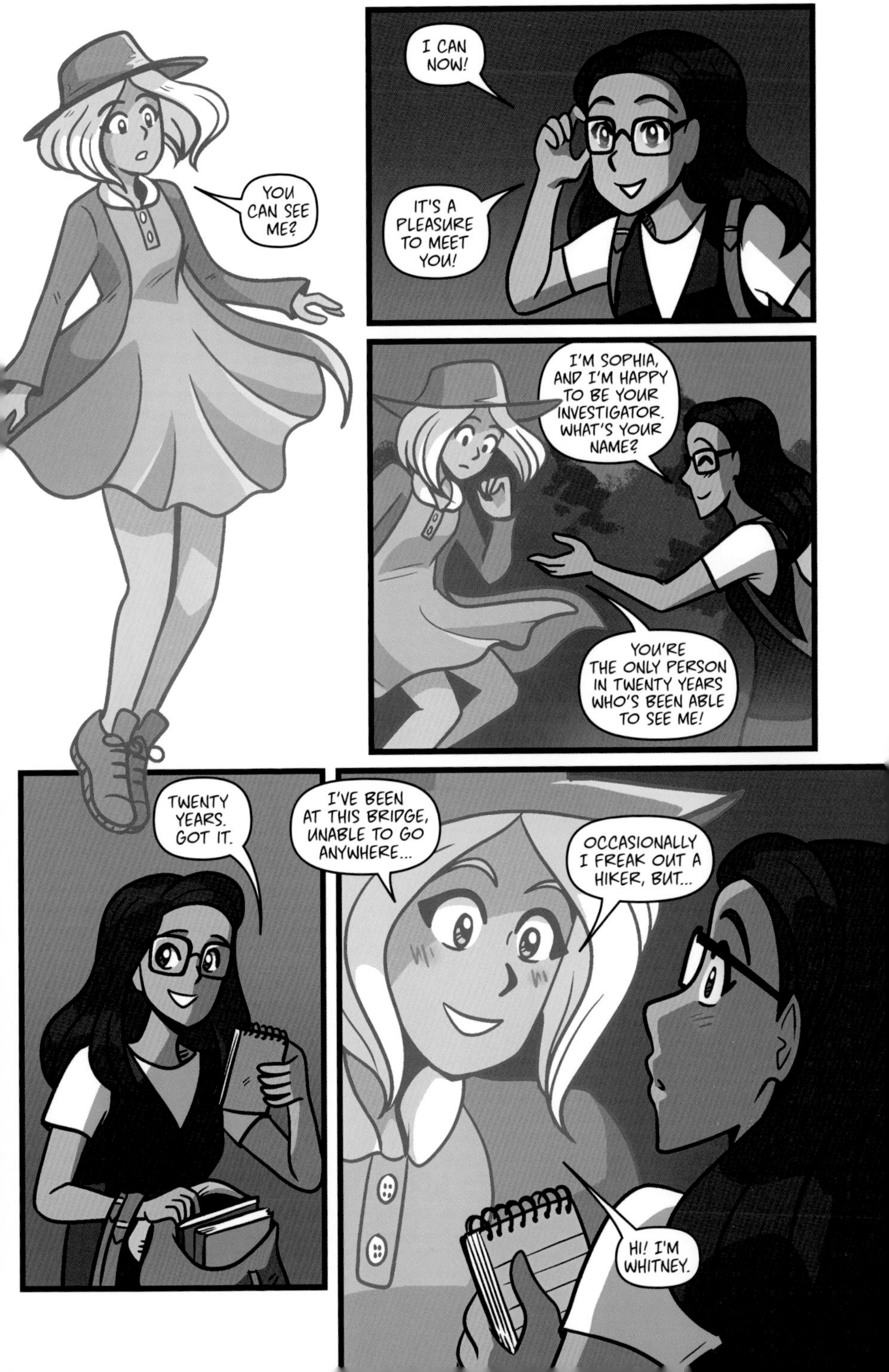
YOU CAN SEE ME?
I CAN NOW!
IT'S A PLEASURE TO MEET YOU!
I'M SOPHIA, AND I'M HAPPY TO BE YOUR INVESTIGATOR. WHAT'S YOUR NAME?
YOU'RE THE ONLY PERSON IN TWENTY YEARS WHO'S BEEN ABLE TO SEE ME!
TWENTY YEARS. GOT IT.
I'VE BEEN AT THIS BRIDGE, UNABLE TO GO ANYWHERE...
OCCASIONALLY I FREAK OUT A HIKER, BUT...
HI! I'M WHITNEY.

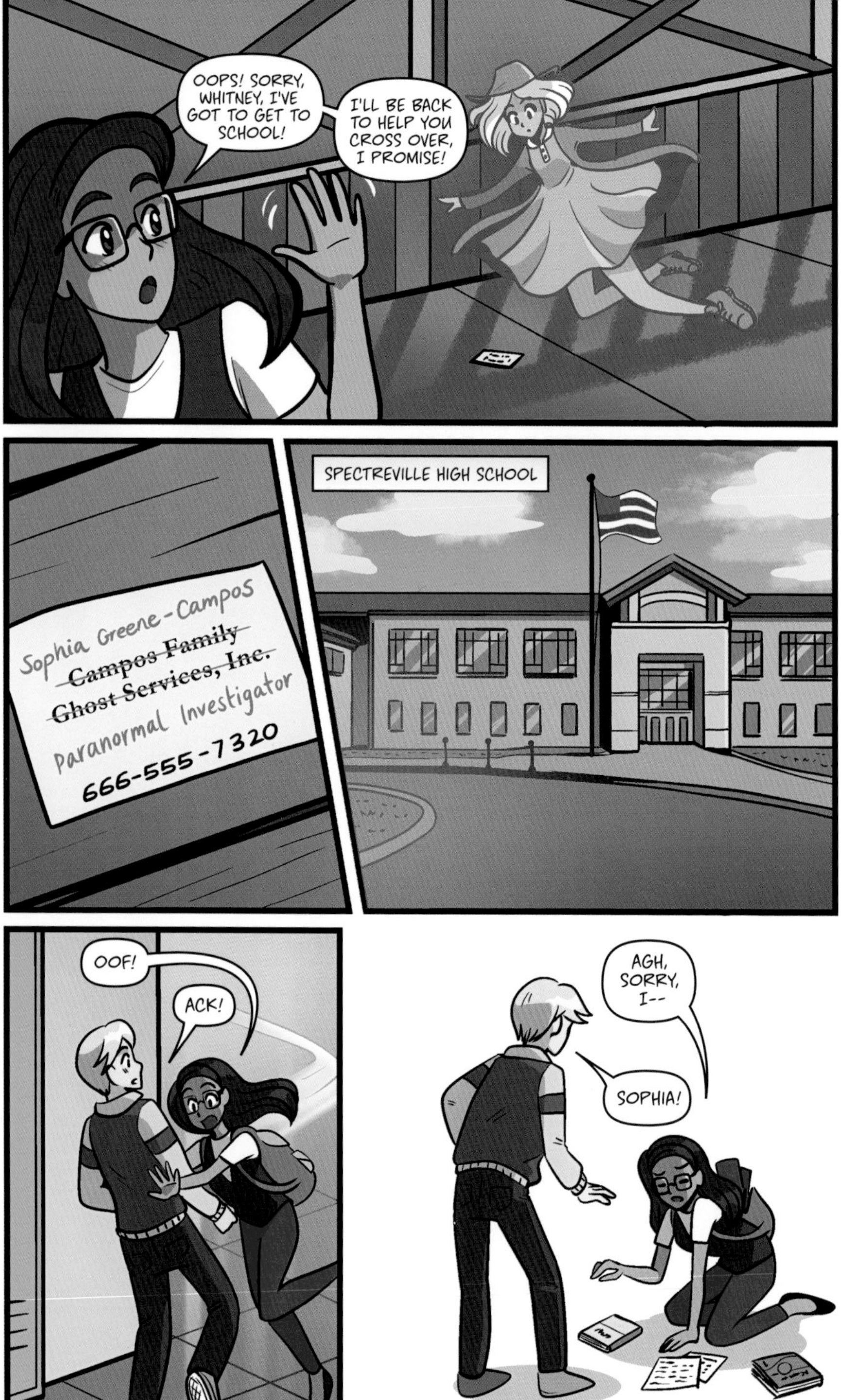
OOPS! SORRY, WHITNEY, I'VE GOT TO GET TO SCHOOL!
I'LL BE BACK TO HELP YOU CROSS OVER, I PROMISE!
Sophia Greene-Campos
~~Campos Family Ghost Services, Inc.~~
Paranormal Investigator
666-555-7320
SPECTREVILLE HIGH SCHOOL
OOF!
ACK!
AGH, SORRY, I--
SOPHIA!

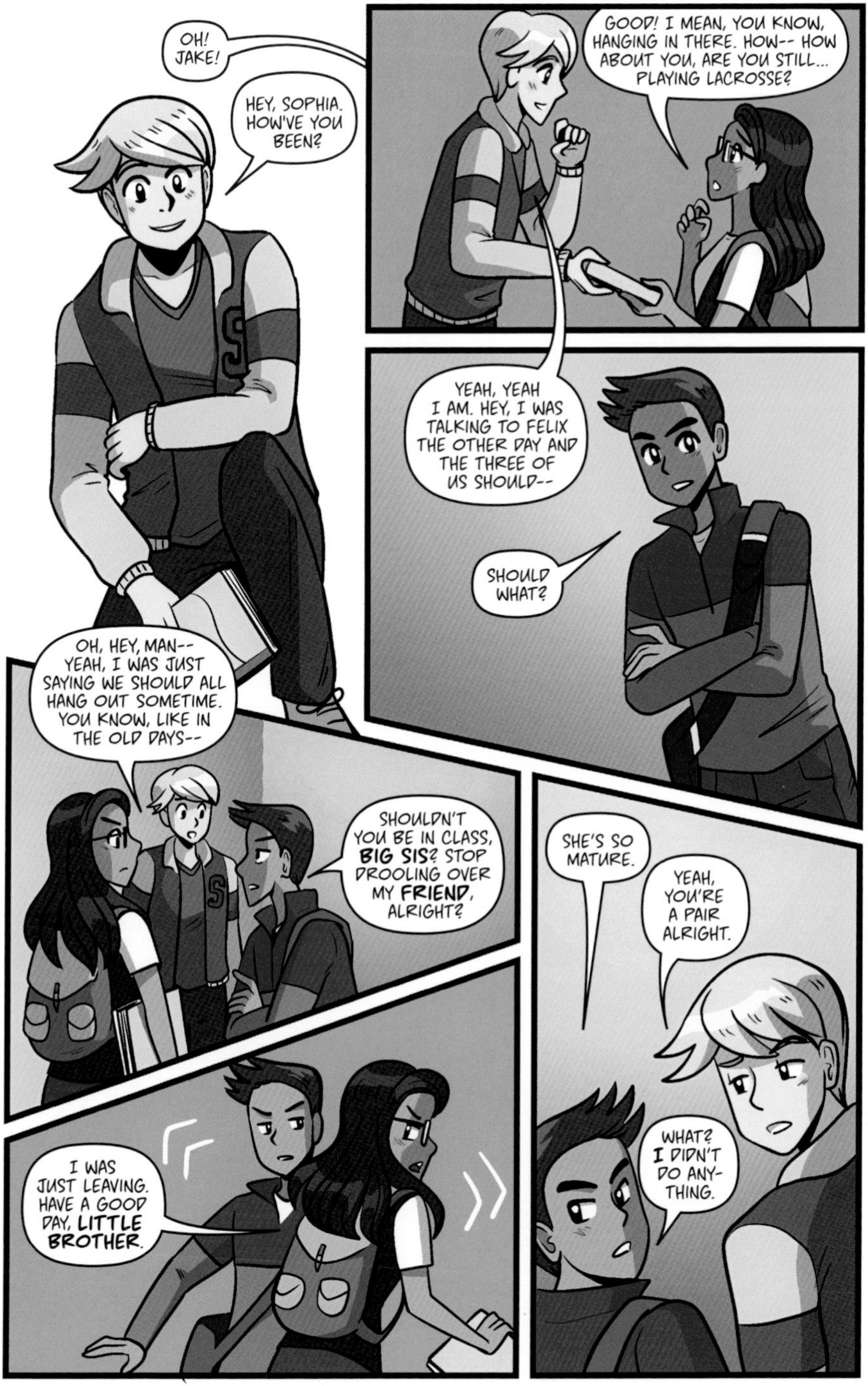
OH! JAKE!
HEY, SOPHIA. HOW'VE YOU BEEN?
GOOD! I MEAN, YOU KNOW, HANGING IN THERE. HOW-- HOW ABOUT YOU, ARE YOU STILL... PLAYING LACROSSE?
YEAH, YEAH I AM. HEY, I WAS TALKING TO FELIX THE OTHER DAY AND THE THREE OF US SHOULD--
SHOULD WHAT?
OH, HEY, MAN-- YEAH, I WAS JUST SAYING WE SHOULD ALL HANG OUT SOMETIME. YOU KNOW, LIKE IN THE OLD DAYS--
SHOULDN'T YOU BE IN CLASS, **BIG SIS**? STOP DROOLING OVER MY **FRIEND**, ALRIGHT?
I WAS JUST LEAVING. HAVE A GOOD DAY, **LITTLE BROTHER**.
SHE'S SO MATURE.
YEAH, YOU'RE A PAIR ALRIGHT.
WHAT? **I** DIDN'T DO ANY-THING.

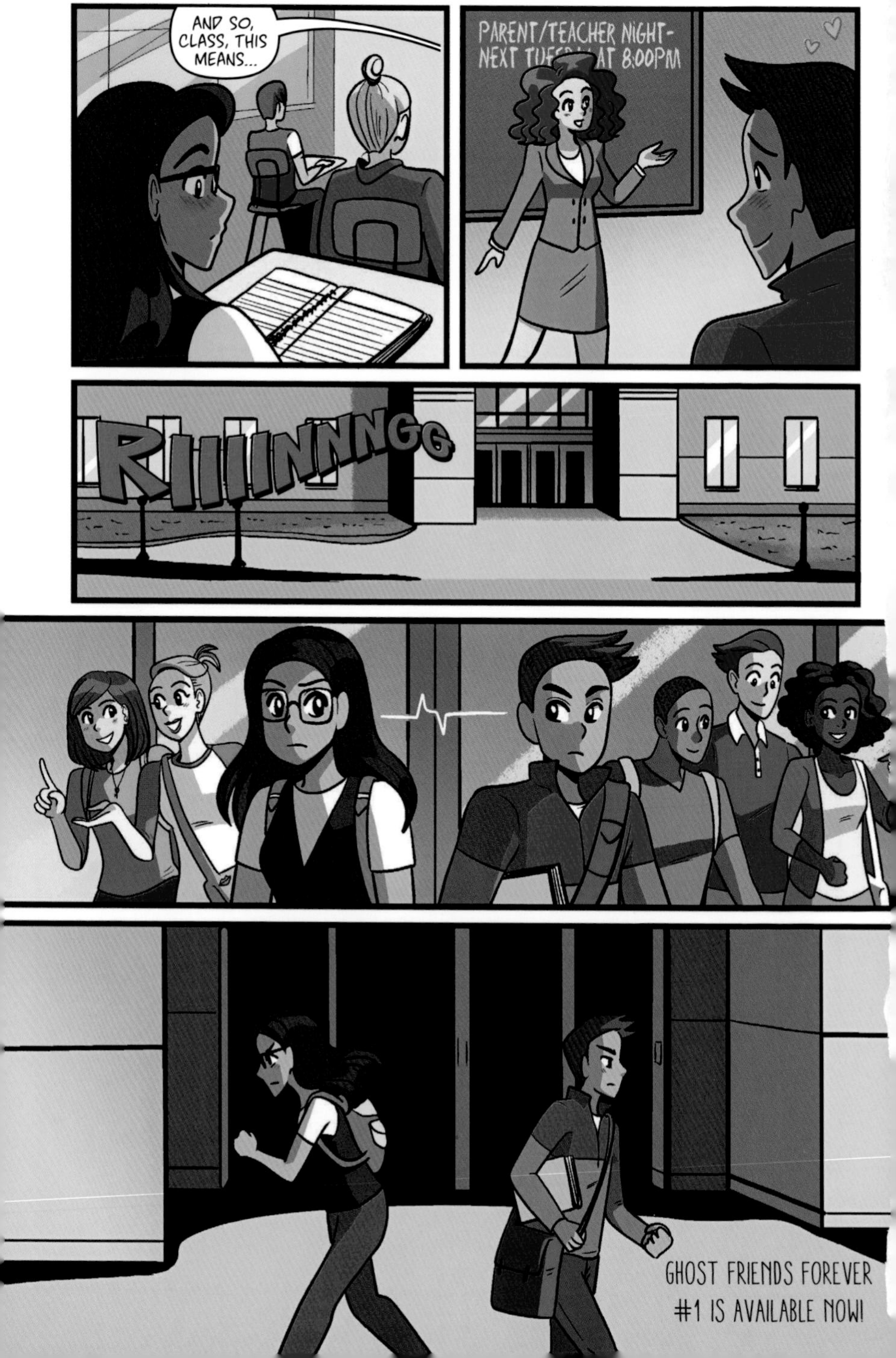

AND SO, CLASS, THIS MEANS...
PARENT/TEACHER NIGHT-
RIIIINNNGG
GHOST FRIENDS FOREVER #1 IS AVAILABLE NOW!